SHORT SHARP SHOCKS

THE SHORT FILMS OF
PAUL KANE

Encyclopocalypse Publications
www.encyclopocalypse.com

CONTENTS

THE TORTURER

PRESENCE

BLACKOUT

LIFE-O-MATIC

For all the hardworking indie film creatives out there, making dreams a reality.

SHORT SHARP SHOCKS

ACKNOWLEDGMENTS

My thanks to Mark and Sean for being interested in publishing this one, and being as big a fans of horror films as I am. To the awesome Anthony Galatis for letting us use the art from the poster of *The Torturer* on our cover. Massive thank yous to the editors and publishers who took these stories in the first place and the filmmakers who brought them to life – who you'll be introduced to during the course of the book. As always, hugs and big thank yous to all my friends in the writing and film/TV world, for their continual help both now and in the past; people like Mike Carey, Pete & Nicky Crowther, Simon Clark, Alison Littlewood, Michael Marshall Smith, Stephen Volk, Tim Lebbon and too many more to carry on listing! You all know who you are. Lastly, a massive thank you to my wonderful better half Marie for loving me and for loving genre TV and film.

CREDITS

Director: Lewis Copson

Script: Paul Kane

Director of Photography: E.T. Williams

Executive Producers: Neil Hewitt-Dudding, Tony Fenn

Associate Producer: Dominic Burns

Producer: Lewis Copson

Editor: David Cork

Sound: Dominic Burns, Rob Jaques, Sam Lennox

Original Score: Keir Ramshaw, 'Kix' by The Real Tuesday Weld

CAST

Stephen Coates: The Voice of the Opportunist

Clare Coleman: The Victim

Daniel Gough: The Opportunist

Catherine Prout: The Friend

Andrew Dennis: The Dog Man

Dominic Burns: The Pub Landlord

Lewis Copson: Friend

Sam Lennox: Friend
Mitzi the Dog: Maxie

THE OPPORTUNITY
THE SHORT STORY

From my hiding place behind the wall I can see the entrance clearly.

Almost closing time. Last orders will have been called. I only have to wait a few more minutes before they start to emerge.

Figures, bathed orange in the glow from the streetlights. They look unreal. I can hear them laughing. Joking. Pregnant with booze.

I stare across, waiting patiently for the crowds to thin. There I see a woman. *My victim.* It looks like… yes, she's with a group, but they're all going their separate ways. She kisses one or two goodbye, on the cheek, on the lips. She begins to walk down the street on her own. They never learn. Coat wrapped around her tightly against the cool breeze, heels clacking on the pavement. When she gets far enough away from the pub then I'll—

She turns.

Someone is calling out to her. Long hair whips round as one of the friends catches her up, a smaller woman whose goodbyes have gone on much longer than hers did. They link arms; she's going to walk home with her.

3

Fuck! My mind is already full of things I was going to do. But now I am denied.

Yet I *must* follow them, keeping a good distance behind. To the untrained eye I am just another late night reveller on my way home. A thrill seeker.

They stroll out of the town, down the side streets where the lights are few and far between – some are not even working at all. I'm too far away to hear the conversation but the sound of their giggling carries on the night air.

I am in luck. The smaller woman points to one of the houses on the other side of the road. The pair embrace, then part, waving all the time.

I follow the first woman now she's alone, closing the gap slightly, but still out of sight. I am in the shadows (I *am* the shadows), my pulse racing. And I can… There's that clacking again, louder now, ringing in my ears.

The opportunity has arrived and I must seize it. The waiting is over at last. I speed up. Can she sense me behind her? I'm still some distance away. If she should turn now…

Someone else is coming along the street. I jump into a garden to hide behind the hedge until they've passed by. A man out with his dog. It does its business on the grass verge.

Finally, he goes away. His interference has cost me dear, though. I have to run, fearing that I've lost her.

But no. I have the woman in my sights again, the clacking leading me to her. I'm catching up, quietly, stealthily. Hand in my pocket on the cheese wire. Don't turn around, please… don't. I don't want to see your face.

She's mere feet away. It's now or never—

And she's spotted me. Shit! No…

"Nicky? Oh Nicky, thank God it's you! I thought someone was following me. Scared me a little bit."

She kisses me then walks on, nearing her house. I stay by her side.

"Just wanted to surprise you," I say.

"Hmm, can't keep away, eh? You know, I wish you'd come out with me and meet my friends one night. They're beginning to think I've made you up."

I laugh. Can she see it in my face? Bathed orange in the glow from the solitary streetlight outside her house. Can she see what I had in mind?

"What have you done with the car?"

"Parked it round the corner," I lie.

She grins. "Right, well… let's go in then, shall we?"

"Sure," I say.

As I tail her up the steps I wonder if I can hold out much longer. Waiting for the right time. The *perfect* opportunity. I don't know how long I can keep up the pretence. Touching her, 'loving' her. When all I really want to do is…

How long before she discovers who I truly am? Before she sees through my masquerade?

She opens the door with her key, striding into the darkness of her empty home. I follow, as I have done all night. As I have done for weeks now. And I know the opportunity will arise at some point. *It has to.* Maybe tonight. Maybe not.

But it will be soon.

The Opportunity
Written by Paul Kane
Based on the short story by Paul Kane

PUB ENTRANCE - NIGHT

We are behind a crumbling wall. We can see
the entrance to a pub late at night from
the point of view of a stalker/killer. The
vision is slightly shaky at first, blurred
even at times, and we can hear heavy
breathing - a mixture of excitement and
expectation.

> OPPORTUNIST (V.O.)
> (in a gruff voice)
> I've been here before, so many times.
> In this situation or others just like
> it. I've known for a long time what I
> was, what I could be, what I shall be
> again.
> In a way I'm an opportunist, I strike
> as the opportunity presents itself;
> whenever that may be. If I wait long
> enough I will get my just reward. It's
> all in the timing, has to be right...
> always has to be... perfect.
> (looks at his watch with a pen-torch)
> I know what's been happening inside
> there. The landlord has rung his shiny
> bell, last orders, last orders... And
> it will be the last. The very last for
> someone. Won't be long now; won't be—

We see figures emerging from the pub,
bathed in an orange radiance from the
streetlamps. They're laughing and joking
with each other, three women and two men.

                    OPPORTUNIST (CONT'D)
                 Here come some of them.

Now we see the figures metamorphose,
becoming cartoon-like, and starting to
glow.

                    OPPORTUNIST (CONT'D)
             Oh... They look so... unreal to me.
             Something not right. Not... They're
             things. Just things. Look at them,
             pregnant with booze. They don't get it
             at all. It's no joke; this is serious.
             If they could only see what I can see.
                 But then, how can they? It's
                          impossible.

The group split up, go their separate ways,
kissing cheeks and saying goodbyes. One
woman stands out from the rest; we focus
on her.

                    OPPORTUNIST (CONT'D)
             Yes! She's the one. My next... victim.
             No, not victim. I liberate. It's
             necessary. The fact that I enjoy it is
             beside the point. Look at her, going
                 off on her own. They never learn.

The woman waves and pulls her coat tightly
around herself. She begins to walk down the
street towards where The Opportunist is
hiding behind the wall. We hear her heels
clacking loudly on the pavement.

                    OPPORTUNIST (CONT'D)
          Yes, that's right. Closer, closer. It
          might be sooner than I thought. Get this
          over and done with, right here and now.

She turns back, hair whipping around,
responding to someone calling her from
behind. It's the other smaller woman, her
friend, whose goodbyes have gone on longer
than hers did.

                    OPPORTUNIST (CONT'D)
                       (frustrated)
          No... leave her alone. She's mine.
                    She's all mine.

The women link arms and start to walk away
from the pub together, laughing and joking.

                    OPPORTUNIST (CONT'D)
          <u>Fuck!</u> I was already there, in my
          imagination. Thinking of the things I
                    was going to do.

We see a series of quick flashes, knife-
edges and blood.

                    OPPORTUNIST (CONT'D)
          And now I've been denied. It seems she
          does have some sense after all. Safety
          in numbers; you never know who might be
          lurking around at this time of night.
          But I don't have any choice. She's been
                        marked.

A mark starts to glow on her forehead, a
death's-head.

                    OPPORTUNIST (CONT'D)
          She already has the tinge of death on
            her, branded like cattle for the
            slaughter. I have to follow her now.
              It's my duty, it's who I <u>am</u>.
                         (beat)

He steps out from his hiding place. We see
the women clacking up the road from a view-
point just over his shoulder.

                    OPPORTUNIST (CONT'D)
                    It's what I do.

<u>STREET - NIGHT</u>

He follows the women down the street,
keeping a reasonable distance from them. We
move up and down more avenues and it's
obvious we're heading further away from the
more central area of town, down the back-
streets where the lights are few and far
between - and some are not even working
at all.

                         OPPORTUNIST
          To the untrained eye I'm just another
             reveler on my way home from a good
              night out. Just another... thrill-
             seeker. And in a sense isn't that
            right? Isn't it the thrill I'm seeking,
             isn't it the overwhelming joy that

comes from doing what I do?
(beat)
No... it's dangerous to think those
thoughts. To enjoy it too much. I'm not
some cheap hack, some nutjob out for a
good time. This is different. This is
different. I'm doing this because—

The women pause and the smallest of them
points to a house on the other side of the
road. The pair embrace, kiss on the cheek,
then part, waving all the time.

OPPORTUNIST (CONT'D)
I'm in luck tonight. My patience and
persistence has paid off. There she is,
alone, as she needs to be. As she
should be. It walks and talks and
thinks and eats and shits and drinks,
but that doesn't make any difference to
me. It's what's inside you that counts.
I know what's inside me, but I need to
see what's inside her now.
There's a compulsion to do so; if I
don't then I might just explode.
I can't fight it. It's useless to even
try...

We hear the clacking of the woman's heels
as she walks on.

OPPORTUNIST (CONT'D)
There, listen to that. A signal to zero
in on, a staccato beat tapping out her
final message to the world. A morse

> code last will and testament, leaving
> her body to me to do with as I please.
> (beat)
> It's time.

The Opportunist is still following his victim, keeping well back in the darkness. His breathing has speeded up again and we hear the whine through his nostrils as he tracks the woman.

> OPPORTUNIST (CONT'D)
> She can't see me. I'm in the shadows —
> I _am_ the shadows. I've become the
> darkness that everyone fears. I'm the
> urban myth made real, given flesh. I'm
> the monster under the bed and the devil
> on the shoulder. It's taken me years to
> perfect my approach. Just because I act
> on instinct, doesn't mean I'm sloppy.
> Far from it. Just because I'm at the
> mercy of chance, that doesn't make me a
> chancer. It's my ally; it's sympathetic
> to my cause... most of the time.

We see another person walking along the street, still from The Opportunist's point of view. It's a man with a small dog, which is straining at the lead.

He makes a point of giving the woman some space, to show her he is not a threat, and even murmurs a friendly hello. The woman nods curtly and carries on walking, giving a brief look back at the man.

The Opportunist casts a quick glance to the right where there's a small garden with a hedge separating one property from the other. He hops into the garden and ducks behind the hedge.

OPPORTUNIST (CONT'D)
And sometimes it puts obstacles in my way. Like him. He wasn't supposed to be here. Or was he?
Fate or fated? Is she or isn't she? Is it to be or isn't it? Just look at him and his stupid mutt.
Probably lives on his own...
That pathetic creature is his only real companion in the whole world. His walks with it the only thing justifying his worthless existence. If I... liberated him too, I doubt anyone would notice.
Or even care. Except the dog. But I don't want him. I've chosen my prey and no-one else will do. It's tempting though, it's tempting... especially as he's holding me up, interfering without even knowing it.

From behind the hedge we see the man pause on the grass verge so the dog can do its business.

MAN
(in a quiet, kind voice)
That's it, Maxie. There's a good boy.

There's a crack as The Opportunist steps on

a twig below him. The man's dog raises its head, looks in the direction of the garden and starts to yap ferociously.

                    MAN (CONT'D)
     What is it? What's the matter, Maxie?

The man begins to walk towards the garden with Maxie straining at the lead again. Maxie is growling the closer they get.

                    OPPORTUNIST
                 (under his breath)
                    Shit.

We pull back behind the hedge until we can't see the man or his dog anymore, just the foliage. But we can still hear them.

                    MAN
     What on earth's got into you?
          (Maxie continues to growl)
     Look, there's nothing there. Have you
     seen another bird? Is that it? Silly
     dog, silly Maxie. You're frightened of
     your own shadow, that's your trouble.
                    Come on...
     (more sternly, or as stern as this man
                    gets)
          I said come on...

Cautiously, we look over the hedge again to see the man and his dog going on their way in the opposite direction. Slowly, The Opportunist comes out from behind the hedge

and looks down the street for the woman.
There's no sign of her.

OPPORTUNIST
Their intervention has cost me dear.
Another time, another time... Damn.
Where is she? I can't see her anywhere.

The Opportunist starts to jog up the
street, then breaks into sort of a run. We
hear him breathing more heavily, and
there's a hint of panic in there too.

OPPORTUNIST (CONT'D)
Come on... Come on. Where are you? Show
yourself. Ah!

In the middle distance is the woman and
we're slowly catching up with her. The
Opportunist pulls back again, fearing that
he might give himself away. He gathers his
composure, his breathing slowing down.

OPPORTUNIST (CONT'D)
Seems I'm not to be denied after all.
The Opportunity is still present.

The Opportunist gets closer and we hear the
clacking of the woman's shoes again. She
glances briefly over her shoulder, as if
she can sense she's being watched, but
still doesn't see anything. She speeds up
slightly.

                    OPPORTUNIST (CONT'D)
         That's right. You know, don't you? The
            cold hands of death will soon be
                        upon you.

We look down and see him pull on a pair of
gloves.

                    OPPORTUNIST (CONT'D)
         And in a way I almost envy you. You're
         part of something you can't even begin
                     to understand.

Now he brings a length of wire out of his
pocket; he winds it around his gloved hands
and snaps it tight a couple of times.

The Opportunist is gaining on the woman,
closing the distance between them now.
She's only feet away. We see flashes of
what's in store.

                    OPPORTUNIST (CONT'D)
         Don't turn around again. Please. I
         don't want to see your face up close. I
                    don't want to—

And now she does turn fully, looking
straight at The Opportunist. But instead of
the horror we're expecting, there's a look
of recognition on her face. Followed by a
smile.

                          WOMAN
         Nick? Nicky... Oh thank <u>God</u> it's you. I

thought someone was following me.
Scared me a bit.

OPPORTUNIST
(out loud)
No, it's only me. Just wanted to
surprise you.

The woman leans in to kiss The Opportunist.

WOMAN
Hmm. So, you couldn't keep away, eh?

OPPORTUNIST
No. Couldn't keep away.

They walk together, the woman looking
straight at The Opportunist and smiling
again. He looks down quickly and we see him
slip the wire back into his pocket.

WOMAN
You know, I wish you'd come out with me
and meet my friends one night. They're
beginning to think I've made you up, Mr
Wonderful.

OPPORTUNIST (V.O.)
(laughs out loud, then we hear his
thoughts again)
Can she see it in my face? Can she see
what I had in mind?

They stop outside another house, a single
streetlamp illuminating the scene.

                    WOMAN
          What have you done with the car?

                 OPPORTUNIST
                  (out loud)
          Parked it round the corner.

                    WOMAN
                  (grinning)
          Right, well... let's go in then,
                  shall we?

                 OPPORTUNIST
                    Sure.

The woman goes up the steps to her house
and The Opportunist watches her.

          OPPORTUNIST (CONT'D) (V.O.)
             (internalised thoughts)
     I wonder if I can hold out any longer.
     Waiting for the right time, the perfect
        opportunity. I don't know how much
          longer I can keep up the pretense.
       Touching her... 'loving' her. When all
             I really want to do is...
                  (beat)
     How much longer before she discovers
       who I really am? Before she sees
              through my masquerade?

She opens the door with a key and beckons
him with a crooked finger.

OPPORTUNIST (CONT'D)
And I follow, as I've followed her all
night. As I have done for weeks now.
And I know the opportunity will arise
soon. It has to. Maybe tonight. Maybe
not...

He trails her inside, into the blackness.

OPPORTUNIST (CONT'D)
But it will be soon.

THE END

THE BACKGROUND TO...
THE OPPORTUNITY

I'm not entirely sure where the inspiration for this story came from, but I've always enjoyed crime fiction and especially anything serial killer-related. I adored *Manhunter* and *The Silence of the Lambs*, so it was probably wanting to do something along those lines but really getting inside the killer's head (hence the monologue) and providing a twist at the end you – hopefully – don't see coming.

It wasn't in the first wave of stories I was writing and sending off to places, most of those were horror or dark fantasy tales like 'Shadow Writer' or 'Astral'; a lot of which ended up in my first collections *Alone (In the Dark)* and *Touching the Flame*. But it was definitely in the second or third batch of them I was working on, and by that time I'd come across a magazine called *Hidden Corners* that was looking for exactly this kind of thing and I'd become friends with its editor Graeme Hurry. Gritty urban stuff essentially, really downbeat. I sold him 'The Protégé' as well, which is another really short crime tale. Both of those ended up in my 2008 collection *Peripheral Visions* from Creative Guy Publishing, which had quite a fraught history itself and went through a few incarnations – but that's another story.

Author of the Bryant and May series, the late, great Christopher Fowler kindly agreed to pen the introduction to *Visions* and said of this story in particular: 'For me one of the most successful tales in this book is "The Opportunity", a short character sketch which owes its powerful punch to a natural marriage of inner thought and outer deed. Trust me, this is a lot harder than it looks.' I'll never be able to thank him enough for those kind words.

When I was thinking about getting back into scripting, after about ten years of not writing any since an introductory course in it at university, this one seemed like an obvious choice because it was something that could be filmed on a small-ish budget (though this ended up being about £2,000 thanks to the generosity of some of the investors) and might do well on the festival circuit. It's also outside, so although it would have to be made on location there wouldn't be any expensive sets involved.

I was teaching a Creative Writing course around the time that *Visions* came out and I was also tinkering with the script for *The Opportunity*. I happened to mention it to one of my students who's also an actress, Clare Coleman. She was going out with a director at the time called Lewis Copson, who'd made some stuff and was interested in seeing the script. One thing led to another and soon Lewis was gathering a team of very talented cast and crew, with Clare in the lead of the girl walking through the streets being stalked. Some of the other people involved went on to have careers in the industry as well, most notably associate producer/sound man Dominic Burns who directed *Cut, Alien Uprising* and *Allies*.

Filming was set to take place at the beginning of 2009 in Matlock (known for its baths and Gulliver's Kingdom, the guys taking advantage of the cable cars there for some of the aerial shots). And around my birthday in February, myself and my better half Marie O'Regan were invited to a night-shoot, which was all very exciting. We got to see the scene where the dog, played by Mitzi, is being walked and senses someone is hiding behind a wall.

Even more exciting was the fact that for post-production singer Stephen Coates from the band The Real Tuesday Weld, was doing the voiceover of The Opportunist himself! And a superb job he made of it as well. When everything was finished, Lewis, Dominic and DP Ed 'ET' Williams took the film to Cannes where it premiered in the Short Film Corner. We even had a screening at the writing class when we were covering scripting. I couldn't have been more delighted with this and the end result, and want to take the opportunity myself (see what I did there?) to thank everyone again for all their hard work.

Oh, and in case you're wondering where you can watch the film, the DVD of it was included in the hardback edition of my crime/psychological terror collection *Nailbiters*, which came out in 2017 from Black Shuck Books (https://black-shuckbooks.co.uk/nailbiters/) and included an introduction from my old mate Paul Finch, bestselling author of books like *Stalkers*, *Stolen*, *One Eye Open* and *Never Seen Again*. It also screened as part of the line-up for HorrorConUK 2023 alongside a live interview with myself, as well as a screening of *Life-O-Matic* and the trailer for the feature *Sacrifice*.

Director Lewis Copson, just before filming.

Mitzi the dog actor guarding The Opportunity *storyboards.*

Storyboard detail.

Storyboard detail.

The main cast (from left to right), Catherine Prout, Daniel Gough, Clare Coleman and Andrew Dennis just prior to filming.

Paul's wife Marie O'Regan (middle) at the night shoot while Paul discusses a scene with Clare at the back.

Lewis and Clare on location

Dog walker Andrew Dennis (left) with Clare.

Director Lewis and DP Ed 'ET' Williams.

Cast and crew shot.

Stephen Coates in the studio recording The Opportunist's voiceover

The Cannes Short Film Corner logo.

At the Cannes Short Film Corner.

Lewis with soundman/associate producer Dominic Burns at The Opportunity premiere.

The launch of the first Nailbiters collection, at the Quad in Derby March 2017

The DVD in the back of the hardback edition of Nailbiters.

HorrorConUK in Sheffield, May 2023 where The Opportunity *screened.*

The HorrorConUK film room.

The crowds at HorrorConUK 2023

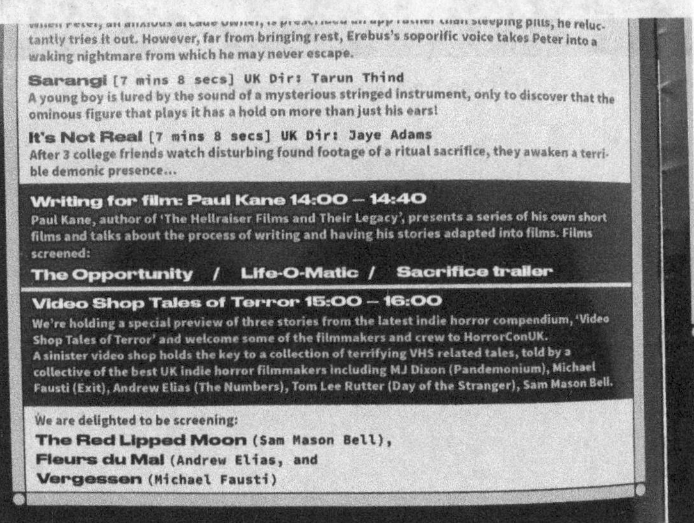

When Peter, an anxious arcade owner, is prescribed an app rather than sleeping pills, he reluctantly tries it out. However, far from bringing rest, Erebus's soporific voice takes Peter into a waking nightmare from which he may never escape.

Sarangi [7 mins 8 secs] UK Dir: Tarun Thind
A young boy is lured by the sound of a mysterious stringed instrument, only to discover that the ominous figure that plays it has a hold on more than just his ears!

It's Not Real [7 mins 8 secs] UK Dir: Jaye Adams
After 3 college friends watch disturbing found footage of a ritual sacrifice, they awaken a terrible demonic presence...

Writing for film: Paul Kane 14:00 – 14:40
Paul Kane, author of 'The Hellraiser Films and Their Legacy', presents a series of his own short films and talks about the process of writing and having his stories adapted into films. Films screened:

The Opportunity / Life-O-Matic / Sacrifice trailer

Video Shop Tales of Terror 15:00 – 16:00
We're holding a special preview of three stories from the latest indie horror compendium, 'Video Shop Tales of Terror' and welcome some of the filmmakers and crew to HorrorConUK.
A sinister video shop holds the key to a collection of terrifying VHS related tales, told by a collective of the best UK indie horror filmmakers including MJ Dixon (Pandemonium), Michael Fausti (Exit), Andrew Elias (The Numbers), Tom Lee Rutter (Day of the Stranger), Sam Mason Bell.

We are delighted to be screening:
The Red Lipped Moon (Sam Mason Bell),
Fleurs du Mal (Andrew Elias, and
Vergessen (Michael Fausti)

Paul in the HorrorConUK programme.

The Opportunity *screening to a packed audience.*

Poster Artwork by Mark Welser

CREDITS

Director – Mark Steensland
Screenplay – Paul Kane (based on his short story)
Executive Producer – Richard Chizmar
Producers – Mark Steensland, Rick Hautala, Lisa Knight
Associate Producers – Chuck Knight, Jeremy Korwek
Editor – Eden Lewis
Special Effects – Mark Kosobucki
Sound – Eden Lewis
Music – Original score by Fabio Frizzi

CAST

Stephen Geoffreys – Harry
Melissa Bostaph – The Weeping Woman
The Children – Fable Bostaph, Sagan Bostaph, Ben Steensland
Kristin Steensland – Harry's Wife.

THE WEEPING WOMAN

THE SHORT STORY

> 'Come not, when I am dead,
> To drop thy foolish tears upon my grave,
> To trample round my fallen head,
> And vex the unhappy dust thou wouldst not
> save.'
>
> — TENNYSON

Well, what could I do? What would you have done in my position? The same thing, unless you're totally heartless.

The woman was right there in the middle of the road. I damned near ran her over myself. If I hadn't had my wits about me she'd have been a red smear on the tarmac. As it turned out, I managed to avoid her, wrestling the Volvo onto an embankment and killing the engine. Thank God there were no vehicles behind me.

That was the first chance I got to look at her properly – before, she was just a blurry shape heading for the bonnet of my car. I guessed she was about forty-five, forty-six tops. Her tawny hair was wild about her head, with leaves and bits of grass clinging to the strands for dear life. As she staggered closer I could see her face was dirty, but floods of tears had struggled through the grime to create a few clean tracks. The patterned dress she wore was ripped in several places.

I got out of the driver's seat, my hands still shaking because of the shock I guess, and was all set to give her a mouthful of the foulest language ever conceived, when I saw the blood. That is, I assumed it was blood. Maroon splotches on her forehead, and as she turned I saw more of the liquid running down her arms. She had no shoes on, either; her feet had been cut to ribbons by the rough terrain.

But that crying noise she made was the worst. I'd never heard such pain in a person's voice before. She was virtually hysterical. Each fresh burst of wailing sliced right through me.

I went up to her. Gripping the woman by the shoulders and looking directly into her eyes, I asked: "Are you all right?" Okay, so that was a stupid thing to say – it was obvious she was far from all right. But I didn't know how else to approach her.

She took a second or so to calm down and speak, though even then the words were almost drowned out by her howling and watery coughs. 'My... Oh Lord... my children... they're..."

She broke down in my arms at this point, waving her hands over to the woods on our right.

"What's happened? Has there been an accident?" The woman carried on sobbing into my shirt. I couldn't get any more sense out of her. I looked up and down the road but didn't see any other cars. Not surprising really, as I'd chosen this route specifically for its lack of traffic. I don't own a mobile, either (can't abide them – unlike the rest of the known world apparently), otherwise it would've been a simple enough matter to call for help. And public phones? Forget it. They were as rare as tower blocks in these parts.

I had no choice. The woman was clearly distraught and her children were in trouble. Placing my arm around her shoulder, I urged her to show me the way...

We walked through the woods a fair stretch, the lady still upset but relaxing a little now that I was in tow. The trees were huge in that place: twisting, gnarly trunks which spawned offspring the higher they went. I recognised the leaves as the same ones she had in her hair.

On the way I started to wonder what might be ahead. Had the family been in a car crash on the other side of the thicket? Perhaps her husband – or partner, I couldn't see a ring – had hit a tree on some deserted lane and she'd been the only person who could scramble out of the wreckage. Her natural instinct would be to find a main road and bring back help. Unfortunately, I was the only person on it at the time.

Then again, she never mentioned a car. Just because she looked like she'd been in an accident, it didn't necessarily follow that she had. Maybe some lunatic had attacked her and her kids while they were out walking, I thought. You read about it all the time in the papers.

I tried asking her again, but she was clearly more interested in getting us both there quickly. A new sense of urgency had taken hold of her. The further we went, the more she would pull on my arm, yanking me onwards. Faster, faster through the lush surroundings.

Until at last we came to the spot.

I saw the bodies from quite a distance away, covered in the same gooey substance as her. Panic raised its ugly head as the weeping woman dragged me nearer and nearer. How could I possibly help them? What had I been thinking? I was no doctor; I'd never even taken a first aid course.

Still, I couldn't let her see that I was scared. She was in a bad enough state as it was without feeding off my anxiety. Actually, the more steps I took the easier it became. A morbid curiosity was overpowering my fears. I needed to see what had happened to her family. A warped compulsion you might say, but a very human one.

When I got there, I found the price of my curiosity too high.

Three corpses in various states of disarray were splayed out on the grass, stripped naked as far as I could tell; it was hard to determine exactly because of all the mess. One was missing its head, a young lad I think. Another was gutted from neck to abdomen, ribs bared, the inside of its belly scooped out, leaving only one or two coils of intestine dangling from the wound. And the last, a woman, had had her limbs removed: torn from their sockets in a vicious, clumsy way.

The dinner I'd eaten at a *Happy Traveller* ten miles back chose that moment to reappear. Doubled over, I spewed the half-digested baked potato onto the ground.

"My children!" screamed the weeping woman, pointing in their direction.

I heaved again, but there was nothing left in my stomach.

"What...?" I started, desperately trying to understand why she'd brought me here. These people were dead, surely she could see that! We should have gone for the police in my car. Or had this happened while she'd been to fetch me? Was the maniac who'd done it still around?

Then I noticed she was pointing not to the bodies, but rather at the woodland beyond. "My children," she repeated in her phlegmy tones.

From behind the trees, springing up from the grass, and swinging down from branches they came: emerging from their hiding places. Strange, embryonic things – dozens of them – with long arms and vitreous flesh. Tufts of tawny hair stood to attention on bulging heads, their eyes little more than dimples beneath thick, curving brows. A split ran from ear to ear on each of them. Mouths that could open much wider than any animal's...

And smothered in blood.

They were on me in a heartbeat. The larger ones held the

others back, like birds after the best crusts of bread. Some of the babies even had to make do with the puddle of vomit on the ground, slurping it up with enormous silvery tongues.

I felt sharp teeth ripping into my legs, my arms. Clawing fingernails digging at my stomach. A couple of my punches hit their mark, but ultimately there were too many of the abominations to tackle.

I fell on my side, a mass of chattering forms all over me. But through the gaps I saw the woman who had led me – no, *lured* me – here. She was still weeping, crying a deluge of tears. Yet I could see a difference.

These were tears of joy and pride. A mother's love for her children.

Happy now that she had once again provided for her young.

The Weeping Woman
Written by Paul Kane
Based on the short story by Paul Kane

<u>EXT. COUNTRY ROAD - DAY.</u>

A typical British summer in the countryside: a slight breeze, birds singing
happily. We see a tiny car approaching on a
distant country road, and close in as it
weaves its way along the winding lanes,
surrounded on either side by fields.

Closer in on the car, a silver estate - a
family car. It's not going very fast, the
driver obviously cautious and taking his
time. Gradually, as the car comes closer
into view, we see more of the man behind
the wheel from the outside: mid-thirties,
hair receding, wearing a shirt and tie.

                                    CUT TO:

<u>INT. CAR - DAY.</u>

Inside the car now and we get a closer look
at the man - he has the beginnings of a
paunch, he looks happy enough though, like
he's on his way back home from work. He's
concentrating on the road, but wipes his
forehead with the back of his hand. There's
a suit jacket already discarded on the
passenger seat.

From a different angle we see, over his
shoulder, that there's an empty child's car
seat in the back. This is obviously not his
usual work car.

Hot, he winds down the window and pulls at the tie —undoing the top button as he does so.

Looking down, he switches on the radio, pushing in the CD that's sticking out. It begins to play a children's nursery song. He chuckles and ejects the CD, bending over to fiddle with the radio itself.

A pop track from the '80s comes on — his era — and he begins to tap on the steering wheel.

CUT TO:

<u>EXT. COUNTRY ROAD – DAY.</u>

We see the car travelling down a slightly wider country lane, heading into a section with trees on either side. We can still hear the pop music, but then it starts to cut out.

CUT TO:

<u>INT. CAR – DAY.</u>

The man bends again, fiddling with the radio to try and get a station. It throws back static.

When he looks up again, through the wind-screen, the way ahead is clear.

He bends and fiddles with the radio again.

This time when he looks up, there's a
figure in the middle of the road. It's
appeared out of nowhere, and we cut away
before we can see it properly.

                    MAN
                   Shit!

He grits his teeth, stamping on the brakes.

                                    CUT TO:

<u>EXT. COUNTRY ROAD - DAY.</u>

We see the car skidding, see how close it
is to the figure. This is all happening
very quickly, adrenaline pumping for the
driver and the audience alike.

We hear the sound of the tires screeching.

                                    CUT TO:

<u>INT. CAR - DAY.</u>

Back to the man as he's still wrestling
with the wheel, his face a rictus of fear.

                                    CUT TO:

<u>EXT. COUNTRY ROAD - DAY.</u>

We see over the shadowy shoulder of the
figure that the car has come to a stop,
only a few feet away. The driver's door

opens and we hear the raised voice even
before we see the man.

ANGLE ON:

                    MAN
        What the bloody hell do you think
                    you're—

The driver as his mouth drops open, his
face switching from angry to concerned in a
flash. And now we see why.

ANGLE ON:

The figure, from the driver's point of
view, starting at the ground and panning
upwards. We see two bare feet, then a
ripped, patterned dress, with blood splattered across the front here and there.

When we get to her face, we see she's about
forty-ish, and her tawny hair is a tangled
mess with bits of grass and leaves in it.
Her face is smeared with dirt, tracked by
the tears she's been crying... and is still
crying. She's distraught. There's blood on
her forehead, too.

When she reaches out a hand, her fingers
are quivering. There are more blood
splotches on her arms.
                    MAN
      Oh my God... Are... Are you all right?

ANGLE ON:

The man's face as he shakes his head, knowing it was a stupid thing to say — the woman's pretty far from all right. To make matters worse, he continues with his idiotic line of questioning:

                    MAN
          What's happened... Has someone...?

                 WEEPING WOMAN
          My... Oh Lord... My children...

                    MAN
          Jesus. Look, what's going on? Has there
               been an accident or something?

He's looking past her, trying to see if there's been a car crash. At the same time he's closing the car door behind him, tentatively coming closer, shocked: but aware that she's desperate for help.

He covers the remaining distance between them.

                 WEEPING WOMAN
          My... my children...

She moves forward now, collapsing into his arms. He holds her, awkwardly at first, then tighter. Then he stands her upright as gently as he can, holding her by the shoulders.

                    MAN
        Hold on... Wait here and I'll call
                  someone.

The woman nods, still crying, as he
retreats to the car. He fishes a phone out
of his jacket pocket.

ANGLE ON:

The phone, with its wallpaper a family shot
of him, his wife and their boy. There's no
signal at all. He holds up the phone,
trying to get one, even walks a little way
down the road.

Nothing.

He looks around, trying to see either
another car or a phone box. He sighs,
looking back over at the crying woman.

                    MAN
          I can't... There's no—

                WEEPING WOMAN
          Please! My children...

She looks towards the wooded area off the
road.

                    MAN
          Look, I can't just...

                    WEEPING WOMAN
                    (more desperate)
                    <u>My children!</u>

The man glances into the back of his car,
at the child's seat. He locks the vehicle
with his key-fob, running over to the
woman, who's now hobbling, obviously struggling to walk. He takes her arm and puts it
around his shoulder.

                         MAN
          Come on then. Show me...

                                        CUT TO:

<u>EXT. WOODS - DAY.</u>

Montage of the pair walking through the
woods, deeper and deeper, past tall,
gnarly, twisting trees. The sun has been
shut out by them, creating a creepier
atmosphere.

                         MAN
          I wish you'd just talk to me, tell me
                what happened to you.

The woman, still crying, says nothing - she
simply points up ahead of her. Then she's
grabbing at his shirt, tugging at it to try
and get him to follow.

                         MAN
                Okay, okay...

More walking through the foliage, to reach:

<u>EXT. CLEARING - DAY.</u>

The man suddenly stops — while the woman
hobbles on ahead slightly, momentum
carrying her forward.

He puts a hand to his mouth.

ANGLE ON:

His point of view, and we see what look
like two or three bodies in the distance,
partially covered by the foliage. From this
far it's difficult to tell what age they
were. A hand juts up out of the grass like
a living flower.

The woman is still hobbling on ahead, and
now she turns, beckoning him.

                    WEEPING WOMAN
             (still crying, pointing ahead)
           Please... Please, my children...

Reluctantly, the man follows her to where
the bodies are.

ANGLE ON:

The man's face as he gets closer and sees
more of the two bodies. He clamps that hand
to his mouth now and we soon see why as
we're shown...

ANGLE ON:

Quick flashes of the corpses, half-eaten
body parts:

The hand that was jutting up, bitten into
halfway down; flies buzz around the wound.

The stump of a neck, the head missing.

A foot in the grass, three of the toes
bitten off, the edges of the wounds ragged.
Internal organs dragged out of a stomach
and scattered.

ANGLE ON:

The man again, who now promptly bends over
and throws up just out of sight. We hear
retching and heaving noises, until there's
nothing left.

When he straightens, the Weeping Woman is
still pointing to the scene, still urging
him to come forward and help.

                    WEEPING WOMAN
                    My children...

                    MAN
            (trying not to be sick again)
                    What...?

> WEEPING WOMAN
> (insistent and nodding towards the
> corpses)
> My children.

> MAN
> I... These people are...

The man looks to the left and the right, over his shoulder. The woman is wailing now, as if crying for the dead.

> MAN
> I can't do anything... They're dead. Don't you understand? Look, we need to get out of here.
> (beat)
> Who did this? Are they still around?

> WEEPING WOMAN
> My children.

She nods a final time and now we follow that nod. Out into the trees, things are stirring in the undergrowth.

ANGLE ON:

Something small, moving fast through the tall grass. Something else up in the trees.

The man looks left, right, above, following the rustling. It's everywhere and nowhere; all around him.

                         MAN
                        What—?

Suddenly the things begin to appear,
springing out of the grass, swinging down
from the trees.

We see one of the 'children' more clearly
now: animalistic, strange, embryonic, with
crooked, razor-sharp teeth.

Another joins this one — then one more on
its other side. They all have tufts of
tawny-coloured hair like their mother.

They open their mouths, as wide and
disturbing as a snake dislocating its jaw.

ANGLE ON:

The man's face — terrified,
uncomprehending.

                         MAN
             I don't... I don't understa—

ANGLE ON:

The Weeping Woman, still crying, but
smiling a weird smile.

                    WEEPING WOMAN
                   (matter of factly)
                    My children.

They leap at the man from all angles, small
flashes of things. He goes down in a heap
and we cut away, only hearing the tearing
and ripping sounds as they kill their next
victim.

We pan back round to the Weeping Woman,
still crying — but these tears are
different.

She's smiling broadly now; the tears are of
pride and happiness at having provided for
her offspring once again.

END CREDITS

THE BACKGROUND TO...
THE WEEPING WOMAN

Like 'The Opportunity' this was one of the second or third clutch of short stories I was writing in the late '90s/early 2000s, when I was just finding my feet. It was inspired by the old urban legends about a driver seeing a woman by the side of the road. I think I'd just reviewed a book about those, plus I'm almost certain someone had been talking about them at a Terror Scribes do I attended; a group of us writers used to get together periodically in a pub (I know, shocker!) and chat about all things horror.

The legend usually goes that a lone, usually male, driver spots a girl standing by the side of the road in a lonely location after the sun's gone down. Fearing for her safety out there all alone, he pulls over and offers her a lift to get home. When they arrive there, he either looks in the rear view or turns around, only to find the girl has vanished. So, essentially, a ghost story.

Me being me, I wanted to do something a bit different.

I'm also a fan of scary kids in books and films, *The Omen* being a prime example. Then again, he is the Antichrist, so what do you expect? The aspects of this story involving the children were probably more influenced by David

Cronenberg's *The Brood* than anything (I've just recently completed a rewatch of all his movies, and as much as I like his later stuff, the early Body Horror entries are always going to be my favourites).

The Weeping Woman in my tale is very much alive, standing there to try and lure said lone driver into the woods where her children can feast. And in the story I describe them as sort of mutated vampire-like things, although the short film that followed brings them back more to the Cronenbergian monsters, which actually are more terrifying when you think about it.

It's a very short short, written for the second *Terror Tales* e-magazine back in 2000, when email was only just getting going. The e-mag was sort of our testing ground for the *TT* website that followed, created by John B. Ford and Simon Logan. It bridged the gap between the small press print magazine and that website, if you see what I mean. Anyway, this size of story was perfect for that format.

I was also very keen to see it published traditionally, however, so with that in mind I figured I'd include it in the line-up of my first ever collection *Alone (In the Dark)* from BJM Press, which appeared in the January of the following year. I even drew a black and white picture to go with it, which you'll find in this book (*Alone* is pretty rare now and quite hard to come by, just to warn you). The story's also been reprinted a couple of times, including in the 10th Anniversary special hardback edition of *Alone* & *Touching the Flame – Shadow Writer* – and the British Fantasy Award-nominated collection *Monsters* from Alchemy Press.

And, again, like 'The Opportunity' when I was looking for tales to adapt into short film scripts that would work on a micro-budget, this one stood out. It's a location shoot, the same as that one – this time out by a road and in a wood – and only requires two main actors, plus the monster kids. The only problem I could see would be the make-ups for those children, and remember this was before CGI was readily available at home. Another reason to make them more humanoid... The script, as you'll have seen, retains the English countryside setting of Spring or Summer, but when this was picked up to be made both those aspects changed. Plus the driver, the Man as I called him in the script, was even given a name: Harry.

Which brings me neatly to how all that came about. Sometime around 2009 when I was thinking about what the next short film would be after *The Opportunity*, I came across a movie on YouTube called *Peekers*, based on the tale of the same name by Kealan Patrick Burke. It had been directed by Mark Steensland and adapted by the late and greatly missed Rick Hautala – and it was disturbing as f**k. I couldn't stop thinking about it afterwards; if you get the chance, go and watch it, but don't expect to get much sleep afterwards.

And so I thought to myself, I've *got* to work with these guys! Mark and Rick had a production company called Chang Shao Trading, so I got in touch and was delighted to receive a very kind and positive reply back. Mark asked to see a few scripts, I believe, but was especially taken by this one – asking if he could transport the action to snowy Waterford Township, Michigan, where they'd film, whilst still retaining the core of the idea and narrative. I had absolutely no problem with that. Over the years I've become less precious about changes that have to be made for audio, film, TV, theatre or comics. It's part and parcel of transferring something from one medium to another, and the original stories are always going to be there for people to read. If anything, it'll make them go and seek them out. Obviously, in this book they're presented together so you don't have to...

When I said yes and signed the contract, Mark basically went off and did the rest, with him, Rick and Lisa Knight producing, and Cemetery Dance's Rich Chizmar as exec producer. To my amazement, they got Tony award-nominee Stephen Geoffreys – from one of my all-time favourite '80s horror flicks, *Fright Night* – to come and play the driver, Harry. Melissa Bostaph, who has since become a friend and tells me that she very often gets recognised for the role, took on The Weeping Woman herself, turning 'My Children, My Children!' into something of a catchphrase (it even ended up on the poster – designed by Mark Welser – and promotional badges). Melissa's children and Mark's kids were also enlisted to play the little monsters, with Mark's wife Kristin playing Harry's spouse at home.

Honestly, the whole thing happened so quickly I don't think there was more than a few weeks between the green-light and having a cut of the movie to show me. The icing on the cake, though, was the involvement of long-time Fulci collaborator Fabio Frizzi, who turned in a perfect score. If you'd have told me when I was a kid watching *Zombie Flesh Eaters* and *The Beyond*, that something I'd written would have music from Fabio I'd have fainted right there on the spot. And by the way, that music also ended up on CD and Fabio is still playing it at his packed out concerts today!

I can still recall how surreal it was to be watching a local news report on Jet-TV over there about the filming, where they mentioned it was written by me. I was with Marie, watching it on the computer, and you couldn't wipe the smile from my face.

The movie premiered at Motor City Nightmares in Detroit, April 2011, which Mark and Stephen attended, and got some really nice feedback from people like Mick Garris, director of *The Stand* miniseries and *Sleepwalkers* ('Paul Kane's twisty and twisted tale is brought to the screen in a faithful and frightening adaptation.') and *Child's Play* director Tom Holland ('*The Weeping Woman* is terrific, an entertaining movie.'), and was even reviewed *by Ain't It Cool*! Doesn't get much better than that.

Mark has, of course, gone on to huge things – writing *Jacob's Wife*, for example, starring the wonderful Barbara

Crampton (who coincidentally starred in *Sacrifice* based on my novelette 'Men of the Cloth' that same year) – but I'll always be grateful to him for having faith in this one. He and Rick also hired me to adapt Graham Masterton's famous horror novel *Tengu* into a feature, which didn't really go anywhere in the end but gave me lots of experience. I'm still using that step outline technique to this day for writing scripts.

A DVD of the film itself was produced to go in the hard-back of the aforementioned *Monsters* collection, which fitted very snugly on the inside back cover.

Director Mark Steensland discusses a shot with Stephen Geoffreys as Harry.

Stephen and Melissa Bostaph performing a scene.

Melissa Bostaph in costume as The Weeping Woman.

A close-up of Melissa as The Weeping Woman.

Tony award-winning actor Stephen Geoffreys.

Melissa looks on as the titular Weeping Woman.

Fabio Frizzi composing the score.

Fabio with engineer Giuseppe.

The CD of the music from The Weeping Woman.

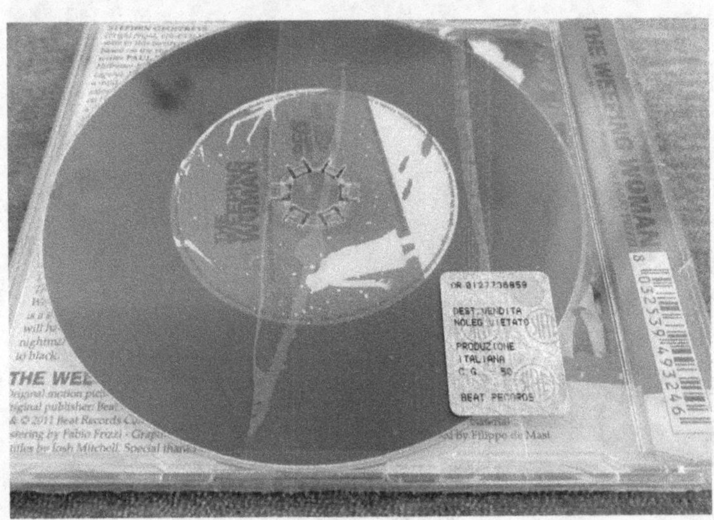

The score on CD.

The Weeping Woman *premiering at Motor City Nightmares in Detroit.*

Stephen Geoffreys (left) and Mark Steensland (right, at the mic) talking about and introducing the movie.

Promotional badges produced for the film with the Weeping Woman's catchphrase on them.

CREDITS

Director: Brad Watson
Screenplay: Paul Kane (based on his short story)
Producer: Brad Watson
Cinematography: John Attwell
First Assistant Director: Michael Watson
Editor: Brad Watson
Art Direction: Heather Winship
Design Consultant: Kay Brown
Costume Design/Stylist/Wardrobe: Caroline Garcia Stauffer
Make-Up Supervisor : Amy Playford
Original Music/Music Department/Main Theme: Brad
Watson

CAST

Robert Carratta: Jon
Joanna Ignaczewska: Anya

WIND CHIMES
THE SHORT STORY

Sunday morning and the city is still asleep.

As he walks down the litter-strewn street, beer cans and bottles from the night before adorning its gutters, he encounters very few people. There is a noticeable lack of traffic on the main road, only one or two cars passing him by as he reaches those familiar wrought iron gates, the black paint peeling with age.

The pathway which runs down the centre of the park stretches out like a duller version of the Yellow Brick Road, and with considerably less promise. The grass on either side is neatly-trimmed and a young couple, arm-in-arm, wearing matching coats and scarves, are throwing a ball for their Labrador to the left of him. Ignoring the laughter, he hunches down in his dark greatcoat and cuts across the sea of green.

He hasn't been walking long when he comes across the place he's looking for, right where it always is. The stone markers are planted in rows, with just enough of a gap between each to allow people to walk down them. Some are large, some small; some are plain crosses or squares, others boasting carved angels playing trumpets. Many are weathered, time and the seasons doing their worst. On the oldest, the names are only just recognisable. On the new, all too legible.

When the rest of the city finally wakes, breaking into the routine of another lazy weekend day, these people will not. They will never wake again.

There are trees scattered here and there, as if to show that even in this place of death and mourning, there is new life. Yet, on this mid-Autumn day, the leaves have begun their descent from their branches, to gather at the trunks, to be swirled around by the light breeze.

He carries on through the graveyard, barely glancing at these. He's heading for another section, one which is separated from the rest by another pathway. There is more colour here, to break up the greys and blacks. Splashes of reds, pinks and whites, where flowers have been left. But the plots are so much smaller than the ones across the way. No massive headstones; just tiny plaques.

The little rectangular graves are covered with cream and brown pebbles. A few have miniature fences around them, others latticed stone or marble marking off individual plots. But more than anything it is the toys that give the game away. Stuffed teddy bears, model cars and trucks, a doll's house lovingly painted (though now more than a little the worse for wear). Then the inscriptions: 'You'll always live on in our memories. Love forever, Mummy and Daddy.'; 'For a special little girl.'; 'You're only a thought away.' The dates show the oldest only to be about three or four.

Jon Cassidy knows them all too well, but doesn't read them anymore. He can't. Not because he's unfeeling, but because he can only hold so much sorrow in his heart. And that has been reserved for one very special plot.

In the relative shade of an oak tree he pauses, stands with his head bowed. Jon takes the small bunch of orange and yellow flowers he has been clutching and places them on the grave, next to a rattle. If there was anyone around to witness this, they would no doubt comment on his pallid skin, his sunken eyes – dry, because there were no more tears left to shed – the way his lip is trembling. Especially as he reads the writing on the plaque there: 'Emma Louise Cassidy. One year was all the time we had.'

More leaves fall from the tree above him, raining down, but he doesn't take any notice. It is only when a sound comes from above that he looks up. There, hanging on one of the branches, is a collection of wind chimes. There are baubles, stars, one even in the shape of a tear – made from glass and silver that catches the early sunlight. But one stands out from the rest, lengths of metal dangling from a brass-coloured angel, more cherubic-looking than any of those in the main graveyard, which looks down sadly on him. It makes a distinctive sound, a tinkling seemingly louder than any of the others.

And when he sees this, Jon realises there are still tears left. There always will be. Eyes wet, and brushing away the consequences with the back of his hand, he whispers, "I'm sorry."

Head bowed again, he begins the long trek back though the graveyard. Gravity feels denser, his body aches. When he reaches the park he finds that families are now gathering. Children play with Frisbees, mothers and fathers cheer them on. It should hurt to see them, but he simply shivers. He feels cold.

In his own way, Jon is just as dead as the corpses buried behind him.

That night Jon sits alone in his flat.

The living room is a shrine to the god Detritus. Around the

armchair where he is slumped lies the evidence of how he has been living his life: the crisp packets, the cans of beer, the empty pizza boxes smeared with grease, bugs crawling in and out and feasting on the leftover food inside.

A snapshot, a moment in time. Taken at *another* time, in another place, it would have been so different. Like the one in the frame on the table next to him, beside the half-empty bottle of malt. Jon and a woman with blonde hair, his arm around her as she holds a bundle of blankets. And just visible, poking out of the top, a round, pink face, features screwed up, eyes barely open. Jon, his shirt untucked and a glass of brown liquid in his hand, picks up the frame and traces the woman's face with his finger, then the baby's.

Jon puts down the photo and picks up his cordless phone. Though he has the number on speed-dial, he presses the buttons anyway with his thumb. Jon remembers the number. After all, it used to be his own.

It rings several times before the phone at the other end is picked up. "Hello," echoes a woman's voice, slightly muffled. "Claire… Claire, it's me."

There's a painful silence and then: "You've got to stop doing this, Jon."

"I—"

"What do you want?" The edge to her voice sends shivers down his spine. He can remember a time when it did exactly the same, but they were pleasurable tingles, more often than not accompanied by colourful winged insects flapping around in his stomach. Today there's just a heavy weight inside there.

"To talk."

Claire sighs. "We've done all our talking. Now I just want you to leave me alone." Yes, leave her alone so that she could pretend none of this had ever happened, that they'd never even met, let alone…

"Please, listen…" Jon's words are a little slurred.

"Have you been drinking?"

Jon stares down at the glass. "A bit."

"For Christ's sake. I'm going now."

"Please don't."

He hears the sound of a scuffle down the phone line, then another voice, a man's voice. *Him*. Jon's replacement in her warped parallel universe. "Give me that. You heard what she said. Claire's moved on. She's trying to make a new life for herself… I suggest you do the same."

There's a loud click as the phone is slammed down on its cradle. An indifferent *burrrrr* wafts over the line: it's dead. Jon lets the phone drop from his grasp, then drains the rest of the whiskey from his glass. He looks down at the photograph, picks it up, and throws it across the room. There's a tinkling sound as it hits the wall. Jon begins to cry again, uncontrollably this time.

When he finally goes over to retrieve the photo – after waking in the middle of the night, soaked in sweat from his alcohol-induced coma – Jon sees a huge spider's web crack across the glass.

It stems from Claire and Emma.

The days blend into each other, but he is back at the grave again soon.

This time, just up from the tree – second row along, at the end – Jon notices another figure out of the corner of his eye. He looks more closely: it's a crouching woman dressed in a black coat, grey skirt, visiting one of the graves. Jon watches as she mirrors his own actions, laying flowers on the top. They are the only two people around in the children's graveyard, the only two who can take such a depressing place this early. Or maybe the only two who have nowhere else to go.

In the end, it doesn't really matter to Jon. He returns his

gaze to Emma's grave. When he happens to look up again, the woman is gone.

There's a slight breeze and above him the wind chimes jangle, the angel still looking down pitifully on him.

The distinctive tinkling sound reaches his ears.

―――――――

That night Jon arrives back at his flat, ignoring his angry landlady who wants to talk to him about the rent increase. He brandishes his bottle in the brown paper bag like a weapon, St George seeing off the fiery dragon. His landlady warns him that she won't put up with that kind of behaviour forever; one of these days he'll come back and find that the locks have been changed. Jon climbs the stairs and says nothing. It doesn't bother him if he's sleeping in a shop doorway by this time next week.

Jon enters his flat, kicking aside the carpet that has ridged up. When he passes the answerphone in the hall he sees that the red light is flashing. *Maybe it's her...* he thinks, clutching at straws. *Maybe she's changed her mind. Maybe we can start over, work through the problems?* He's willing if she is.

Eagerly, Jon presses the button and it beeps. When he hears the deep, throaty voice, his heart sinks again. "Jon, it's Michael. Look, I know you've been going through a lot and I sympathise, I really do. It's just that we're really going to need those completed proofs soon. Otherwise it could mean—"

Jon presses the button again, turning off the drone. Next he deletes the message. *If only you could do that in the real world – delete then record over the top,* he thinks. Wipe out whatever has made you sad, broken you, left you clinging to the drain for fear of spiralling down it.

It's a nice fantasy, but reality isn't like that – and Jon knows what he has to do to blot that out. He wanders into the kitchen, passing dirty pots piled high in the sink, a half-finished loaf of bread – now rock hard – and a tub of butter with the lid off, and grabs a mug from one of the cupboards overhead. He takes his bottle out of the brown paper bag, pours a generous amount into the mug, and takes a swig.

Jon's shoulders slump. He wonders whether he'll wake at all tomorrow, and thinks it's probably best if he doesn't.

And yet here he is again, back at the graveyard.

It's like he's become stuck in a loop, the plot of some silly science fiction anthology show. The same thing over and over again until it drives him insane. He isn't far away from that now anyway.

At the graveside, Jon is lost in his thoughts. The wind chime – Emma's wind chime – jangles softly above. Jon starts when he hears the voice, but only because he didn't notice the woman approach, didn't even realise she was in the graveyard.

"Oh, I'm sorry," she says when he jumps. "I didn't mean to…"

Jon composes himself, tells her it's okay, that he was miles away. He recognises her as the person he's seen here before, but never up close, never *this* close. She has copper hair which falls in ringlets and grey eyes: a strange combination but one that works remarkably well. He wouldn't describe her as a natural beauty but she certainly has something. Jon can't help but stare. She catches his eye and he looks away.

"It's very beautiful," the woman says.

"I'm sorry?" Jon follows her finger, to the wind chime above Emma's grave.

"I-I was thinking of maybe getting one myself."

Jon nods, unsure of how to respond to this. They lapse into silence. For the longest time nothing is said. The woman's eyes drop to the floor again and she turns as if to walk away and leave him to his thoughts. Suddenly, Jon realises he doesn't want that.

"There's... there's a reason people leave them there," he blurts out.

She stops and turns back towards him. "To remember."

And that's true. She almost gets it, Jon can see that. But the children here will be remembered with or without them. "It's more than that," Jon tells her. "They say when someone..." He pauses, realising what he's going to say will sound really stupid. "No, forget it."

"Go on... please," she encourages him, facing Jon fully now, the wind blowing a strand of that springy copper hair across her face. "I want to know."

"It's just that some people say when someone dies, their spirits drift on the wind."

She comes closer again, even nearer than before – towards the grave.

"And..." Jon continues, "and some say when the wind chimes jangle like that it's as if they're talking to us."

She joins him, then looks up again at the branches. "Do you believe that's true?"

"I don't know. But I like to think so."

She considers this for a moment, cocking her head, listening to the wind chimes – listening to one in particular. "I wonder what they're trying to tell us."

Jon shrugs.

"You're here quite often, aren't you?" she says to him.

"I come as often as I can."

Her eyes fall again, but this time she reads the plaque in front of her, mouthing the inscription. Jon feels a stab of pain in his heart and bites back the tears. He can't lose it now, not here, not in front of this stranger. Better to wait till he gets home again, better to wait till he has a drink in his hand. He grits his teeth, gaining some kind of control over himself.

To deflect the attention away, Jon asks, "The grave down there, is it—"

He sees her stiffen, eyes narrowing.

"I'm sorry. I shouldn't have asked."

Then, almost a whisper, she says, "My son, Joshua."

"I'm really sorry."

She looks at him and he sees that she wasn't being defensive at all; she was trying to fight back the grief, just like him. "So am I... And your daughter... a year. No age at all."

Jon shakes his head. "No. How old was—"

"Four months." Now a tear does escape and trickles down her cheek.

"Jesus," says Jon, not feeling any guilt because of where he is. He finished with religion a long time ago, even before Emma, and in spite of the 'angel' hanging above her (Claire's idea). "So many children. So much pain."

She pulls back from him, readying herself to head off again. "I should be going."

Jon nods and she walks away, casting a single glance over her shoulder. He watches her leave, then something forces him to set off after her.

"Wait!" he calls out, and she stops.

"Yes?"

"Please don't," begs Jon. "Go, I mean."

The force of the plea holds her in place like a tractor beam. They look into each other's eyes and see something of themselves there, the heartache reflected back.

"Would you like a cup of coffee?" he asks her and immediately wishes he hadn't. What is he, fifteen or something?

She bites her lip, then says, "I'm not sure—"

"I thought we could... talk." Jon attempts a smile.

"I really shouldn't."

"Please." That word again, so small but so powerful. She gives a slight tip of the head. They begin walking together, away from the grave and up along the path. "My name's Jon, by the way."

"Abi," the woman replies.

At first the conversation is awkward and stilted. They sit opposite each other at a table in a quiet café, the only other person there an old man in the corner reading his newspaper. Abi has been stirring her tea for about five minutes when he breaks the silence.

"Will someone be waiting for you, then?" Once again, it's the kind of thing that's said and you wish you could take it back instantly. Too nosey, too forward.

Abi comes out of her daze. "Someone…? Oh, I see." She shakes her head. "You?"

"My wife," says Jon, then adds quickly, "ex-wife… Well, she's barely spoken to me since…"

"It happens a lot," states Abi with all the conviction of one it's happened to. "All they can see when they look at you is…"

Jon rubs his forehead. "No, it was my fault, you see. Claire, she was at her sister's for the evening. I should have checked on Em more often. But the monitor was on; I thought it would be all right."

"What happened?" asks Abi, watching him intently.

"Fell asleep, didn't I." Jon slams his fist on the table. "Idiot. Fucking idiot!" He draws the attention of the man in the corner and the waitress, but they both look away when he glances up. "Sorry."

"No need," Abi assures him.

Jon breathes out. "By the time Claire got back it was too late to do anything."

"It wasn't your fault."

Jon jabbed a finger into his chest. "I was the one looking after her."

"Yes, but it could have happened anytime. It *does* happen anytime." Abi gazes into her still swirling teacup. "That's what people kept telling me. Took a long time to realise they were right."

Jon is starting to grasp that they have more in common than he first thought. Not just the end result, but the way.

His voice is softer when he asks, "Joshua?"

Abi nods sombrely. "Tuesday afternoon. 2 o'clock to be precise. God, look, I even know the exact time."

Jon wishes he even had that. But all he has is a rough estimate.

"Joshua was having a nap but… but he never woke up."

"And since then you've blamed yourself, haven't you."

"There was no-one else *to* blame," she snaps. "Mark wasn't even home. He couldn't understand. No one can." Abi cries, the tears running a race down opposite cheeks. Instinctively, Jon reaches out and takes her hand. He squeezes it.

"Not true."

Abi looks at him, her mascara a mess, then she pulls her hand free.

"I have to go."

"Abi—"

She rises swiftly. "Thanks for the coffee, Jon." But before he can stop her she is out through the door, out of his life again. Jon slumps back into his seat and sighs heavily.

Another day, and he is at the graveyard again.

The sky is grey, there's little trace of the sun. If he's honest with himself, he's been coming here the past few days as much in the hopes of seeing Abi again as to visit Emma, though he's loathe to admit it to himself. But she never returned.

Out of curiosity, Jon finds himself at Joshua's grave today. To all intents and purposes, it is just the same as all the others, but the words on the inscription mean something since he has met Abi: 'Joshua Hill. Now at Peace."

He hears the clacking of heeled boots behind him, then Abi's voice: "I can remember the day Joshua was born." He doesn't turn, partly because he doesn't want to scare her off again, partly because he wants to hear this. "Mark was there holding my hand, and his face... I don't think anything could have upset him at that moment. We were a family and... and now, now it's all gone."

When he hears her sobs, Jon has to look around. They're wracking her body, she's almost hunched over with them. He reaches out a hesitant hand, then decides to just put his arms around her. She doesn't resist, but holds onto him like a ship-wrecked sailor might cling to a rock.

"Why did this have to happen to us, Jon? Why is life like this?

"I don't know," he says honestly.

A chill wind blows through them and Abi shivers.

"Come on, let's get you out of the cold." Jon puts an arm around Abi and walks her up towards the park.

The sound of the wind chimes jangling follows them – but one in particular, one louder than the rest.

Jon and Abi sit at the kitchen table, the half-empty bottle of brandy between them, the rest of the space being taken up by papers scattered over the surface. Abi still has her coat on; she is looking around at the state of Jon's kitchen.

"I'm sorry about the... What can I say, I'm a pig."

"I've seen worse." Abi picks up a manuscript from the

table, examining it. Jon takes it off her and tosses it aside. "Is that what you do, write?"

Jon laughs. "I *read*, believe it or not. For a publishing house."

"Sounds interesting."

"It really isn't. They send me all these cheesy romance books. You should see some of it, things that would never happen in a million years." Jon takes a swig of his drink.

"It won't help," she tells him.

"I know, but it dulls the pain for a while."

"Only for a while."

Jon ignores the last comment. "C'mon, drink. It'll do you good."

Abi takes a sip from the mug in front of her. "But it won't bring them back."

"Nothing ever will."

This time it is Abi who reaches across and takes Jon's hand. He looks up, surprised and she gives him the closest thing to a smile he's seen on her lips.

"I think I'd better be going," she tells him, getting to her feet.

"So soon?"

Abi nods. "But I'll see you again. I'm not that hard to find." She walks around the table and kisses him on the cheek. "Thank you."

"For what?"

"For listening. For understanding."

Then she is gone again. He hears the slam of the front door. Jon brings the cup to his lips, his hand hovering there. But he doesn't drink.

In fact he places it back down on the table again.

And it begins from there.

The more he sees of her, the more he wants to. Jon takes her to the café, they walk through the park together, have dinner at Jon's flat – which he makes the effort of cleaning, just for her. They talk, and they talk. If he'd read it in one of the novels they were still sending him to work on, he would have dismissed it as unbelievable. Yet this is his life now, as real as anything he's ever experienced, the joy or the pain. Jon barely notices the passing of the months, but the length of the grass and the flowers in bloom rather than just on the graves tell him it is spring; a time for new beginnings. Even the tree above Emma's grave is now in full leaf.

As they stand there together he ventures, "Abi?"

"Yes?"

"Something's been worrying me."

She looks scared, frightened of what he might say next. "What is it?"

"Do you ever wonder if what we're doing is wrong?"

"Wrong, how?"

He shakes his head, not sure how to explain. "I don't know. It's just… these past few months, with you. I'm starting to feel things I really shouldn't. I'm starting to feel happy again and I don't know if I have the right."

Abi touches his face. "What happened was terrible. There isn't a day goes by when I don't wish I could see Joshua again. But how long can we go on punishing ourselves, Jon?"

"I just can't help thinking—"

"I know." She leans in close to him. "But the alternative scares me so much more. I-I don't want to lose you either."

Then she kisses him softly on the lips. When she pulls away, he promises, "You won't."

That night they make love, their movements slow and loving, comforting even. Outside, the gusts of wind rise and fall to the rhythm of their bodies. When the release comes it's like they've both been waiting for this since their individual tragedies.

And in the distance, though neither of them can hear it, comes the sound of a distinctive jangling.

Jon is reading through one of the manuscripts when Abi knocks on the door to his flat.

She's almost hysterical, and he can't make out what she's trying to say at first. Then he hears the word 'late' and it hits him all at once.

"There's no doubt?"

"I took a test," Abi informs him. "And even if I hadn't I've been throwing up in the mornings. What are we going to do? Jon, I'm scared."

He holds her, feels her trembling. "Shh. Don't love. It's going to be okay. Really, it's all going to be okay."

Jon starts to tremble too.

It all happens so quickly.

Suddenly they are looking at bigger places, discussing mortgages. Abi puts her house on the market, but there's still nothing in their price range without putting themselves in debt. It's worth it, though, when they see the perfect home; in a nice little neighbourhood, down a cul-de-sac, away from everything.

They marry at the registry office, honeymoon at the coast.

Abi swells up like a balloon, gets heartburn most nights and her back aches, but Jon rubs it for her. Neither of them talks about the future, only the here and now. That's all that counts.

Their son is born in the early hours of the morning at The Royal hospital in the centre of town. There are no complications and the baby is healthy.

"We have a son, Abi," says Jon as the baby is handed over to her.

"Do you have any thoughts about a name?" asks the midwife.

"Yes... Yes, we're going to call him after his father. Jonathan." She smiles.

"Jonathan Joshua," corrects Jon, before kissing her, then the new-born child in turn. A photograph is taken to mark the occasion.

Jon stands in front of his daughter's grave. He has brought more orange and yellow flowers which he places on the mound. A peace offering more than anything.

"I know I haven't been around as much as I used to be. I'm sorry. But Em, you have a little baby brother. His name's Jonathan. J.J. And I, well, I just wanted you to know that I won't be making the same mistakes with him as I did with you. Besides, he's got his big sister to watch over him, hasn't he."

The wind chime above begins to jangle and Jon looks up, cocking his head. "Emma?" The wind chime jangles more loudly now, then suddenly falls silent. Jon opens his mouth to speak, staring upwards. He lets his head fall and walks away.

If he'd looked more closely, he would have seen that the angel now had its hands covering its eyes.

Jon lets himself into his house with a key and steps into the hallway.

"Abi? Abi, are you there, sweetheart?"

He takes a look in the living room, but there's no-one there. His eyes fall on the framed picture, on the table next to the chair. It shows him, Abi and Jonathan together after the birth. Then he spots the clock. It's 2 pm.

A strange feeling hits him, like an icy wind – Jon shivers. "Abi... Abi?"

Climbing the stairs two at a time, he makes for the bedroom. Opening the door, he sees his son laying by the window in his cot. He isn't making any noise, isn't moving in fact. He rushes over, bends, but can't hear any breathing. No breath except his own.

"Jon." The voice behind him. He spins around.

"Abi, quick, call for an ambulance. Jonathan—"

"Jon, it's better this way. Better than waiting for it to happen again," she tells him. And there's something about her face, an odd glint in her eye. "Now he'll be at peace. Now he'll be with Joshua, with Emma."

Jon can't quite take in what he's hearing. He grabs Abi by the wrists. "What have you done? WHAT HAVE YOU DONE?"

But she doesn't answer him. Doesn't speak again. Not even when he shakes her. Not even when the police and the ambulance arrive.

It's dark and Jon watches her being taken away. He sits on the steps, head in his hands. Someone puts a blanket around him because of the chill.

He feels numb. Dead inside.

Sunday morning and the city is asleep.

The trees are completely bare and Jon is standing in front of another grave, next to Emma's. He is wearing a dark coat, dark glasses.

The inscription reads: 'Jonathan Joshua Cassidy – J.J. Taken before his time. He will speak to us on the wind.'

Jon lays down another bunch of flowers. "I'm sorry," he says, voice wavering. "Daddy's so sorry. I should have listened."

He looks up to the branch, to the second wind chime, a second cherub placed next to Emma's. It seemed fitting. He pulls up his coat as the wind begins to rise.

Then he makes his way down the path towards the park, the sound faint behind him...

Of two wind chimes, jangling in perfect unison.

Wind Chimes
Written by Paul Kane
Based on the short story by Paul Kane

<u>EXT. PARK/GRAVEYARD - DAY</u>

One or two people are walking dogs along a
path, through big old park gateposts.
Although worn, these are not neglected.
The path leads further in, to a graveyard
at the far end of the park. Trees are
dotted here and there, yellowing leaves
falling.

We move amongst the graves, some with large
headstones, some adorned simply with
crosses.

Further in is another section of the graveyard. Here, splashes of colour break up the
gloom. Flowers are laid on many graves -
smaller graves, adorned simply with
plaques.
Some graves are topped with pebbles of
varying colours, some with squares of rock.

There are fenced graves here and there.
Most have toys on them — teddies and
rabbits, cars and trucks. Every grave is
awash with flowers.

The dates on the graves show us they belong
to children, none over the age of three or
four. The inscriptions bear mute witness to
their parents' sorrow and loss.

A man, JON, stands next to a very small
grave, shaded by a large tree.

Dressed in a large overcoat, he holds a
bunch of orange and yellow flowers as he
stands with his head bowed. He doesn't
notice the leaves falling around him.

He places the flowers on the grave, his
pale face marking his sorrow.

ANGLE ON:

The inscription: 'Emma Louise Cassidy. One
Year Was All The Time We Had.'

Jon chokes back a sob.

We hear tinkling, and the camera moves up
to reveal a collection of wind chimes
hanging from the lower branches of the
tree.

Some are in the shape of silver and glass
tears, some stars, some baubles. But one
stands out from the rest. Lengths of metal
dangle from a brass-coloured angel, head
buried in its arms with sorrow.

Jon looks up at that particular wind chime.

> JON
> I'm sorry.

He walks back through the park area, looking
at the families gathering on the grass to
play, or just walking hand in hand.

<u>INT. HOUSE - NIGHT</u>

A very cluttered living room. Clothes and books litter the space, CDs that haven't been put back on their shelves, plates on the floor encrusted with food. The light is low in there, coming from one solitary wall lamp.

JON is sitting in an armchair, shirt untucked, glass of scotch in his hand. The bottle is on the table by the side of him.

It's half-empty.

On his lap is a framed photograph he's staring at. It shows him and a WOMAN with blonde hair, smiling. She is cradling a baby in her arms. He traces the woman's face with his finger.

Then Jon picks up a cordless phone resting on top of some books by the side of his chair.

He stabs a number he knows by heart.

                    CLAIRE (O.S.)
                 (slightly muffled)
                      Hello.

                      JON
               Claire... It's me.

CLAIRE (O.S.)
You've got to stop this, Jon.

JON
I...

CLAIRE (O.S.)
What do you want?

JON
To talk.

CLAIRE (O.S.)
We're done talking. Enough now.

JON
(slurred)
Please... Listen...

CLAIRE (O.S.)
You've been drinking.

JON
A little.

CLAIRE (O.S.)
I'm going, Jon.

JON
Please don't—

MAN'S VOICE (O.S.)
(gruffly)
Here, give me that. You heard what she
said. Claire's moved on. She's trying

> to make a new life for herself. I
> suggest you do the same.

There's an audible click as the phone is put down at their end. There are tears in Jon's eyes.

He lets the phone drop and we can hear the dialling tone: it's dead.

Jon drains the rest of the scotch in the glass, looks down at the photograph, then hurls it across the room. We hear the glass shattering. He sobs uncontrollably, covering his face with his hand.

We focus on the picture where it has landed on the floor. There's a huge spider's web crack stemming from the woman and the baby.

<u>EXT. GRAVEYARD - DAY</u>

JON is crouching by the grave next to the tree.

He stands, and notices another figure out of the corner of his eye: ABI. She's dressed in a black coat, grey skirt, and is visiting one of the graves a little further down.

He watches as she lays her own flowers down, then returns his gaze to the plot in front of him. A long shot shows us that

they are the only two people in this children's graveyard at that time of day.

When he turns back, the woman is gone.
There's a slight breeze again and the metal
dangling from the angel wind chime above
jangles.

<u>INT. JON'S HOUSE - NIGHT</u>

JON comes in through the front door, brown
paper bag in his hand; the light is
flashing on his answerphone so he presses
the button.

> MICHAEL (O.S.)
> Jon, it's Michael... Look, I know
> you've been through a lot and I
> sympathise, really I do. But we're
> going to need those completed proofs
> soon. Otherwise it could mean—

Jon presses the button again, cutting him
off. Then he erases the message.

He wanders into the kitchen, which is just
as untidy as the living room. There are
unwashed dishes in the sink, a half
finished loaf of bread on the work surface,
the butter left out.

He puts down the bag, picks up a dirty mug
and rinses it in the sink.

Then he takes a bottle of whiskey out of

the brown paper and opens the top, pouring
himself a generous amount. He has his back
to us and we see his shoulders slump.

<u>EXT. GRAVEYARD - DAY</u>

JON is staring at the grave, a familiar
pose to us now. He is lost in his own
thoughts as the wind plays with his hair.
The wind chime is jangling quietly.

      ABI
     (from behind)
    It's very beautiful.

Jon starts, then turns around. The woman
from the other day is standing there: ABI.
She has long dark hair and green eyes,
which are a little red and sore.

      JON
     I'm sorry?

Abi points to the wind chime, which
continues to jangle.

      ABI
   I... I was thinking of maybe getting
     one myself.

Jon nods.

Abi drops her eyes to the ground and turns,
as if to walk away and leave him alone again.

JON
(suddenly)
There's... there's a reason people
leave them there.

The woman stops and turns back.

ABI
To remember.

JON
It's more than that. They say when
someone dies, their spirit drifts on
the wind.

Abi begins to walk towards the grave.

JON (CONT'D)
And... And some people say when the
wind chimes jangle like that it's as if
they're talking to us.

Abi now joins him.

ABI
Do you think that's true?

JON
I don't know... But I'd like to
think so.

She considers this for a moment, head
cocked, listening to the wind chime. Jon is
watching her. Then Abi's eyes drop to the

plaque in front of her. She reads the
inscription to herself.

                    JON
          The grave down there... Is it—

He sees her visibly stiffen and drops his
head.

                 JON (CONT'D)
          I'm sorry, I shouldn't have asked
                    about—

                    ABI
               (breaking in)
          My son, Joshua.

                    JON
          I'm really sorry.

                    ABI
          So am I. And your daughter... a year.
          No age at all.

                    JON
          No. How old was...

A tear tracks down Abi's face

                    ABI
               (voice cracking)
          Four months.

                    JON
          God.

He looks around the graveyard.

                    JON (CONT'D)
          So many children, so much pain.

                    ABI
          I should be going.

Jon nods again and Abi walks away, casting
a single glance over her shoulder. He
watches her for a moment or two, then sets
off after her, catching up.

                    JON
          Wait!

                    ABI
          Yes?

                    JON
          Please don't... Go, I mean.

He smiles, tentatively — but it's infec-
tious. Abi's eyes brush the ground, but
then meet his and she smiles back.

                    JON
          I'm Jon.

                    ABI
          Abi.

<u>INT. CAFE - DAY</u>

JON and ABI are at a table in a quiet café.

The only other person there is a man in the
corner reading his newspaper. Abi stirs her
tea, lost in thought.

                    JON
        Will someone be waiting for you,
                    then?

                    ABI
            (coming out of her daze)
            Someone...? Oh, I see.

She shakes her head.

                ABI (CONT'D)
                    You?

                    JON
        My wife... Ex-wife... She's barely
            spoken to me since...

                    ABI
        Happens a lot. All they can see when
            they look at you is...

                    JON
        No, it was my fault, you see. She was
        at her sister's for the evening. I
        should have checked Em more often. The
        monitor was on but I fell asleep in
        front of the TV. By the time Claire got
            back... it was too late.

                    ABI
            It wasn't your fault.

                    JON
          I was looking after her.

                    ABI
        It could have happened anytime.
      It does happen anytime. That's what people
      kept telling me. Took me a long time to
          realise they were right.

Jon begins to grasp they have more in
common than he first thought.

                    JON
                 Joshua?

                    ABI
      Tuesday afternoon, 2 o'clock, to be
      precise. He was having a nap, but...
            but he never woke up.

                    JON
      And you've blamed yourself ever since.

                    ABI
      There was no-one else to blame. Mark
          wasn't even home. He couldn't
                understand.
                  (beat)
              No one can.

Abi sniffs and two tears run in parallel
down her face.

Instinctively, Jon reaches over and takes
her hand. He squeezes it.

                    JON
                 Not true.

Abi looks at him again, then pulls her hand
free.

                    ABI
               I have to go.

                    JON
                   Abi—

                    ABI
        Thanks for the coffee, Jon.

Abi gets up to leave.

Jon rises too, but before he can stop her,
Abi's already out through the door. He
slumps back down into his seat and sighs.

<u>EXT. GRAVEYARD - DAY</u>

Another day and JON is at the graveyard
once more. The sky is grey; there's little
trace of the sun.

He finds himself walking down the path to
visit Joshua's grave.

To all intents and purposes it is just the
same as all the others, but the words on
the inscription mean something to him now
he's met ABI: 'Joshua Hill, Now At Peace.
Forever In Our Hearts'.

There are footsteps behind him, the click-
clack of heeled boots.

                    ABI
I can remember the day Joshua was born.
Mark was there holding my hand, and his
   face... I don't think anything could
 have upset him right at that moment. We
  were a family and... and now, now it's
              all gone.

Jon turns just as Abi bursts into tears. He
steps up and puts his arms around her,
holding her.

                    ABI
  (through the tears, into his shoulder)
 Why did this have to happen to us? Why
           is life like this?

                    JON
    I don't know. I don't know.

A chill wind blows straight through them
and Abi shivers.

                    JON
  Come on, let's get you out of the cold.

As he walks her up towards the park, the
wind chime starts to jangle on the tree.

<u>INT. JON'S HOUSE - NIGHT</u>

ABI and JON are sitting at the table in the

kitchen, a bottle of half-empty brandy
between them, papers scattered across
the top.

Abi is still wearing her coat. She looks
around at the state of the kitchen.

                    JON
          (taking a gulp of the brandy)
     Sorry the place is in such a state.

                    ABI
          I've seen worse.

She picks up a manuscript that's lying on
the table and examines it.

Jon takes it off her and tosses it to the
side.

                    ABI
     Is that what you do, write?

                    JON
          (laughs)
     I read... For a publishing house.

                    ABI
     Sounds interesting.

                    JON
     It isn't. They send me all the cheesy
     romance books. You should see some of
     it, things that would never happen in a
                million years.

Jon takes another swig of his drink. She
watches him.

                    ABI
          It won't help.

                    JON
     I know, but it dulls the pain for a
                   while.

                    ABI
          Only for a while.

This time it is Abi who reaches across the
table and takes Jon's hand. He looks up,
surprised. She smiles again, but catches
herself; the smile fades.

                    ABI
     I think I'd better be going.

                    JON
          So soon?

Abi nods, gets up.

                    ABI
     But I'll see you again. I'm not hard to
                    find.

She leans over and kisses him on the
cheek.

                    ABI
          Thank you.

                    JON
                 For what?

                    ABI
           For understanding... and for
                  listening.

She starts to walk away and Jon just
watches sadly. He looks like he's about to
say something but doesn't.

The front door slams and he looks at his
drink. He's about to bring it up to his
lips, but changes his mind and puts it down
on the table instead.

<u>MONTAGE SEQUENCE</u>

We see ABI and JON back in the café talking, walking through the park, chatting,
getting to know each other better. And we
see them having dinner at Jon's, the
kitchen now tidied up.

It's almost springtime; the time for new
beginnings. And now they're at the graveyard, first at Joshua's plot, then Emma's.
The tree above them is in full leaf.

Jon has his arm around Abi's shoulders but
the support is most definitely mutual — her
arm slung around his waist as she leans
into him.

<u>EXT. PARK - DAY</u>

JON and ABI are on a bench watching the families walking by. The couple are holding hands.

JON
Abi?

ABI
Yes.

JON
Something's been worrying me...

She suddenly looks scared and shuffles forward onto the edge of the bench.

ABI
What is it?

JON
Do you ever wonder if what we're doing is wrong?

ABI
Wrong how?

Jon shakes his head, not sure how to explain what he means.

JON
I don't know. It's just... these past few months, with you. I'm starting to feel things that I really shouldn't. I'm starting to feel happy again. And I don't know if—

Abi sits back and faces Jon.

                    ABI
Jon, there isn't a day goes by that I
  don't long to hold Joshua one more
   time, touch his face... But how much
      longer can we go on punishing
   ourselves? I think we're entitled to a
       little happiness now maybe.

                    JON
        I just can't help thinking—

                    ABI
   I know. But the alternative frightens
  me so much more. I... I don't want to
                lose you.

He nods, smiles, and leans in to softly
kiss her.

                    JON
        You won't. I promise.

They smile, comforted, and kiss once more.

<u>INT. JON'S HOUSE - NIGHT</u>

The door opens and JON is carrying ABI over
the threshold. He pauses on the doorstep to
kiss her.

                    JON
   Welcome to your new home, Mrs.
                 Cassidy.

She rests her head on his shoulder and he
proceeds to carry her up the stairs.

INT. BEDROOM - NIGHT

ABI and JON are in bed making love, their
movements slow and loving, comforting more
than anything. Jon gazes into Abi's eyes
and they hold each other.

Outside, we can hear the wind rising,
rustling through the trees.

And the far away jangling of the wind
chime.

INT. BY BATHROOM DOOR - DAY

JON knocks on the bathroom door. We can
clearly hear the sound of someone being
sick.

> JON
> Abi, are you all right? You've been in
> there ages.

There's no answer, so he knocks and calls
again. Finally the door opens and ABI is
standing there with a worried look on her
face.

> JON (CONT'D)
> Something you ate?

She shakes her head.

> ABI
> I'm late this month.

Abi waits to see what his reaction will be; she looks terrified. Jon just takes her into his arms and strokes the back of her head.

> ABI
> I'm scared, Jon. What if...?

> JON
> Sshh. Don't, love. It's okay. It's going to be okay.

She hugs him back, so tight her fingers are digging into his shoulders. We see Jon's face over her shoulder. He's petrified.

> JON (CONT'D)
> It's all going to be okay.

<u>INT. DELIVERY ROOM - DAY</u>

An average delivery room, ABI is giving birth with JON by her side. Her face is screwed up, forehead dripping with sweat.

The tall MIDWIFE is telling her to:

> MIDWIFE
> Push, Mrs. Cassidy. You're doing very well. Not much longer now.

Jon is right next to her, holding her hand.

                    JON
      You're nearly there, love. A couple
                   more...

Abi bears down and pushes again, blowing
out with each heave. The scene slips into
slow motion and we hear the sound of each
breath, long and loud. Then this is broken
by the crying of a baby. The midwife holds
the child up for Abi and Jon to see.

                  MIDWIFE
      Congratulations, you have a healthy
                 baby boy.

Jon smiles so widely it looks like his face
will split in two. The baby is handed over
to Abi, who cradles him gently.

                    JON
      We have a son. Abi, we have a son.

                  MIDWIFE
        Any thoughts about a name?

                    ABI
      Yes, yes we do. We're going to name him
                after his father.

She smiles up at Jon and he kisses her,
then kisses his newborn baby.

<u>EXT. GRAVEYARD - DAY</u>

JON stands in front of his daughter's

grave. He has brought more orange and
yellow flowers and places them over the
grave itself.

                    JON
     I know I haven't been around as much
     lately as I used to be. I'm sorry. But
     Em, you have a little baby brother. His
     name's Jon. And I just, well, I just
     wanted you to know that... and to know
     I won't be making the same mistakes
              with him as I did with you.
                   (beat)
     Besides, he's got his big sister to
          watch over him, hasn't he?

The wind chime starts to jangle and Jon
looks up. There's something about it this
time and he cocks his head.

                    JON
                 (whispers)
                   Emma?

The wind chime rattles much harder, then
falls silent. Jon, mouth open, stands and
stares at the angel. Then he lets his head
fall and walks away from the grave.

<u>INT. JON'S HOUSE - DAY</u>

JON lets himself into the house with a key
and steps into the hallway.

                    JON
Abi? The strangest thing just happened.
                 I think...

There's no reply.

                JON (CONT'D)
Abi? Are you there, sweetheart?

He has a look in the living room, but
there's nobody there. His eyes fall upon a
framed picture, on the table next to the
chair. It shows him, ABI and the baby
together. He smiles.

Then he spots the clock. It's 2 pm. And the
calendar is ringed: it's a Tuesday.

                    JON
                 (worried)
              Abi? Abi...

Jon climbs the stairs two at a time and
opens the bedroom door. The baby is in his
cot but isn't making any noise. Jon walks
over to him.

                    JON
               Jonathan...

He bends, but he can't hear his son breathing. In fact the only breathing is coming
from down by the side of the bed.

It's Abi, she's crawled and hidden there.

She's staring at him but not really
seeing him.

                    JON
     Abi... What is it? What's wrong?
        Please... Please don't...
              (shouting)
                 Abi!

                    ABI
               (flatly)
           He's at peace.

                    JON
              (confused)
         What are you talking about?

                    ABI
     And he'll be forever in our hearts.

Jon walks round and sees the pillow in her
hands. He rushes over and grabs her by the
shoulders.

                    JON
               (angry)
        Abi, what in Christ's name have you
                 done?

Abi is simply staring at him.

                    ABI
      You understand... You're the only one
         who can. He'll speak to you now.
                 (beat)

> He'll speak to you, Jon.

Jon lets go and takes a step back, his face a mixture of emotions: grief; horror; and some pity as well.

We close in on Abi's face, wide-eyed and staring. Fade out to be replaced by:

<u>EXT. OUTSIDE HOUSE - NIGHT</u>

ABI in the back of a police car, to be taken away. There are flashing lights all around. JON follows its trail as it drives away.

He breaks down on the steps and begins to cry.

> RADIO VOICE OVER
> (fade in)
> ...are not releasing any more details about this tragic story, but it is believed that the woman's first baby also died in suspicious circumstances five years ago. And that up until a year ago she had been receiving counselling for the loss.
> (beat)
> On to other news now...
> (fade out)

<u>EXT. GRAVEYARD - DAY</u>

The trees are bare again. JON is standing

in front of another grave, situated right next to Emma's.

We read the inscription: 'Jon Joshua Cassidy. Taken Before His Time. He Will Speak To Us On The Wind.'

Jon lays down another bunch of flowers across the grave.

> JON
> (crying)
> I'm so sorry. Daddy's so sorry.

He looks up to the branch above, where a second wind chime has been placed next to Emma's.

Jon pulls up the collar of his coat as the wind begins to rise. Then walks away down the path towards the park.

Just as both the wind chimes start to jangle.

FADE OUT RUN CREDITS

THE BACKGROUND TO...
WIND CHIMES

Now, I can definitely remember where the idea for this story came from, such was the impact it had on me. I was visiting a friend I'd made on my History of Art, Design and Film course at university, and we went for a walk around where she lives. It was a gorgeous autumn day and she took me into a nearby park, where there were the usual families scattered about, kids having fun on the slides and swings, a pond with ducks and so on.

We strolled down the path, and to my surprise – because I'd never visited this particular park before – only seconds away from all this, slap bang next to it actually, was a children's graveyard. I'm not quite sure what the reasoning behind it was, especially as grieving parents had to walk past all that (I couldn't see another way in or out) to pay their respects. Or perhaps that was exactly the point, showing that life does go on, that there are still children enjoying themselves, having fun. Perhaps it was so the spirits of the children weren't alone just with each other, the dead? I don't know...

But a story began forming in my mind, especially when we toured around the various items that had been left by the tiny graves, like teddy bears, toys and... wind chimes. Tied to the trees all around us were wind chimes, and this immediately connected with something I'd once heard – because that's how writers' minds work. It was a belief about the dead being able to whisper on the wind, so perhaps – I thought to myself – that was why all those wind chimes had been hung there. So the parents of such young kids might be able to more easily hear them in the wind.

But what kind of things might they say? Could it be that a few are trying to warn us about something bad? They do say the dead can see further than us.

I wrote the story pretty quickly when I got home, and already had a market in mind for it. The famous Dead by Dawn horror film festival was now publishing yearly anthologies to go along with the event, and I'd been trying to get into one of those for a little while. It wasn't until I'd written 'Wind Chimes' and submitted it to editor (and festival organiser) Adele Hartley, that I finally managed it and I snuck into Vol. 3 of *Read by Dawn* in 2008.

I think it was around this time that I first met Brad Watson, who became one of my best mates in the industry (director of, most recently, *Hallows Eve, Miss Willoughby and the Haunted Bookshop* – starring Kelsey Grammer – and *The Siege*). It was at a huge convention down in London where we were interviewing people like Scream Queen Christa Campbell (who has since gone on to be executive producer for movies like *Hellboy, Angel Has Fallen* and *Rambo: Last Blood*) and also got to meet the legend Christopher Lee before he passed away. Brad and his producer Janice Willis had just made a feature called *Asylum Night,* which Kim Newman had said some very nice things about. We all got chatting and I offered to review it as well – I think for *Gorezone*, but don't quote me – and was equally impressed. The movie subsequently ended up on The Horror Channel…

Then, over the next few years, we met up with Brad and Janice quite a bit and they asked if I had anything they could take a look at with a view to making a short and/or a feature. I'd already scripted 'Wind Chimes' by this point, which again I figured might make a decent low-budget short, so I showed them that and sent a few other things for possible features. One feature they were interested in doing was *Arrowhead*, my post-apocalyptic Robin Hood novel, because Brad had already made a book trailer for that – and indeed it got so far down the line that test footage was filmed… but sadly it wasn't to be. Same goes for the potential feature of *Lunar* that I scripted, although I still live in hope about both of these.

What did get made, though, was *Wind Chimes*.

As with *The Weeping Woman* just before it, Brad took the script and simply ran with it – even taking on a producer, editor and composer role himself (he's a wonderful musician as his home performances on the piano during lockdown attest). He made it and brought it out through his own company Filmic Media, casting Robert Carratta as Jon and Joanna Ignaczewska (from *Wallander* and more recently *Hidden*, *Casualty* and *The Crown*) as Anya – changing the name from Abi in the story. Both give truly magnificent performances.

I included the original short story in my PS Publishing collection *The Butterfly Man*, which was launching at FantasyCon in Brighton in 2012. So Brad and I decided to hold the launch of the short film there too, which was screened on the Saturday night of the convention to much applause. A DVD of the film was subsequently produced for the hardback edition of my Spectral collection *GHOSTS*, which included an Edward Miller (Les Edwards) cover. That was launched at the World Fantasy Convention, also in Brighton, in 2013.

A scene being set up in Jon's living room.

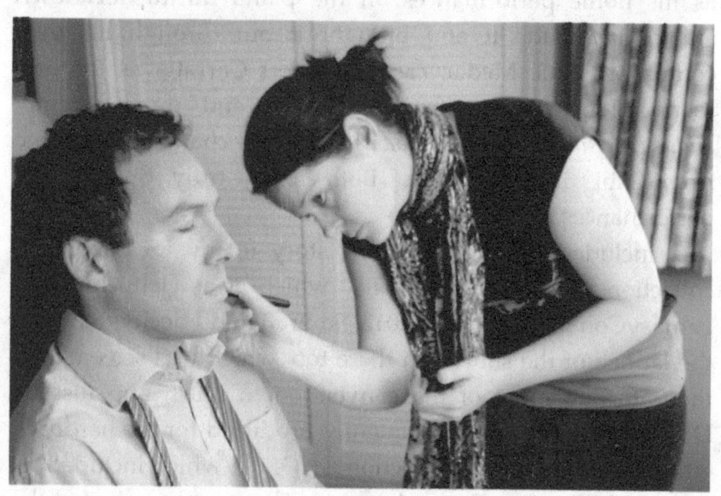

Make-up artist Amy Thornton with Robert Carratta, playing Jon.

Director Brad Watson and Robert discuss the scene.

The scene in Jon's living room being shot.

Brad Watson.

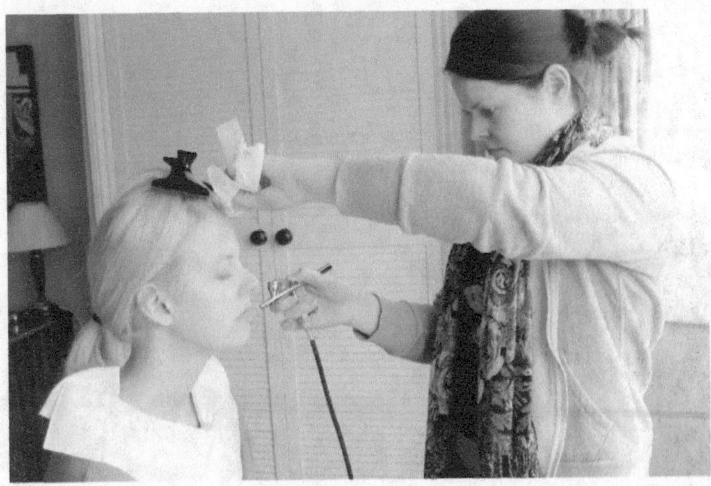

Joanna Ignaczewska, playing Anya, being made up by Amy Thornton.

*Brad (middle) with Robert and Joanna, about to shoot the beach scene – part of
the montage.*

The beach scene being shot.

And afterwards, Brad enjoying a well-earned ice cream.

Shooting the café scene.

Joanna about to shoot the scene in Jon's kitchen.

The kitchen scene.

Joanna at the mirror during the finale.

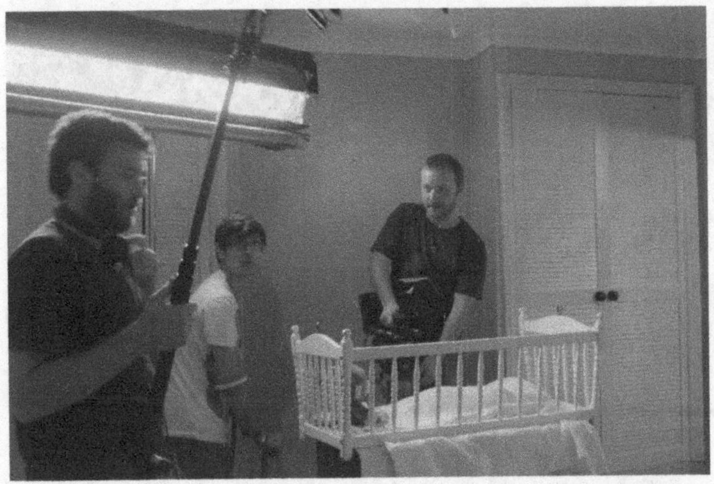

Preparing the cot for the shocking finale.

Robert in the make-up chair once again.

And…action!

Paul introducing the screening of Wind Chimes *at FantasyCon 2012 in Scarborough.*

*The launch of the GHOSTS collection, World Fantasy Convention 2013 –
Paul with Nancy Kilpatrick (middle), who wrote the introduction, and cover
artist Edward Miller (Les Edwards, far left).*

*Paul at the GHOSTS launch with author of The Silence Tim
Lebbon (middle) and creator of Afterlife Stephen Volk (far right).*

The gorgeous Edward Miller/Les Edwards cover art of GHOSTS.

The DVD of Wind Chimes *in the back of the hardback edition of* GHOSTS.

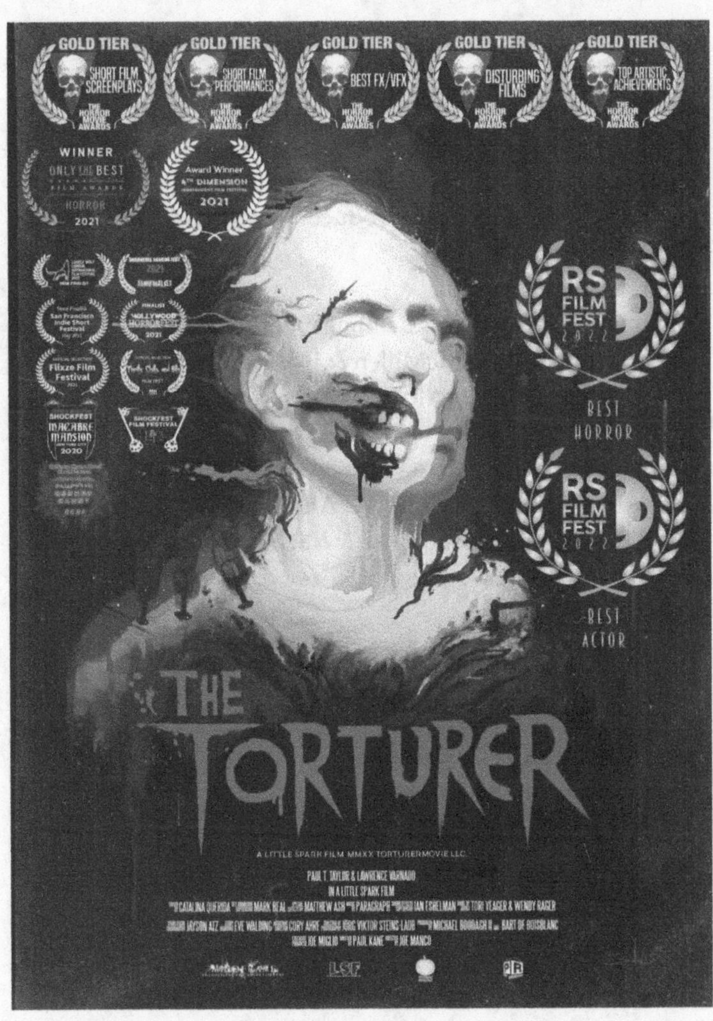

GOLD TIER
SHORT FILM SCREENPLAYS
THE HORROR MOVIE AWARDS

GOLD TIER
SHORT FILM PERFORMANCES
THE HORROR MOVIE AWARDS

GOLD TIER
BEST FX/VFX
THE HORROR MOVIE AWARDS

GOLD TIER
DISTURBING FILMS
THE HORROR MOVIE AWARDS

GOLD TIER
TOP ARTISTIC ACHIEVEMENTS
THE HORROR MOVIE AWARDS

WINNER
ONLY THE BEST FILM AWARDS
HORROR
2021

Award Winner
4TH DIMENSION
INDEPENDENT FILM FESTIVAL
2021

San Francisco Indie Short Festival

FINALIST
HOLLYWOOD HORRORFEST
2021

Flixxe Film Festival 2021

SHOCKFEST MACABRE MANSION 2020

SHOCKFEST FILM FESTIVAL

RS FILM FEST 2022
BEST HORROR

RS FILM FEST 2022
BEST ACTOR

THE TORTURER

A LITTLE SPARK FILM MMXX TORTURERMOVIE LLC.

PAUL T. TAYLOR & LAWRENCE VARNADO
IN A LITTLE SPARK FILM

Poster Artwork by Anthony Galatis.

CREDITS

Director: Joe Manco
Screenwriter: Paul Kane (based on his own short story)
Producers: Michael Boodagh II, Bart de Boisblanc, Nathan Gershon
Line Producer & Executive Producer: Joe Miglio
Music: Paragraph Taylor
Editor: Catalina Querida
Production Management: Catalina Querida
Art Department: Tara McMillen & Eve Walding
Make-up: Sassy Yeager Albee, Kelsey Briones, Wendy Rager & Tori Yeager
Special Effects: Matthew Ash & Steven Daniel Ellis
First Assistant Director: Cory W. Ahre
Sound Department: Jayson Atz & Michael Boodagh II

CAST

Paul T. Taylor: Andy Brooks
Lawrence Varnado: The Torturer
Robb Hudspeth: Sarge
Richard Houghton: Dr Campbell
Lance Parker: Officer Smith
Kristin Keith: Girl with the Big Eyes
Nathan Gershon: Motorcyclist

THE TORTURER
THE SHORT STORY

I'm not sure how long I've been here. A few days, a week maybe? It feels like a lot longer. I've not seen a soul since I arrived, either; shoved inside by rough hands like some kind of animal. I didn't see the men – I assume they were men – who grabbed me, kidnapped me. I know it sounds like a cliché, but it really did all happen so fast. And it was dark, too. As dark as it is here in this… cell. Yes, I suppose that's what you'd call it. One tiny window lets in a little light, just enough so I can make out what the place looks like. Four stone walls surround me, slimy to the touch. It's damp in here and smells of faeces and urine. Mostly mine. There's no bed, so I have to sleep on the cold floor. At night I feel things crawling over me, insects and I think rodents of some kind as well. Needless to say, I've slept very little of late.

My stomach lets out a cavernous growl. I clutch at my noisy abdomen but it does nothing to stop the rumbling. Hardly surprising as I've not eaten so much as a scrap of food since my incarceration. I sometimes wonder if they've forgotten all about me, the people who put me here. Or left me to die for some reason I can't even begin to fathom.

If so, then I'm not the only one.

Even now I can hear distant crying. It might be coming from the cell next to mine, I can't tell, but the very sound of another human being gives me some hope. I've tried banging on the wall and the locked metal door – which must be at least several inches thick – to elicit a response, from either my captors or from the poor unfortunate who shares my fate. But I never receive a reply.

It's like you can feel yourself going insane, in stages. No, not insane. *Not yet!* We were never meant to be alone like this, imprisoned. It's inhuman.

I pace up and down in the limited area allotted to me, trying to think things through clearly; to work out why I'm here. I'm not rich, am I? I don't think I'm famous, so no one will pay a ransom for me. Nobody bears me any kind of grudges that I can recall.

Perhaps it's just an arbitrary thing. My being here could be a random act. Wrong place at the wrong time. Terrorists trying to make a point by snatching the first person they came across.

If only they'd let me go. I wouldn't tell anyone. What the hell do I know to tell anyone anyway? Oh Jesus, why won't they just let me go?

The footsteps are loud. Because of the absence of any other noise (apart from the muted crying), I hear them instantly. The soles of heavy shoes beating out a rhythm down the corridor. Closer, closer. The tapping gets louder... then stops.

I think someone is outside my cell. I've been praying for this moment for days, yet now that it's here I'm backing away from the door. Why am I so scared? I've done nothing wrong. Have I?

A metallic jangling, keys rattling: lots of keys. How many prisoners are there here? One key is being inserted in the lock. Thrust in hard and turned ferociously. It makes a sound akin to nails on a blackboard. I quiver involuntarily.

The big door opens, but the corridor is as dimly lit as my cell. I can just about discern two large shapes, possibly the men who threw me in here. Smudged figures, black upon black, come into the chamber. I make myself small in the corner, but they still find me and lift me up. They ignore my protests and my feeble blows bounce ineffectually off their hardened bodies. Even if I wasn't weakened by lack of sustenance, I doubt whether I'd be any more of a match for them.

I'm pulled through the door and my feet scrape along the uneven ground of the corridor. I look up in the vain hope that I might see a face, something to give me a clue. But their countenances are still deep in shadow.

"Why are you doing this?" My question disappears along the length of the hallway to be repeated over and over by a vague imitator. There's no answer forthcoming.

They kick open the door to a side room and deposit me unceremoniously inside. The men have vanished, leaving the door wide open. This is my chance to escape! But as I limp as fast as I can to the exit, the way is blocked by another person. He walks into the room, and brings the stench of evil with him.

Reaching around just outside the door-frame, he finds a light switch. Instinctively, I look up as the naked bulb comes on. The blaze of sudden light sends me blind. I see whiteness, then purple dots cartwheel across my field of vision. I bring a hand up to shield my eyes and blink rapidly. It takes a good few minutes for me to adjust to my new... illuminated state.

Slowly, I look around the room, and things start to come into focus like props in a low-budget movie. It's slightly larger than my cell – though not much – and there's a table in the centre with two chairs on either side of it. The furniture isn't fancy; it's practical. The kind a carpenter might have in his workshop.

Then my eyes come to rest on the man, a thickset fellow with a wide neck. He appears to have no cheekbones to speak of and two sloping pencil-thin eyebrows meet in the middle of his brow. Below these are a pair of dark brown, almost black, eyes – framed by octagonal glasses with thin metal rims. The glasses seem to magnify not only his pupils, but also the power they have to gaze deep into my very soul.

His hair is greying at the temples. It looks like a military cut that has grown out some. And he is dressed in a black shirt and trousers. In his left hand he holds a clipboard.

When he speaks his voice is flat, almost toneless: "Please, take a seat."

I don't know how to react to this, but in the end I obey. With all the grace of a world-weary traveller, I slump down in one of the hard wooden chairs. If nothing else, I may get some answers now.

I wait for him to sit opposite in the other chair. He doesn't. He hovers above me, scrutinising as an owl does with a mouse before the kill.

"Splendid. Now we can begin." His expression of indifference turns into a sneer. "Please tell me your name."

"What?"

"Your name. Quickly."

"Andrew… Andy Brooks."

The man stops to write something down on his clipboard. "You know why you're here, of course."

I shake my head.

"Oh, come now. You *do* know, Mr Brooks. Think."

I had done nothing *but* that since I got here. I was no closer to understanding any of this than when I started.

"No? All right, if that's the way you want it. Tell me how you came to be here."

"Your people grabbed me and—"

"Before that. Tell me what you were doing before that. What you have been doing for the last few months, the last few years."

He seems impatient, as if he knows this information already. I open my mouth to answer him – and nothing comes out. I'm horrified to discover I can't remember anything before they seized me. Where had I been? On the street? In my house? (My *house*? I can't even remember where I live.)

The man bends over me, expecting an answer. I want to give him one, desperately; it doesn't seem prudent to do otherwise. But my mind's a complete blank. I know this, truly I do. It's just temporarily out of reach. No matter how hard I try, I simply can't access it.

"Well, Mr Brooks?"

"I'm sorry, I—"

He swings the clipboard around, missing my head by centimetres, then slams it down on the table.

"Not good enough. Who do you work for?"

"I-I don't remember. What's all this about?"

'It's very simple. You tell me which side you're on. Make life easy for yourself." He walks past the back of my chair and I feel his hands on my shoulders.

"I'm not on anyone's side."

His grip tightens, his fingers inching towards my neck. "We're all on one side or the other," he says. "I'm not a patient man. You should know this. I've been hired to do a job, and that's exactly what I'm going to do, Mr Brooks."

Despite his proximity, I can feel the anger welling up inside me. Just who the hell does he think he is?

"Listen, where am I? What do you want from me?"

"I've told you that already." His dispassionate voice is getting to me.

"When am I going to get something to eat?" My humble attempt to sound assertive.

"When you answer my questions. Who do you work for and what have you done?"

"What have I—" The hands close around my neck, forcing a puff of breath out of me. I try to prise the fingers from around my throat, but the grip is like iron. My windpipe is being crushed and I hear myself coughing, wheezing. I can feel the pressure building up behind my eyes. If I don't get air soon I'll—

Then he shoves my head forward so that it collides with the edge of the desk. My forehead throbs wildly and a wetness is running down my cheeks. The liquid is too thick to be tears and I realise it can only be my own blood. My vision becomes blurred again and this time I black out.

In my dream I see people standing around me in a darkened cell. Like the men who came for me, they are just silhouettes at first. One of the number steps up to point at me, except... except his hand is hanging off! It dangles from his arm on a piece of loose flesh, the forefinger raised as it spins round. And now he's stepping closer, into the light. Oh God!

I'm roused by someone slapping my face. It is my interrogator.

"It's not polite to pass out in the middle of a conversation," he says.

My head is aching fit to burst, and when I swallow for the first time it feels like his hands are still at my throat. Hot bile rises and I turn to the side to spit it out. I can't turn far, mind, because my arms are strapped to the back of the chair. Also, my shirt has been ripped open at the front to reveal a sweaty and pale chest.

"Do you remember what we were talking about before you 'dropped off'?" I attempt to nod, but think better of it. The man continues anyway. "Good. My question still stands. Who do you work for?"

"Told you." My voice sounds strange, slurred. "Don't remember."

"I refuse to believe that." He stands back and picks something up off the table. It takes me a moment to work out what it is: a length of black plastic wire with a frayed end. The man coils an amount of it around his hand and leaves the rest to droop over his fist.

The Torturer smiles. Then he brings the wire across my

exposed skin like a whip. A white-hot fire runs along its tip and burns my chest. I feel pain like I've never experienced before. A cut opens up just below my collarbone. Two more strikes follow in quick succession: one across my stomach, the other just shy of my neck.

I writhe forward on the seat and groan. I convince myself not to scream; it's hard but necessary. I won't give him the satisfaction. Biting on my bottom lip helps a little.

"We'll try again. Tell me what you know."

Panting, I look into his eyes – those hard nuggets of coal. "My name is And... Andy Brooks. I don't remember any more."

Another swipe, across my hands this time.

"Tell me." He doesn't shout, but his speech is louder; frustration begins to emerge.

"N-Nothing to tell."

The slashing goes on until my torso is raw. I say nothing to him. How can I, when I don't know what he wants? As a last resort he starts on my face. I can't even begin to describe what this is like. My head rocks from side to side with each crack.

Eventually, he is forced to let me go. I'm vaguely aware of being carried back to my cell, but before I leave I think I see someone else in the torture room with the man. Then again, I can't be sure of anything in my state.

They leave me be in that dismal cubicle and I can do nothing but lie on my back, trying to will the agony to die down. It doesn't, of course.

I don't know how, but I fall asleep right there and then. Maybe it's the exhaustion, or the body's way of healing itself. I don't know. Don't care.

Anyway, I'm back in the place with the mutilated man. There are more people gathered around him, not just men, but women and children too. Their wounds are abhorrent. I see one girl, she can't be more than twenty-five, with a long piece of metal sticking out of her side, ragged and sharp. It's in much further than any foreign object should be. How can she still be alive? I ask myself.

Another sufferer – I can't tell their sex – is creeping along the floor. At first I think they are looking for something, but then I see they have no legs. Something has torn this being clean in half and organs are spilling out onto the stone as they move.

Yet irrespective of their injuries, they are all coming towards me, pointing. Are they warning me of something behind?

I roll over on my front in the night and the soreness of the cuts snap me sharply awake. Someone is looking at me from inside the cell. I can't see them, but I'm sure of it.

No, it can't be... Just a leftover image from the dream.

I listen for the crying. There it is, much louder now. In spite of this, I still can't work out the source. Is it coming from next door, or a world away?

It isn't long before the men come for me again. I put up very little resistance, even less than last time. As they drag me through the doorway, I turn back to see if anyone is in the cell. Unfortunately, my throat hurts too much and I'm yanked past so quickly that I only catch a glimpse of something intangible.

Back in The Torturer's lair, I am relieved of the last remnants of my clothing: tattered shirt, trousers, socks and underwear. I'm then chained to the wall by clasps I didn't notice were there before. My arms are out horizontally straight at my sides and my legs are spread wide. The chains are short; they don't allow me to sag forwards. This uncomfortable position pulls the flesh tight over my chest, intensifying the tenderness of those lacerations.

The men leave me alone with the lights off. I can hear things moving in the room. They make too much noise to be rats. Something touches my leg. A brief sensation, but enough to make me jump. Then it's travelling up my thigh, something with short legs: a spider?

No, it's a hand. I can tell that now.

More fingers join it. They pick at my cuts, squeeze my skin, pinching and kneading. A multitude of eager, grabbing hands all over me, covering my legs, my arms, my face. I want to shout out, tell them to stop. But I know that they won't. The smothering hordes progress; more stroking of digits. What do they want from me?

The light comes on suddenly. I am alone in the room. No hands, no fingers. It was all just a trick. But how could they disappear so quickly? I cast such thoughts from my mind as The Torturer enters.

"Good morning, Mr Brooks." I can see no emotion in his face today. But the fact that he got nothing from me yesterday has done little to dampen his resolve. "I trust you slept well. I'm sorry we had to get you up so early, but we've got a lot to do and so little time in which to accomplish it."

Little time? Does that mean somebody is looking for me? Or is he referring to the short amount of time he has left before I 'expire'?

He walks over to me, hands in his pockets.

"Perhaps you might see reason today. If not, well..." He deliberately tails off, allowing my imagination to do its worst.

"Yesterday was a mere taster of the pleasures to come. But it would be better for all concerned if you just co-operated."

"Please... *Please*, I've done nothing to you."

"Nothing to me personally, no. But it's not as simple as that, Mr Brooks. When I'm called in, people expect results. Nothing more, nothing less. And I always get them. You *will* tell me what I want to know. In the end they always do."

"How can I tell you anything when I don't even remember?"

He ignores me completely and strolls over to the other side of the room. The Torturer stands there for a minute, nodding to himself, then comes back across. As he makes his way to me, he takes a small plastic bag out of his pocket. I can't see what's inside, but it jangles like the ring of keys that open my cell door.

"I ask you once more: who do you work for and what do you do?"

I can only drop my head and sigh. There is more rattling. I look up in time to see him go to my left hand. He takes a number of small objects out of the bag and clasps them tightly. The Torturer drops the bag and produces a hammer from his other pocket.

When he grips my middle finger and pushes one of the small objects under the fingernail, I realise they are long, thin arrows of metal – possibly thick pins or nails. In any event, the point is sharp and scrapes the nerves of my fingertip.

But it isn't until he strikes the nail with his hammer that I really feel it. Holding my finger up, he bangs it right in there, embedding it well below the surface until it almost splits the fingernail.

I find it impossible to look away, even as he does the same thing again and again, planting more shafts of exploding torment beneath my tissue. As a stone causes ripples in a lake, so the pain that starts off in my fingers cascades throughout my entire body. It's like something is trying to burrow its way into my hand and up my arm: a small creature with sharp teeth, feeding on my anguish.

"How's your memory now, Mr Brooks? Anything coming back to you?" I can hardly comprehend his words. All my concentration is devoted to blocking out my own suffering; it isn't easy. In fact it's impossible. Every twitch of my hand, every spasm, aggravates the pain.

He waits for an answer I cannot give, leaning in to hear my gasps in case I should whisper some important piece of information.

The Torturer bangs his fist on the wall next to my head. "You disappoint me."

Over his shoulder I can see people in the far corner of the

room. It's only a momentary flash, but I see them: the figures from my dream. Then they are gone.

"I-I don't—"

"Who do you work for? Who? Who? WHO?"

"Don't r-remember."

"What are you? What do you do? What? What? WHAT?"

He is shouting the last part of each question. As he barks the words out at me, spittle flies from his mouth and lands on my cheek. I can smell his rank breath, like curdled milk left out in the sun. He will get nothing from me.

"Very well." I watch him go out of the room, slamming the door behind him.

The space around me becomes unreal, melting into a puddle on the floor, and I am lost to the world for some time. Yet I do not dream.

The next thing I know, a coldness strikes me in the face. The icy water, thrown by Him, draws me back to reality. The Torturer is holding a bucket. There are a few more lined up next to the table legs. On the table itself just behind him is a black bundle of cloth and a glass of brown liquid.

The pins in my fingers have awakened as well, jabbing me with fresh darts of distress. However, the nerves seem to be going numb and it hurts much less than it did before.

"Do try to remain conscious. It makes my job so much harder when you keep dozing off like that." The calmness has returned to his voice. I can't work the man out. He swings from polite to vicious without warning. Initially, he struck me as a sadistic individual, but now something tells me it's just a means to an end for him, all this... torture.

He turns his back on me and unrolls the cloth across his table. More jangling noises, but heavier. I surmise these are the tools of his trade.

When he turns round again, he proves me right, though I wish to God I hadn't been. He's thumbing a large blade six or seven inches long. It's pristine and glints in the light from the bulb above.

"Do you know how long a person can remain alive during a torture session, Mr Brooks?" I remain silent. "Neither do I, but I suspect we might find out together."

He approaches with the blade raised.

The next few hours are a blur of blood and barbarity. First The Torturer slices pieces off my legs and arms – thin slices like he's carving a Sunday roast. He uses a variety of brutal tools, including one that reminds me of an apple peeler. Long strips of skin are pulled back, allowing the wine-coloured liquid to flow. Muscles and tendons are exposed to the air as he continues to ask me the questions, "Who are you? What were you doing before you came here?" over and over, ad infinitum, until the repetition itself becomes a kind of torture for me.

The cuts and defacement of my body don't bother me that much (strange, I know). I believe I'm past my pain threshold already. But I soon discover that is not so.

The Torturer picks up the glass of brown liquid, and I assume he is taking a break for a drink. I'm mystified when he pours a small amount into his cupped hand. But all becomes frighteningly clear as he rubs the vinegar into my open wounds.

Like a man possessed, I buck against my constraints. My screams are loud and piercing in my own ears. All the things I have endured up to this point are overshadowed by his new game.

Again I feel a gloom descending upon me. I can't take much more and my eyelids beg to be closed. Another bucket of freezing water is hurled in my face. He won't let me escape that way, into oblivion. But to some extent I am grateful, for the water does at least wash a little of the condiment out of my sores.

"Tell me what I want to know, Mr Brooks."

I mumble something incomprehensible. He takes it as "I don't remember", the same answer I have given all along.

"So you have said repeatedly, and I don't doubt that you believe it… up to a point. But both you and I know that the truth is up there." He points to my head. "You've convinced – brainwashed – yourself into believing what you're saying. 'I don't remember.' You don't *want* to remember, Mr Brooks. Can't you see that?"

I manage a mouthful of words, but only in hushed tones. "If you know… then tell me."

"I can't do that. You have to figure it out for yourself. Christ, people like you make me sick. You're scum."

"But—"

"And still you resist. Why do you think that is? Why do you think I am doing this? It's not for the good of *your* health!" He allows himself a wry grin.

"D-Don't know," I utter. The figures at the back of the room have returned. Watching them, I feel an uncontrollable fear. Those poor, poor people. Oh God, look at them. Wretches with broken limbs and bloody faces: one small girl clutches at a teddy bear soaked in her own gore; an old woman staggers forwards, her chin a pulped mess; a young man with blond hair is missing part of his left shoulder, the meat torn away somehow.

"You *do* know, admit it. Think very carefully, now. Who do you work for?"

I gaze past The Torturer and he looks back at the spot where the people are gathering.

"They know. Don't they, Mr Brooks?"

Why am I nodding? Because he's right. *They* know, I'm positive of it. But how can The Torturer see the crushed souls from my dream? Who now number at least thirty; the room appears to be swelling to accommodate them all.

"I ask again, who do you work for?"

A name pops into my head: Hobson's. I don't know what it means, so I keep my mouth shut.

"Look at them, Brooks," he says, dropping the niceties of 'Mr'. Even after all he's put me through, I find this one small detail significant. "Would it surprise you to learn that their blood is on your hands?"

"No! That's not true!"

"You, Brooks, are a murderer."

What is he talking about? I'm no killer. I haven't got the stomach for it. I just couldn't. The crowd comes up to join The Torturer at his desk. All are pointing like they were in my dream. They blame me, I can see it in their dead eyes.

"And aren't they right to blame you?" The Torturer asks, reading my thoughts.

"No, I... don't think—"

"You don't think, you don't remember. I know that you *do*."

"How..." I find strength from inside, desperation driving me to ask, "How do you know all this about me, when I don't?"

He smiles again. "You know the answer to that, too."

Riddles, all riddles. The Torturer revolves now and busies himself with his implements for a final time. He chooses one to use: a stainless steel scoop.

Flanked by the ravaged collection of corpses, he sweeps forwards. They urge him on, pointing and pushing. I am more fearful of them than of him. It terrifies me and I don't know why.

"M-Make them go away!" I look from The Torturer to the faces around him, around me.

"You are to blame for their deaths, Brooks. Yes? YES?"

I scream at him: "No! It wasn't my fault. I swerved to

avoid the car… It was on the wrong side…" My breath is quick and shallow. "I had to turn the wheel to avoid it, then I couldn't… I lost control."

"Did you, or did you not, kill them?"

"Yes, you bastard. Yes!"

The people nod quietly to themselves, content with my admission. I remember now who I am, who I work for, and why I tried to forget.

"Please make them go away," I beg The Torturer.

"There are none so blind as those who will not see. First, tell me what I need to know. I need to hear you say it. Then I'll make the faces disappear."

I tell him.

And as he moves closer, bringing the instrument up to my eyes, I see his face change. It is as if someone is holding up a mirror to me. His visage has become a reflection of my own.

I hear the crying again. It is very loud, very near. I am not at all surprised to discover that I am the one shedding the tears. Before I have time to ponder this, though, I am plunged into darkness.

Permanent darkness.

———————————

I am woken by sounds at my cell door. A banging noise. Someone is breaking in. Someone has found me, albeit too late. They are calling my name.

And they are inside. I cannot see them, cannot see anything anymore, but I hear what they are saying:

"Somebody turn on the light, I can't bloody well see a thing."

"Watch your step, there's water everywhere."

"Good Christ! Sir, I think we've found him, here in the garage. He's behind this partition."

"Oh my… Look at him. I think I'm going to—"

"Has he done this? Fuck! I think he's done this to himself. Smith, don't just stand there, fetch the paramedics. Right now!"

"What's all this stuff? Clothes-line, nails, hammer... and he must have half the cutlery drawer in here with him. Shit! His eyes, he's taken his eyes out!"

"Dr Campbell, your patient's in here."

"What's that smell? Can you smell that? I think it's vinegar."

"Oh Lord in Heaven, no. I had a feeling something like this would happen. I tried to warn them at the hospital. Told them he wasn't ready to go home yet. And when he missed his appointment today..."

"Why's he done this, Sergeant?"

"It's that guy who was in the motorway pile-up last August. You remember, the driver for Hobson's Coaches. It was in all the papers. Right, Doc?"

"He blames himself for the accident. A lot of people died. Holidaymakers: men, women, children."

"That still doesn't explain—"

"It's textbook. He's tortured himself mentally for months, but it seems that wasn't enough. Thank God his neighbours heard the screams. Otherwise..."

"Smith! Where are those bloody paramedics?"

The voices drone on – does someone mention the words 'fantasy' and 'withdrawn'? – but I take no notice. I can see something now. How can that be? I know The Torturer stole my eyes. Nevertheless, I see the host of dead people pointing in my mind. My accusers.

He lied. They haven't gone away at all! They never will.

But what about The Torturer himself? He *has* gone, at least for now. The voices in my cell have chased him off.

Yet I can't help wondering, deep down inside, if he will return one day.

The Torturer
Written by Paul Kane
Based on the short story by Paul Kane

<u>INT. CELL TWILIGHT</u>

Darkness, and the first thing we're aware
of is the sound of dripping water.
Gradually we see the details of this place,
thanks to a tiny window letting in the
smallest fraction of light. The walls are
made from stone, slimy and glistening. A
rat makes its way along the cold, stone
floor and we follow its journey. It stops
to sniff at the air, then scuttles away
when it hears something else moving in the
blackness at the back of the cell.

We can barely make out its shape at first,
then a hand slams down on the floor. Slowly
the figure drags itself into view: a man,
gaunt and ill-looking. His clothes are
dishevelled, heavy bags under his eyes. His
stomach lets out a groan and he clutches it.

The sound of crying joins the dripping
water, but it's not sorrowful - it's borne
of fear. He places his head against the
wall to hear better. Then bangs his fist
against a heavy door. It's completely
useless, of course.

Next comes the sound of footsteps, in the
distance at first, then louder, louder,
until... They're right outside the door.
There's a jangling of keys, lots of keys.
One is shoved into the lock and makes a
sound like fingernails on a blackboard when
it's turned.

The door swings open with a crash against
the wall.

Two big men in silhouette are standing
there. The man in the cell tries to crawl
away but they grab him by the leg and drag
him across the floor.

They pick him up and he tries to fight
them, but his blows simply bounce off the
bigger pair. They drag him out through the
doorway by the arms, ignoring his cries. We
never see their faces.

<u>INT. INTERROGATION ROOM NON-SPECIFIC</u>

The guards kick open another door and the
man is thrown unceremoniously into a second
room, which is just as dark as the first.

                    MAN
          Why are you doing this?

But his question falls on deaf ears; the
men have gone.

He looks back at the doorway, now tantalis-
ingly open. He considers escape for a
moment, licking his lips. As he begins to
move towards the door, though, a figure
steps into the frame and bars his exit.
The camera lingers on his form, still
indistinct, just a shape against the light
of the outside corridor.

The newcomer reaches a hand into the room
and feels around on the wall for the light-
switch. He flicks it on.

A bare bulb illuminates the room and the
prisoner screws up his eyes. Opening them
slowly, the blurred features of his
surroundings come into focus: a wooden
table, with two chairs — one on either
side. Finally, he looks at the man who has
turned on the light.

He's a thickset fellow with a wide neck,
and appears to have no cheekbones to speak
of; two sloping pencil-thin eyebrows meet
in the middle of his brow. Below these are
a pair of dark brown, almost black, eyes —
framed by octagonal glasses with thin metal
rims. His hair is greying at the temples.
It looks like a military cut that has grown
out a bit. And he is dressed in a black
shirt and trousers. In his left hand he
holds a clipboard.

TORTURER
(almost toneless)
Please, take a seat.

He points at the far chair. The prisoner is
reluctant at first, but then obeys.
Wearily, he slumps down into the seat. He
looks up, expecting his jailer to sit opposite him. He doesn't; he hovers above him
like an owl with a mouse before the kill.

                    TORTURER
          Splendid, now we can begin.
                   (sneering)
            Your name. Quickly.

                      MAN
            Andrew... Andy Brooks.

The man writes something down on his
clipboard.

                    TORTURER
        You know why you're here, of course.

Brooks shakes his head.

                    TORTURER
        Oh, come now. You <u>do know</u>, Mr Brooks.
                     (beat)
                    Think.

                    BROOKS
             I... I can't remember.

                    TORTURER
         All right, if that's the way you want
         it. Tell me how you came to be here.

                    BROOKS
           Your people grabbed me and—

                    TORTURER
          Before that. Tell me what you were
          doing <u>before that</u>. What you have been
          doing for the last few months, the last
                    few years?

Brooks frowns, concentrating, wanting to
tell him. He opens his mouth... but nothing
comes out.

                    TORTURER
          Where do you live? What's the street
                name, the number? Hmm?

Brooks shakes his head, exasperated.

                    BROOKS
                I'm sorry, I—

His interrogator swings the clipboard
round, missing Brooks' head by centimetres,
then slams it loudly on the table.

                    TORTURER
          Not good enough. Who do you work for?

                    BROOKS
          I... I don't know. What's all this
                    about?

                    TORTURER
          It's very simple. You tell me which
          side you're on. Make life easy for
                    yourself.

He walks around the back of Brooks' chair
and puts his hands on his shoulders.

                    BROOKS
          I'm not on anyone's side.

His grip on Brooks' shoulders tightens and
we see him wince. The Torturer's fingers
inch towards Brooks' neck.

                  TORTURER
        We're all on one side or the other...
        I'm not a patient man. You should know
        this. I've been hired to do a job, and
        that's exactly what I'm going to do, Mr
                    Brooks.

                    BROOKS
          (mustering up some courage)
        Listen, where am I? What do you want
                  from me?

                  TORTURER
          I've told you that already.

                    BROOKS
        When am I going to get something
                  to eat?

                  TORTURER
        When you answer my questions. Who do
        you work for, and what have you done?

                    BROOKS
          What have I—

The hands tighten around Brooks' throat,
forcing a puff of breath out of him. He
starts to choke, bringing up his hands,
clawing at The Torturer's fingers — all to
no avail.

Brooks is wheezing now, can hardly catch
his breath. Just when it looks like The
Torturer is never going to let him go, he
shoves Brooks' head against the side of the
table.

Brooks raises his head once, blood trick-
ling down his forehead, then he collapses
onto the table.

FADE TO BLACK.

<u>INT. CELL NIGHT (BROOKS' NIGHTMARE)</u>

We're inside Brooks' dream — or should that
be nightmare. There's a group of people
gathered around him in his cell. Like the
guards, they are just shadows at first.

Then one steps up to reach out, except the
man's hand suddenly comes off and dangles
on a piece of loose flesh. He's coming
closer, and closer.

Brooks opens his mouth to scream.

<u>INT. INTERROGATION ROOM NON-SPECIFIC</u>

The Torturer is slapping Brooks' face,

bringing him around. We can only see a
headshot of Brooks. Slowly, but surely, he
wakes, shaking his head and wincing once
more at the pain.

> TORTURER
> It's not polite to pass out in the
> middle of a conversation.

Brooks turns his head and moans. Then he
tries to move and finds he can't. We pan
down to see his arms have been strapped to
the back of the chair. His shirt is wide
open, revealing a pale and sweaty chest.

> TORTURER
> Do you remember what we were talking
> about before you 'dropped off'?

Brooks attempts a nod, but it hurts too
much.

> TORTURER
> Good. My question still stands. Who do
> you work for?

> BROOKS
> (slurred)
> Told you... Don't remember.

> TORTURER
> I refuse to believe that.

The Torturer stands back and picks something up off the table. He coils it around

his hand and we suddenly realise it is a
length of black plastic wire, but he's
holding it like a whip.

The man smiles sadistically... then slashes
Brooks across the chest.

Brooks writhes in the chair, howling with
pain. A wicked red welt has appeared on his
chest and there is some blood as well. Two
more strokes follow in quick succession,
one across his stomach, the other just shy
of his neck. Brooks pitches forward on his
chair, as far as his bonds will allow him,
but he doesn't cry out. There is a look of
determination on his face as if he won't
give The Torturer the satisfaction, and
he's biting his bottom lip to help with the
agony.

                    TORTURER
     We'll try again. Tell me what you know.

                     BROOKS
         (panting, looking his tormentor in
                     the eye)
         My name is And... Andy Brooks... I
              don't remember any more...

The Torturer swipes Brooks again, this time
across the knuckles on the backs of his
hands. They weep red tears.

                    TORTURER
                  (still evenly)
                   Tell me.

                     BROOKS
                N-Nothing to tell.

There's a succession of slashes, one after
the other, shown as quick shots. We are
tight on The Torturer's face; there's a
glint in his eye that tells us he's actually enjoying this. When we return to
Brooks, his torso is raw.

As a last resort the man starts on Brooks'
face. His head rocks with each fresh crack
of the whip.

Brooks lolls in the seat and The Torturer
realises that he's going to be forced to
end this session there. The two guards
arrive, undo Brooks' bonds and carry him
out of the room, his feet scraping along
the floor as he goes.

He's tossed back into his cell with a
thump. Brooks just about has the energy to
raise his head once, then blacks out again.

<u>INT. CELL NIGHT (BROOKS' NIGHTMARE)</u>

He's back in the room with the mutilated
man. But the other people are starting to
come into focus now. Not just men, but
women and children too.

One girl, she can't be more than twenty-
five, has a long piece of metal sticking
out of her side, ragged and sharp.

A little boy turns and we see that half his
face is a bloodied pulp.

One final person — their sex indistinct —
is dragging themselves along on the floor
by their arms, the bottom half of their
body in darkness.

When they haul themselves even further into
the shot, we see that they have no legs at
all. Organs slip out onto the stone floor
as they crawl along.

The person stops and reaches out a hand,
moaning.

<u>INT. CELL TWILIGHT</u>

Brooks rolls over and the pain snaps him
sharply awake. He lets out a cry, but we're
not sure if it's because of the wounds or
the dream. We can hear the crying coming
from another cell again.

There's a shape in the corner of his cell.
The briefest of outlines; a figure. Brooks
shakes his head and looks again.

He sees only shadows on the stone wall.

INT. INTERROGATION ROOM NON-SPECIFIC

Brooks is brought back into the dark interrogation room by the men - we're still not
given a view of their faces - but this time
his shirt is gone. We can see the marks
left by the vicious whipping on his bare
chest.

The guards chain him up to the far wall by
clasps, arms outstretched. But the chains
are short and don't allow him to sag.

The men leave Brooks alone with the lights
off. He waits, watching the open doorway —
the escape route mocking him... then
suddenly stiffens and looks down.

Something is crawling up his leg. In the
half-light he can see what look like
spindly legs, a spider's legs. But they're
big: bigger than a tarantula. The 'spider'
carries on crawling up and we cut back to
see the terror on Brooks' face. He daren't
shake his leg, daren't even move in case it
bites him.

Then we see that it isn't a spider at all.
It's a hand... clutching at his trouser
leg, using it to pull itself up. More
fingers join it, then hands — on both legs.
They're pawing at him, reaching higher and
higher.

                    BROOKS
                  (terrified)
                    No...

The light comes on suddenly, we're given no
warning. It takes a second or two for
Brooks' eyes to adjust again. When he looks
down he sees that the hands have vanished.

And The Torturer is standing at the door;
he doesn't have the clipboard.

                   TORTURER
    Good morning, Mr Brooks. I trust you
    slept well. I'm sorry we had to get you
    up so early, but we've got a lot to do
      and so little time in which to
              accomplish it.

He saunters over towards Brooks, hands in
his pockets.

                   TORTURER
    Perhaps you might see reason today. If
               not, well...
                   (beat)
      Yesterday was a mere taster of the
      pleasures to come. But it would be
    better for all concerned if you just
               co-operated.

                    BROOKS
     Please... Please, I've done nothing
                  to you.

                    TORTURER
   Nothing to me personally, no. But it's
   not as simple as that, Mr Brooks. When
   I'm called in, people expect results.
   Nothing more, nothing less. And I
   always get them. You <u>will tell me what
   I want to know.</u>
                    (beat)
   In the end they always do.

                    BROOKS
      How can I tell you anything when I
         don't even know myself?

The Torturer ignores him completely and
strolls over to the other side of the room.
He stands there for a minute, nodding to
himself, then comes back across.

As he makes his way towards Brooks, he
takes a small plastic bag out of his
pocket. We can't see what's inside, but it
jangles like the keys that opened the cell
door.

                    TORTURER
      I ask you once more: who do you work
         for and what do you do?

Brooks drops his head and sighs. There's
more rattling. When he looks up again he
sees The Torturer at his right hand.

He's holding one of the objects from the

bag, a thin sliver of metal, possibly a pin
or nail.

Holding it between thumb and forefinger, he
places it under one of Brooks' fingernails.
Then he produces a small hammer from his
other pocket.

Seeing what is about to come, Brooks
panics.

> BROOKS
> (begging)
> No, wait, please...

But it's too late. We see the hammer drawn
back, but are denied the actual sight of
the nail going in. We just see The
Torturer's face, then Brooks screaming in
agony.

After the fact, we see the metal shard
embedded in there. As The Torturer takes
another one and does the same thing
again...

And again... And again...

When we cut back to the hand, there are
pins underneath each of Brooks' nails — a
couple of which look like they are about to
split or fall off. It's a wince moment
designed to make the audience feel his
pain.

TORTURER
How's your memory now, Mr Brooks?
Anything coming back to you?

Brooks' hand twitches involuntarily and he
cries out with each movement, the pain
shooting up his arm. His cheeks are wet
with tears.

The Torturer waits for his answer, leaning
in close to Brooks' face. Then he bangs his
fist on the wall just behind Brooks' head.

TORTURER
You disappoint me.

BROOKS' P.O.V.

Over The Torturer's shoulder, he sees
blurred shapes — because of the tears.
They're figures: the figures from his
dream.

When he blinks again, they're gone.

BROOKS
I-I don't—

TORTURER
Who do you work for? Who? Who?
(shouting)
WHO?
BROOKS
Don't r-remember.

> TORTURER
> What are you? What do you do? What?
> What?
> (shouting)
> WHAT?

Brooks remains silent.

> TORTURER
> Very well.

The Torturer strides out of the room and slams the door behind him. Brooks nods forwards, his eyes drooping.

The pain is too much for him and he blacks out again.

<u>INT. INTERROGATION ROOM NON-SPECIFIC</u>

Brooks is woken by a bucket of freezing cold water hitting him in the face. He lets out a yelp and shakes his head, then shivers slightly.

There are more buckets lined up next to the table leg. But on top of the table there's a glass filled with brown liquid and a bundle of black cloth.

Brooks winces, looking over to his hand, the one with the pins under the nails — it's obvious that the pain in it has awakened when he did.

TORTURER
(calm again)
Do try to remain conscious. It makes my
job so much harder when you keep dozing
off like that.

He turns his back on Brooks and attends to
the bundle on the table. We can't see
what's in it yet, but there is more
jangling.

Then The Torturer moves to one side and
finishes unrolling the bundle. In velvety
pockets are the tools of his trade, a
hideous array of shiny metallic torture
implements, glinting in the light from the
bare bulb.

He takes out a large blade about six or
seven inches long and thumbs the end of it.

TORTURER
Do you know how long a person can
remain alive during a torture session,
Mr Brooks?

Brooks says nothing; his petrified face
says it all.

TORTURER (CONT'D)
Neither do I, but I suspect we might find
out together.

He approaches Brooks with the blade raised.

INT. INTERROGATION ROOM NON-SPECIFIC

Montage sequence with close-ups of The Torturer cutting Brooks' flesh, slicing strips from his arms, using a variety of tools, including one that looks like an apple peeler.

Blood flows, making it harder to see the specifics of what he's doing. Intermixed with these shots are glimpses of The Torturer's face and close-ups of Brooks' screaming mouth.

The questions are repeated over and over:

TORTURER
Who are you? What were you doing before you came here?

Just when we think it's over, The Torturer fetches the glass of brown liquid from the table. He raises this so it looks like he's going to take a drink - then he throws the contents at Brooks, who bucks and contorts in agony.

TORTURER
Vinegar, Mr Brooks. Just a plain, old condiment...
(beat)
Simple, but effective.

It looks like Brooks might pass out again, so The Torturer throws another bucket of

cold water over him. At least it washes
away some of the vinegar.

TORTURER
Tell me what I want to know, Mr Brooks.

BROOKS
(mumbling)
I don't remember.

TORTURER
So you have said repeatedly, and I
don't doubt that you believe it... up
to a point. But both you and I know
that the truth is up there.

The Torturer taps Brooks' forehead.

TORTURER
You've convinced — brainwashed —
yourself into believing what you're
saying. "I don't remember." You don't
<u>want to remember, Mr Brooks. Can't you</u>
<u>see that?</u>

BROOKS
(whispering, though it takes effort)
If you know... then tell me.

TORTURER
I can't do that. You have to figure it
out for yourself. Christ, people like
you make me sick. You're scum!

                         BROOKS
                          But—

                        TORTURER
And still you resist. Why do you think
that is? Why do you think I am doing
this? It's not for the good of <u>your</u>
                        <u>health!</u>

The Torturer grins wryly.

                         BROOKS
                      D-Don't know.

                        TORTURER
You <u>do know</u>, admit it. Think very
carefully, now. Who do you work for?

Brooks gazes past The Torturer.

                        TORTURER
              What are you looking at?

Brooks sees the men, women and children
there again at the back of the room. This
time, his tormentor follows his gaze.

                        TORTURER
Ah, I see... They know. Don't they, Mr
                        Brooks?

Their numbers are increasing, filling the
room almost. The Torturer faces him again.

To his own surprise, Brooks finds himself
nodding.

TORTURER
I ask again, who do you work for?

Brooks frowns as if he almost had it, the
answer that would release him from his
bonds. But it's gone again. He stays
silent.

TORTURER
Look at them, Brooks! Would it surprise
you to learn that their blood is on
your hands?

BROOKS
No! That's not true...

TORTURER
Yes. You, Brooks, are a murderer.

The figures are reaching out. No, we can
see now that they're pointing. Pointing at
Brooks.

BROOKS
I... I could never...

TORTURER
Haven't the stomach for it? I admit, it
takes some doing. But you'd be
surprised how easy it can be sometimes.

We see close-ups of the crowds' eyes —

their pointing fingers. Accusing Brooks,
blaming him. The Torturer casts another
look back, then faces Brooks.

TORTURER
And aren't they right to blame you?

BROOKS
No, I... don't think—

TORTURER
You don't think, you don't remember. I
<u>know</u> that you do.

BROOKS
How...
(struggling with the words)
How do you... know all this about me...
when I don't?

The Torturer laughs.

TORTURER
You know the answer to that, too.

The Torturer turns and busies himself with
his implements on the table a final time.
We hear the jangling of the metal... But
also something else. The crying has
returned, faint but noticeable.

When The Torturer turns round again, he's
holding a steel scoop in his hand.

The ravaged collection of corpses are

flanking him as he moves forwards. Brooks
seems more frightened of them than of The
Torturer himself.

He looks at the man, pleadingly.

                    BROOKS
            M-Make them go away.

                    TORTURER
        You are to blame for their deaths,
                Brooks. Yes?
                (shouting)
                    YES?

                    BROOKS
            No. It wasn't my fault.

                    TORTURER
            Yes it was. Admit it.

                    BROOKS
        No, I swerved to avoid the car... It
            was on the wrong side...

                    TORTURER
                    Go on.

                    BROOKS
        I had to... turn the wheel to avoid it,
        then I couldn't... I lost control...

                    TORTURER
        Did you, or did you not, kill them?

                    BROOKS
                 (reluctantly)
          Yes, you bastard. Yes!

The people nod, apparently content with his
admission.

                   TORTURER
          You remember now, don't you?

                    BROOKS
          Yes... God in heaven, yes...
                    (beat)
          Please, make them go away.

                   TORTURER
          There are none so blind as those who
          will not see. First, tell me what I
          need to know. I need to hear you say
          it. Then I'll make the faces disappear.

He leans in closer and Brooks whispers
something to him. The Torturer smiles.

                   TORTURER
                 (satisfied)
          Good. Very good.

As he pulls his head away slightly, we see
the pair in frame together. Then close-ups
of The Torturer, Brooks, The Torturer...

Until the features of The Torturer begin to
change, until they become like those of
Brooks.

The crying is much louder now — and with a
chilling realisation we discover that it is
coming from Brooks. The Torturer, now
wearing Brooks' face, holds up the scoop.
He brings it closer to his victim's eye.

Blackness, accompanied by a squelching
noise and a faint scream.

<u>INT. GARAGE NIGHT</u>

Blackness still.

Then a rattling sound. A metal door swings
upwards and open. It's a garage door and in
the open space are two large figures; for a
second we can't see them properly, they
look like the guards who brought Brooks to
the interrogation room...

MAN'S VOICE
Someone turn a light on, I can't see a
thing...

A light is switched on; a single bare bulb.
And we see that the two men are police. Who
move further into the garage.

FIRST YOUNGER POLICEMAN
Mr Brooks... Mr Brooks, are you there?

Another man enters through the garage door,
placing his hand on the stone wall. He's
dressed in ordinary clothes.

SECOND OLDER POLICEMAN
Watch your step, there's water
everywhere.

The first policeman is at the rear of the garage, he turns to look behind a partition and steps back, holding his mouth as if he's going to be sick. The second policeman rushes up to have a look.

SECOND OLDER POLICEMAN
What's all this on the floor...?

We see him stepping over a length of black clothes-line, a hammer, some nails.

FIRST YOUNGER POLICEMAN
Jesus Christ... Jesus Christ I think...
Has he done this to himself? Shit, look
at his eyes...
(beat)
He's taken out his eyes....

SECOND OLDER POLICEMAN
Don't just stand there, Smith, call for
the bloody paramedics.

Smith is happy to get out of the way.

SECOND OLDER POLICEMAN
Dr Campbell, Dr Campbell... I think
we've found your patient.

The man at the door comes into the garage and joins him at the back.

DR CAMPBELL
Oh no. I had a feeling something like
this would happen. I tried to warn them
at the hospital. Told them he wasn't
ready to go home yet. And when he
missed his appointment today...

SECOND OLDER POLICEMAN
Can you smell that? I think it's
vinegar... And he's got half the
cutlery drawer in here with him.

FIRST YOUNGER POLICEMAN
Sarge? Why's he done this? I don't
understand.

SECOND OLDER POLICEMAN
It's that guy who was in the motorway
pile-up last August. You remember, the
driver for Hobson's Coaches. It was in
all the papers. Right, Doc?

DR CAMPBELL
He blames himself for the accident. A
lot of people died, holidaymakers: men,
women, children...

FIRST YOUNGER POLICEMAN
I still don't...

DR CAMPBELL
It's textbook. He's tortured himself
mentally for months, but it seems that
wasn't enough.

> ### SECOND OLDER POLICEMAN
> Smith, where the bloody hell are those
> paramedics?

INT. INTERROGATION ROOM NON-SPECIFIC

The room is empty and dark. Gone are the table, chairs, chains. Only Brooks remains, head down, slumped in the darkness, as we found him at the beginning...

But then the people from the crash come again, emerging from the blackness.

They form a circle around Brooks. He looks up and we get a quick glimpse of his sightless eyes.

> ### BROOKS
> No... No, you promised... You promised!

The figures continue to close in on Brooks, closer, closer, pawing him with their hands... Until they swamp him completely.

And The Torturer's laughter rings long and loud in our ears.

> ### FADE OUT RUN CREDITS

***NOTE** - An alternative method of presenting the scene with the policemen and doctor could be to just have a black screen and voices, because Brooks has lost his eyes.

THE BACKGROUND TO...
THE TORTURER

'The Torturer' is the story that's been with me the longest, dating back even to before 'The Opportunity'. It was one of the first tales I wrote for the small presses, back in the '90s, and one of the handful I'm most proud of. I've certainly got the most mileage out of it! It's been turned into a comic script, which artist Ian Simmons provided images for (we still hope to finish and publish this one day), a play, and the character of The Torturer himself has cropped up in other tales, from my PL Kane crime novelette 'Graffitiland' (this was where I finally named him: Mr Waterhouse) and Controllers story 'The Scoop', to the third novel in the *RED* trilogy, *Deep RED*. I've also been recently toying with the idea of giving him a back history in a short story, but it won't be anything like you're expecting.

The idea for the original came from those kind of twisty psychological crime stories and films where you're just not quite sure what's going on or which way is up. What might at first look like a supernatural event in 'The Torturer' – the ghosts or resurrected versions of my character Andy Brooks' victims – ends up being something a lot more frightening, or at least I hope so. I was also hugely inspired by, oddly enough, a couple of SF TV shows. There's an episode of *Star Trek: The Next Generation* where Picard (the always excellent Patrick Stewart) is interrogated for information, the second of a two-parter called 'Chain of Command'. Then there's a *Babylon 5* episode where Sheridan (Bruce Boxleitner) is given the same treatment, 'Intersections in Real Time'. Those really stuck with me, mainly due to the stellar performances of those involved.

Frustratingly, I had quite a bit of trouble getting the story published once it was written. I tried everywhere with it, and finally placed it in a small press magazine that went belly up before it could appear. Sigh. So I thought 'sod this for a game of soldiers' and included it as a new story in my second collection *Touching the Flame* from Rainfall Books in 2002. I now do that with any shorts I can't place, save them up as new pieces for collections.

Given how well the story leant itself to other media and formats, it was perhaps inevitable that I'd end up turning it into a film script. Again, though, I had a hard time getting it off the ground – perhaps because of the effects involved? I remember Marie arranging for a meet with a director down in London (this was back when Marie and I were just good friends as opposed to having been married now for many years). He bought us lunch, we talked, he came up with ideas on how to shoot it, then everything just fizzled out, as these things sometimes – or even often – do.

I tried to get people interested several more times over the next decade or so, then eventually gave up... until along came a Texas-based company called Little Spark Films. I should probably explain that I wrote a Sherlock Holmes/*Hellraiser* crossover, with Clive's permission, which came out in 2016: *Sherlock Holmes and the Servants of Hell*, published mass market by Solaris/Rebellion. It became a bit of a fan favourite, and Derek Neal created a puzzle box based on the red and black cover; he sent me one and I now have it on display in the house. Sold by Configuration Boxes, it inspired a short promotional video which saw Holmes and Watson with the box in question, filmed by… none other than Little Spark (they did a few of these, including a *Nightbreed*-inspired one).

This put me in touch with director Joe Manco and producer Catalina Querida, the husband and wife team behind LSF, and we've all been friends since. They're currently heavily involved in work for Troma. I asked if they might be looking for short film scripts to make, and when they said yes I sent them *The Torturer*. They fell in love with it straight away, optioned and bought the script, then set to work making it a reality – which involved raising the ten grand needed to make it.

Every now and again they'd send me updates on how they were getting on, including make-up effects tests (there was a particularly gruesome one involving the metal nails in the fingers), publicity stuff (they used some of Ian's b/w Torturer images to help with this) and eventually auditions. It was all very exciting.

I can recall vividly the day that I was told who would be playing Andy and The Torturer, namely Pinhead from *Hellraiser: Revelations*, Paul T. Taylor (thereby retaining the *HR* connection) and Lawrence Varnado from *Breaking Bad* and *Sin City: A Dame to Kill For*. A read-through then a shoot followed, and the guys posted behind the scenes photos from all this, including other members of the cast like Robb Hudspeth, Kristin Keith and Nathan Gershon in costume/make-up. This was around the same time that the feature of *Sacrifice* was filming too in Norway, so it was all really surreal for me – and I couldn't get to either of the sets!

A lengthy post-production followed, which included bringing on board musicians Paragraph Taylor and the band ManifestiV to work on the soundtrack and artist Anthony Galatis to come up with a final poster. During this time many people were very supportive of the project, not least the Clive Barker Podcast and *Hellraiser* Podcast guys. And to my surprise, the finished thing ended up being around 40 mins instead of the 20 mins I'd envisaged – but worked much better. There was even some talk of it being a pilot for a potential TV show eventually.

When Joe and Catalina began sending the film off to festivals, around 2020, it started winning awards. *Lots* of awards. Including: Five Gold Tiers at the Horror Movie Awards, Only The Best Film Awards, 4th Dimension International Film Festival and Best Horror and Best Actor at the RS Film Fest 2022. All culminating with the movie heading for streaming in the US and UK, on the likes of Tubi, Plex and Amazon Prime! Last I heard it was available to stream in over 100 countries, which is quite the accomplishment.

I couldn't be prouder of everyone involved in this and there are definitely plans for us all to work on stuff again in the future – so, watch this space!

Concept artwork by Ian Simmons for the comic book version of The Torturer, *used to promote the film campaign.*

A page of the comic book version of The Torturer *— used in the preparation period of the movie.*

The original poster used during the prep period.

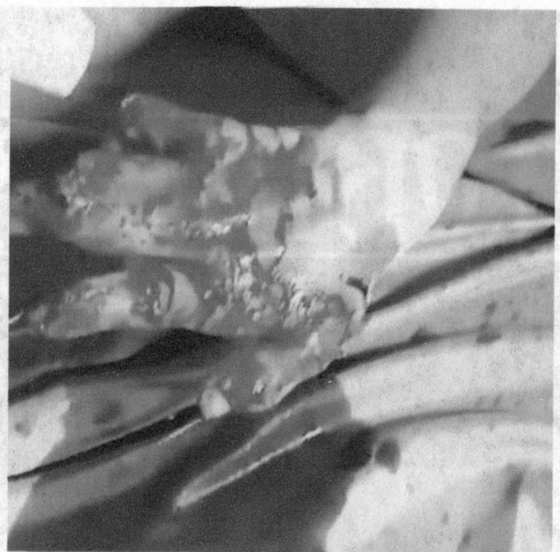

An effects test for the nails under the 'nails scene.

Star Paul T. Taylor (Andy Brooks) and director Joe Manco in a short video to raise funds for the budget.

The table readthrough with the cast, including Paul in the middle.

The Torturer himself, Lawrence Varnado, going through his lines in the readthrough.

The stars of the film, Lawrence and Paul T. Taylor.

The cast and crew of The Torturer.

Paul T. Taylor at the start of filming.

Jörg Viktor Steins-Lauß on the set of The Torturer.

Nathan Gershon as a motorcyclist victim with Catalina Querida, co-founder of Little Spark Films.

Filming what became known as 'All Ghouls Day' on set, with Nerd Scum's Cory Ahre on the clapperboard (photo credit Will Gwin).

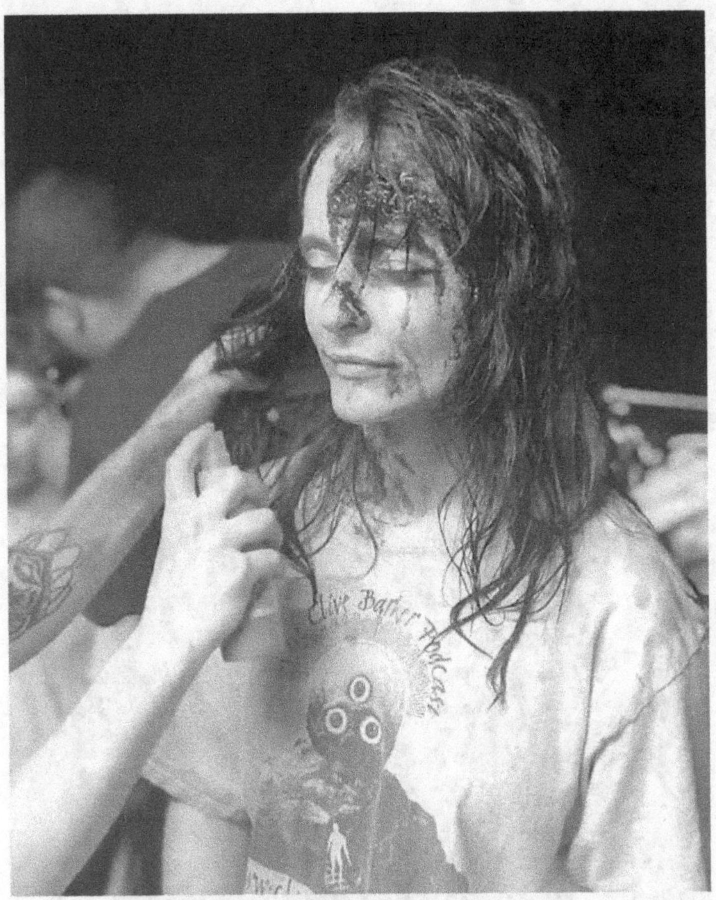

Kristin Keith being made up on set as Girl with the Big Eyes.

On the set of The Torturer.

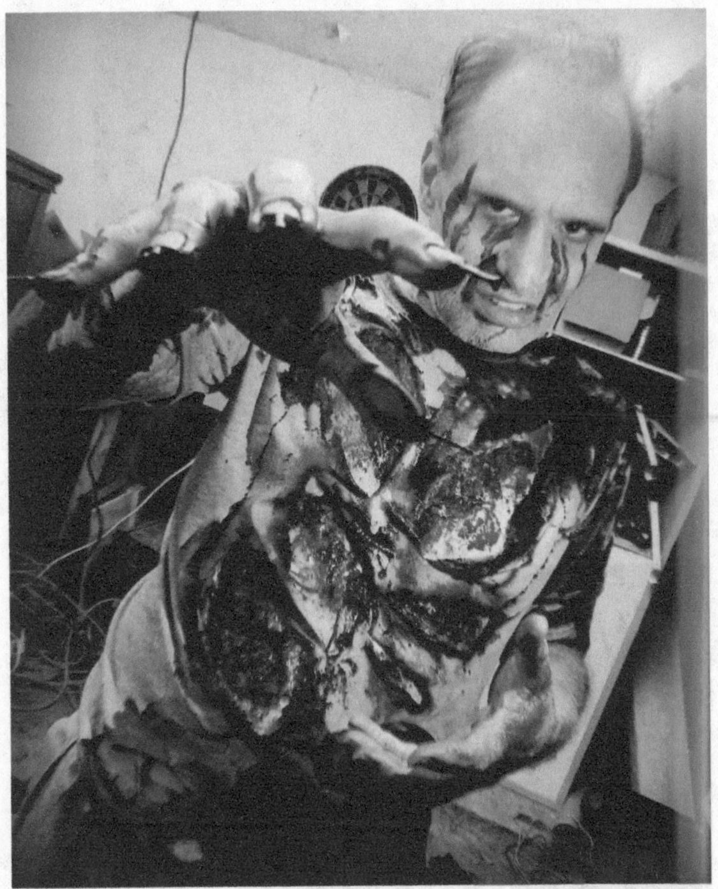

Paul T. Taylor in full tortured mode.

Robb Hudspeth, playing Sarge in the finale.

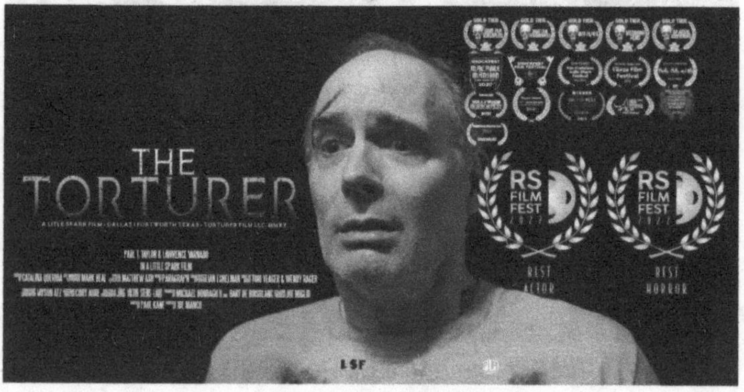

Variant poster with laurels.

The trailer finally dropping online.

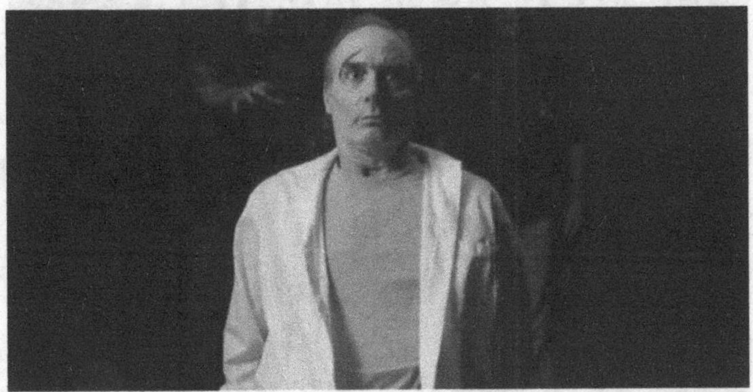

A still from The Torturer *trailer.*

Anthony Galatis' The Torturer *artwork at Shockfest Film Festival, hosted by Elvira – the poster itself was projected in Times Square.*

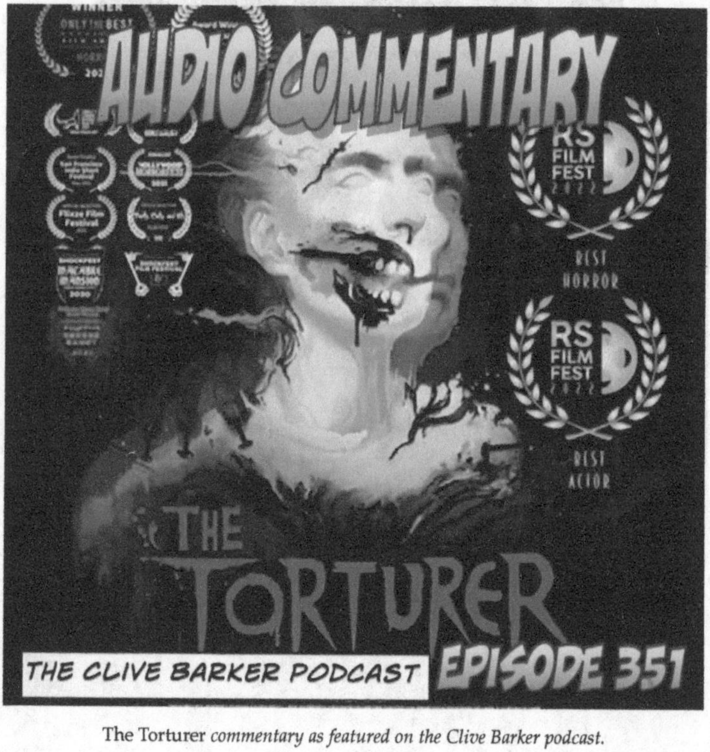

The Torturer *commentary as featured on the Clive Barker podcast.*

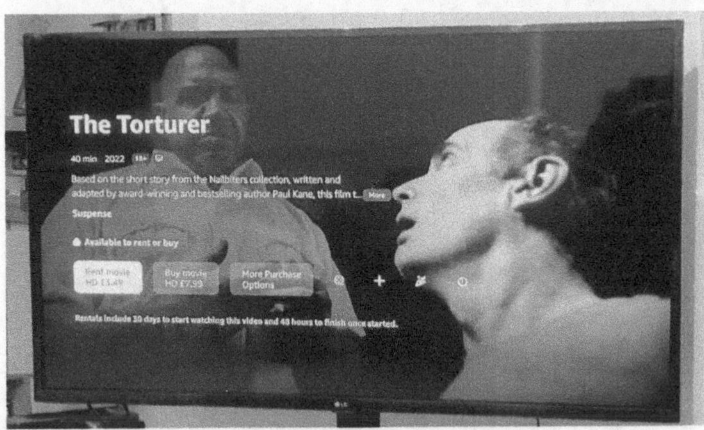

The Torturer drops on Amazon Prime in the UK.

Director Joe Manco with the poster for the film.

CREDITS

Director: Dave Morgan
Screenwriter: Paul Kane (based on his own short story)
Producers: Dave Morgan, Neal McAndrew

CAST

Annabel Entress: Annette
Caitlin Bradley: Hayley
Andrew Abrahamson: Terry
Vin Hawke: James

PRESENCE

THE SHORT STORY

Life is sweet; it's what he used to say.

He'd borrowed it from his grandfather, who had said those words on his deathbed. What Terry used to say, but couldn't anymore. He was gone. Had been gone for a good three months – not that any week, day, hour, minute or second of those months had been what you could call good.

Not for her, not left behind like this. Annette Griffiths gave a small laugh, which held no humour at all. Left behind; what a strange phrase. Like she was the loser in some kind of race. Or, more accurately, a marathon – where the runner in front had suddenly sped up; then turned a corner, out of sight.

Would she ever catch up to him? Perhaps, someday. But not in this life, because it wasn't any kind of race you *wanted* to finish, let alone win.

Annette stood and stared at the boxes and bags in front of her on the landing. It wasn't much to show for a life: a person's belongings reduced to so much detritus waiting to be taken to charity shops. Although it was nice to think that someone, somewhere, would get the benefit of clothes and books which were of no use to her.

Just reminders of the stabbing pain she still felt.

Of no use to Terry, either. Not now. Not anymore. Never again... She bit her lip, fighting back tears that were threatening to break free from the corners of her eyes. Annette shook her head. She'd done enough of that; *too much*. Time to pull herself together, be strong. Become the person that she'd pretended to be since—

She'd played the part in public, and especially for little Hayley. There was no sense both of them being in bits. Hayley had always been a daddy's girl, Terry's little princess. In a lot of respects it might even have hit her daughter harder than it had Annette, but then she'd always been quite a nervous child. Annette had just got her back to school a couple of weeks ago, and only then by bribing her that they might venture to Central Parks when the weather finally turned warmer. It would do them both good to spend more time together, especially away from here. Try and get back to some kind of normality, whatever that meant.

There you go again, sorting things out, she said to herself. *Trying to fix things.*

Terry had always called her the practical one, while he was more emotional – probably where Hayley got it from. He'd often go off in a huff if they had an argument – which only happened rarely, it had to be said – while she'd want to just fix things again, finally resorting to tears when she got nowhere.

Not many saw the softer side of Annette. Perhaps only Terry had really seen it.

Her eyes pricked again.

Try not to think about it. Think about something else, like the day you met – introduced by a mutual friend at Uni – or your wedding day, how handsome Terry had looked with his wavy brown hair, how beautiful he said you'd been in your dress.

Try not to think of that other day, try not to hear the phone's shrill ring. And of course, suddenly she was there again, picking it up, questioning the sense of the caller.

"No... that can't be... You've got it wrong... He was only

here half an hour ago." Like that made a difference, like you couldn't be here one minute, gone the next. It was the way of the world. Life and...

He'd gone out for a walk to the shops, that's all. He got so bored these days since he'd lost his job and couldn't find another. He'd been a salesman, used to travelling, so being cooped up indoors for too long drove him crazy.

It had happened as he'd been about to cross the street to the newsagents, to pick up one of his monthly magazines. One of those writing ones, a life-long ambition (in a life which hadn't been that long) he was hoping to turn into a profession now he had some time on his hands. Always the creative soul. Not that he'd done any actual writing yet, just read about it, just talked about it. Well, no writing that she knew about anyway... "I want to help bring in some more money," he'd told her, the redundancy package he'd got being what it was – and almost exhausted. "Then you wouldn't have to do so much of that book-keeping stuff of an evening."

She'd always been good with figures, always seen them in her head, been able to work out sums. Solving problems. But old school, jotting things down on paper. Actual book-keeping, in an actual book. In spite of the fact she knew how to use them, she had no time for computers and programs that would do this for her. Where was the fun in that? It was something... there was that word again... *practical* she could do.

But Terry had found a way to help with the money, hadn't he? In a roundabout fashion. A life insurance policy that meant he had to be—

She'd pictured the scene in her mind so many times, like something out of a medical drama. Terry lifting his foot, about to take a step off the pavement, then screwing up his face, clutching at his head, doing a swan dive any premier league footballer would be proud of.

The reality was almost definitely much, much worse. Terry had probably vomited – one of the early signs, apparently –

maybe even fitted. Nobody would tell her. Not the owner of the paper shop, who'd eventually spotted Terry – how many people had simply walked by? Annette wondered – not the paramedics who were summoned. It was something she really didn't need to know, but which she would often ponder.

She'd always imagined they'd go together. Old farts on a beach, sat on a bench, watching the tide roll in and get sucked back out again. And waiting, simply waiting. Or in bed, a kiss on the cheek, a switching out of the light. A closing of the eyes. Then both waking up in... wherever it was you ended up. *If* you ended up anywhere. In her fantasy, they'd both go to that place together. Heaven possibly, where they'd sit on clouds and drink champagne with the angels all day, who'd congratulate them on lives well led. Tell them what good people they'd been, how they'd helped and cared for others... well, done what they could. They gave to charity when they could afford it.

Gave to charity shops. Annette's eyes found the bags and boxes once more.

No, don't think about that. Think about...

Too late, her mind had spun on – fast-forwarding to that replay of the day it happened. *The* day. The *only* day... Now she was with the fat, balding doctor and he was telling her all this stuff about brain haemorrhages; preparing her, she guessed. Saying it was more common than she thought, that they accounted for 13% of all strokes (unlucky for some, eh?); that people like President Roosevelt and Richard Burton had died of the same thing (she remembered thinking *What?* And then *what?*); saying it could happen at any age, that any of us could go just like *that*. And he'd clicked his fingers, actually clicked them. She could still hear that noise, same as she could the telephone.

Click!

Oblivion. Nothing on the other side. There couldn't be. If

she wasn't with him, hadn't gone at the same time to that paradise land up above, then how could she believe in—

"Are you all right?" he asked her. The most stupid question in the history of stupid questions. How could she be all right? How could she ever be all right again? Yet she'd found herself nodding. The tears hadn't come then. Not yet.

Not even when she'd had to identify the body, been ushered inside that cold room which looked like it'd had all the colour leeched from it. She walked stiffly, like a zombie. No… don't mention zombies. There was no coming back from this; her husband wasn't going to sit up and try to eat her brains. This was real life. Real death, too.

They'd opened that metal door, and she remembered thinking it was like some kind of huge filing cabinet for corpses. "Griffiths, Griffiths... give me a second. Ah yes, here we are, under the G's. As in G for Gone."

Even as they pulled back that cloth covering his face, right up to the last second, she'd hoped they'd made some kind of mistake. That this was somebody else's spouse, someone else's problem to fix.

"Is this your husband, Mrs Griffiths?" the man had asked – she couldn't even remember what that one looked like.

She'd wanted to shake her head. *Of course* this wasn't Terry, because her husband was alive and well. She'd only seen him a couple of hours ago, called goodbye to him as he'd gone out through the front door – oh, how she wished she'd gone downstairs, left what she was doing (she couldn't remember what it was now, nothing important, certainly not as important as seeing your husband alive for the last time, kissing him, holding him while he was still warm). Wished she'd rushed downstairs and begged him not to go: "What do you need that stupid magazine for anyway? I need you more."

But it wasn't the leaving that had done this, not the leaving of the house at any rate. Could have happened while he was sitting on the sofa. She couldn't blame that; couldn't blame anything. There *was* nothing to blame.

People just don't die like this, she remembered thinking. They die in car accidents, of terminal illnesses that drag on for months, years even. They're stabbed by muggers. Or lost at sea. But not this, she couldn't get her head around *this*.

Again, she'd found herself nodding. It was him, even though it wasn't. Even though the colour had drained from him, just as it had the room.

The rest had been a bit of a blur: being driven home, sitting with a neighbour who'd been dragged into this – old Mrs Bell, who'd rubbed Annette's shoulders and said "There, there" at regular intervals; then Hayley arriving home, having walked with her friend and her mum, as per usual on Thursdays, Annette still not crying even as she had to break the news to her daughter about what had happened.

Next, all the arrangements for the funeral, done on autopilot – the service itself at the local church, during which she remembered picturing God, white flowing beard like Father Christmas, hand curled into a gun shape and pointing, aiming at Terry, then thumb coming down like a hammer.

Going through the motions.

She remembered the snow on the ground, though. A watery sun straining to break through the clouds above, but offering no warmth even if it could. A handful of friends and relatives standing around the grave. And the coffin, so small she wondered how Terry could possibly be inside that box.

How his stuff could possibly be inside those in front of her now.

It was a couple of weeks after that, on Terry's birthday (as opposed to his much more significant *death*day), that she began to cry. It had been inevitable really; sooner or later something had to give. She'd waited for Hayley to go into a coma at last, after crying *herself* to sleep again. It had finally sunk in that Terry was never coming back, that she couldn't fix things no matter how practical she was. And she'd wept all night, then been forced to put on the act for Hayley the next morning – everything's okay, *you* can break down but not Mum – and so it had gone on for a month or more until she thought there were no tears left in her.

The pricking again; there *were* tears left. Perhaps it had still been too soon to clear all this stuff away. And she still had a few bits and bobs left in the room Terry liked to call his study – really it was the little bedroom. A room she hadn't even dared enter until today.

No, it was the right time. There were too many reminders, too many things to trip her up – making her more likely to cry in front of Hayley. Annette went back into Terry's study, started to clear the last remnants of him from the room. Not in the spiritual sense, because she didn't believe in all that; if his physical form was no longer here, that meant *he* wasn't here; if he wasn't around to touch, to hold, then how could she truly 'feel' him?

In the study, especially, there had been so many things associated with Terry. He'd spent so much time in here since they'd 'let him go' from work.

Was that what she was doing? Letting him go? Or trying to?

As she was flitting about, however, she caught the corner of the desk. There was a beeping noise, and she realised she'd knocked the mouse sitting on top of the mat. Suddenly Terry's computer sparked into life. Annette started, then frowned. It took her a moment to realise that the thing must have been on standby all this time, that Terry had never had a chance to switch it off. Why would he, when he was only intending to be a short while?

Annette couldn't help herself, she sat down in the chair and gazed at the screen – wondering whether she might find something, the last thing he wrote perhaps, a story he might have been working on and never told her about, let alone showed her. But instead she found herself looking at a page on a website.

Terry's page on a social networking site – something he'd set up when he decided to begin writing. "It says here it helps to have some kind of online presence," Terry had told her, looking up from his magazine one day.

A photo of him taken on holiday several years ago – when Hayley was just a toddler – stared back at her. He looked so happy, so at peace.

Her eyes were misting again, but she fought it. In spite of herself, Annette took hold of the mouse, clicking the link that would take her to his wall. Perhaps he'd been on that before he—

The browser took her to the login page. The site had obviously logged Terry out after a certain amount of time. Annette struggled to remember his email and password, but it didn't matter because the computer had remembered them. She logged in, navigating to his opening page, then clicked on his wall.

The saltwater was welling as she saw some of the messages, from well wishers hoping Terry'd had a nice Christmas with his family, hoping he had a lovely birthday. Virtual friends from various parts of the globe, who didn't know Terry wasn't around anymore to read their posts.

She continued scrolling downwards, then stopped. There was the final message from Terry, left on the day it... On *the* day, the *only* day.

It's so cold and dark now. I don't like it.

It had been at the beginning of winter that day, it was true. Temperatures were plummeting, the nights were drawing in. Several of Terry's friends – he had thirty or so, she noted, though no family – had liked this comment, some had even agreed that they didn't care for the new season very much either.

The only thing was it had been the middle of the morning

when Terry went out for his final walk. Okay, it hadn't been bright sunlight, but you could hardly describe it as dark. Then Annette noticed the time, and a breath caught halfway up her throat.

The message had been left around midday, around the time she was identifying Terry in the morgue.

There was a pinging sound and Annette jumped in her seat, the breath suddenly shaking loose, but another catching again just as quickly. When she'd had a second or so to compose herself, Annette traced the source of the noise. The messages part of the taskbar was lit up, flashing excitedly, finally gaining someone's attention now that she'd logged in.

Annette hovered over it with the cursor, half of her wanting to see, the other half terrified of what might be in there, lurking. A message from a secret lover, perhaps? No, Terry wasn't like that; never had been. She could have put him in a room full of naked women and he'd just have tried to cover them up because he thought they were chilly.

So what...?

Annette could stand it no longer: she clicked on his messages. There were several, but not incoming as she might have thought. These were all in his outgoing folder. Who the hell had been using her husband's... her – yes, say it – *dead* husband's account? She'd get to the bottom of it, whatever happened. Personally see to it that they hurt as badly as she did right now.

They were messages from Terry, but then they would be if someone had hacked him. And they were to her account, the one he'd insisted on setting up for her so she could be his first friend on there ("It'll be like a snowball effect, you'll see..."; not much of a snowball, thirty people). She clicked on the first, dated a day after he'd suffered the collapse:

Hello... Annie? Annie, sweetheart... are you there? Please. I'm so, so scared.

She ground her teeth together, breathing in and out now

through her nose. Tears were escaping, but they were tears of fury not sadness. At the person who'd done this, who was leaving such cruel messages – what, because they thought it was funny? Bloody sickos!

She forced herself to look at more:

Please... please Annie, talk to me. I need to hear your voice. I'm so alone.

Darlin', where are you? I'm lost... I'm not sure what's happening to me.

For the love of Christ, please say something! Answer me!

That last one sounded angry, like he thought she was ignoring him. That was it, she was going to call the police, see what they had to say about—

Darlin', it's me. It's really me. I don't know what's happened or why you won't talk to me. But... Look, I can prove it. Remember the juggler. The one we saw on our first date, when we were walking through the city?

Annette's blood ran cold. How could whoever this was know about that? Yet it was right there in front of her, in the final entry dated about a fortnight ago.

He was rubbish, remember? Dropped all his clubs and we laughed, so hard?

That was when we—

—kissed for the first time, while we were laughing, the message finished for her.

Annette swallowed hard, got up and backed away from the desk. No, it couldn't be. Somebody was messing with her. But, well, they'd never told anyone that story. It was theirs, alone. That moment when they'd both first felt it.

Click!

Annette ran from the study, only just finding the toilet in time. Throwing up her lunch into the pan, then standing, stumbling into the bathroom and splashing her face with water.

She looked at herself in the mirror, dyed black strands of hair glued to her cheeks. Annette stood up straight, chin set firm. Her husband must have told *someone*, maybe when he'd had a few on one of his trips (though he'd always rung her, hadn't he, every night, completely sober... he'd always found a way to get through to her, so... No... no, no, no, no, no). Annette marched back into the study, sat down again, then logged out of Terry's account, before bringing up the page to log into hers. The information for that had been saved, too. Lucky for her Terry was in the habit of doing that. Lucky for the hacker, as well?

Annette got the same pinging noise when she visited her page. Her one friend – Terry – made her late husband's collection look vast by comparison.

She found the last message he'd left and opened it, hitting REPLY.

I don't know who this is, she typed, **but I'm going to find out. You're evil and I'm going to make sure you pay for what you've done.**

When she logged out again, her hands were shaking. She powered down the computer, gathered together the rest of Terry's belongings, and put them in the boxes and bags. Annette took them downstairs one at a time, placing them in the garage for now.

She said nothing to Hayley when she collected her from school, just nodded and murmured "A-huh" at the appropriate moments as the seven-year-old talked and talked about her day. Annette did the same as they had dinner that night, just stared into space as Hayley went on and on about some game they'd played in one of her classes.

"And then Bobby Townsend said this... And then Kerry Wolter did that..." Annette let it all wash over her. She was still back in the study, with the computer.

She waited until Hayley was in bed, until the girl was asleep, then she crept into the study and powered up the machine on the desk. Her heart was racing, she could feel it pounding in her chest.

There was a reply to her message. What now, an apology? Whoever it was could stick it up their—

Annette stared at the message back from 'Terry'.

Sweetheart, it *really* is me, it began. **I don't know how or why, but I'm able to talk to you this way. It's been very... confusing. It's only the thought of you maybe replying that's kept me going.**

Annette huffed, but read on.

I know what you're thinking, how do you *know* it's really me? Okay, if the juggler didn't prove it, how about this...

Annette's mouth fell open, her jaw locking. *No, no!* She rose again, breathing quickly in and out. How? How could this person know that? Their secret that they'd kept all these years? That they'd *definitely* not told anyone. In her imagination now, it was the bald, overweight doctor delivering the news to her, rambling on and on, occasionally mentioning the word ectopic: "It's more common than you think, especially during the early stages. Could happen to anyone, happened to people like Mary Shelley, Marilyn Monroe, Bess Truman and—"

There was another pinging sound. A live chat box had just appeared in the bottom right-hand corner of the screen. Terry wanted to talk to her.

Annette bit her lip, so hard she thought she would make it bleed. This couldn't be happening. This was crazy. She was going mad. No, how could she be? She was too damned rational for that. The only logical answer was that Terry had found a way again. Perhaps in this day and age, where technology was worshipped and people turned their backs on religion and the church (the same as she had done), it was the *only* way to come back. If you could chat to someone on the other side of the planet like this, then why not *the* other side?

And, she reasoned, weren't human beings electrical by nature? Neurons were just electrical cells transmitting information, weren't they? Thoughts and sensations. A computer was a kind of electrical brain, so...

Maybe, just maybe, there *was* a ghost in this machine.

Slowly, she sat back down, opened the chat box, and said hello to her dead husband.

Over the course of the next few months, over the next couple of years, they 'talked' as often as they could, sometimes chatting all night, just like they used to do when they first got together. It was a strange continuation of their union, and she'd wondered all the time whether it was a healthy one (as well as still questioning her sanity during her more wobbly moments), but it sort of worked. And if this was the only way to have Terry back... There was still that closeness, they'd still argue on occasion and he'd go quiet. Then she'd return to the computer after the flood banks had broken, wanting to fix things, wanting him to talk again – in a weird reversal of when he'd first appeared on here. And suddenly he'd be back.

Necessity had transformed him into the writer he'd so longed to be, only it was poetry that turned out to be his forté. He'd often leave love poems for Annette in her messages folder, there for her to find when she logged back on; forcing the pricking at the corners of her eyes for a different reason.

She'd share everything, just as before. Annette told him about her work – she'd begun advertising in the local paper again, taking on clients. She'd repeat – often parrot-fashion – what Hayley had told her about her day, too. Post photos and video clips so he could see how much his princess was growing, beginning with that trip she'd promised the girl to Central Parks.

Every now and again, Terry would also go quiet when she did this. But she knew why: because he couldn't be with them both. Because he couldn't give them hugs, his body six feet under in the cemetery. It might have been why he'd made Annette promise not to tell Hayley.

>**She can't know about any of this**, he'd typed. **I'm not sure she could handle it.**

He was probably right.

Annette had asked him quite a few times to describe what it was like where he was, what might be waiting for her when she passed over.

>**It's difficult to explain**, Terry said once. **It's like being in some kind of limbo. In a sort of fog or something. A thick mist. It's all still so confusing. But I don't think this is normal, sweetheart; what's happened to me. I don't think this happens to everyone, y'know?**

Annette nodded, not really understanding at all.

But as much as they tried to fool themselves into thinking things were okay, there was something missing. And the more time that passed, the more that became apparent.

Sooner or later, something had to give.

———

November 20th – almost three years after Terry's passing.

Annette sat back down at the desk, as she had done every night for two weeks, checking to see if he'd been 'online'.

Nothing again.

There'd been nothing since that last message, short and to the point:

>**I know**, it had said.

Annette bit her lip again, remembering. It had been ironic, because she'd had to build herself up to sitting down that day. Hadn't known quite how to broach the subject to Terry. Turned out there was no need. He was already well aware of James, of how when she'd met her latest client – a freelance photographer, weddings, christenings, proms, that kind of thing – there had been that spark. *The* spark. Terry already knew about how, after they'd met up for coffee those few times, that spark had turned into a crackle, then a bolt of lightning that hit her and left her head spinning. Sometimes, although she'd never experienced it herself – her and Terry had been friends first, then the rest had followed later – but just sometimes it could happen like that.

Click!

That was it, they'd clicked. It could happen to anyone at any time. Anthony and Cleopatra, Jackie and John F, William and Kate... She'd had no control over it, and she'd fought it. Oh, how she'd tried to fight it! But he was in her thoughts all the time; she'd be doing the washing or hoovering, and he'd just pop up. That smiling face, silvery-blond hair.

Plus it was mutual, he'd even asked if he could take her photograph on one occasion. Said she was the most beautiful woman he'd ever laid eyes on. It sounded like a cheesy pick-up line, but somehow Annette knew that James meant it.

It was when things started to get too serious, when they'd almost kissed, that she'd had to stop seeing him socially.

"It's Terry," she'd said, and he'd nodded. Hadn't tried to force the issue. James knew she was a widow, knew that he was competing with her late husband's memory. But that was just it, he wasn't simply competing with a memory. He was competing with Terry himself.

Ashamed, and knowing she'd never kept a thing from Terry the whole of their marriage, she realised she had to tell him. But how? It would break his heart... figuratively speaking.

All that agonising about it, and when she'd finally plucked up enough courage, Terry had said those two short words:

>I know.

How, was anyone's guess; they hadn't even talked yet or anything. Nevertheless, there could be no other interpretation of it. Terry knew everything. Deep down, Annette *felt* that he did. And now he was gone, had disappeared – in spite of her frantic messages to him, trying to fix things:

Can't we talk about this, sweetheart? Please? Why won't you answer me?

As she sat down again that unseasonably warm November morning, she was expecting much of the same. A blank message box, the light on live chat dull rather than bright. But, just as she was about to get up and make herself a cup of tea, there was a pinging sound.

"Terry!" she said, hardly able to keep the joy from her voice – and not wanting to anyway. Then she typed the same thing into the bottom right hand box of the page.

>**Yes, it's me,** he gave as a reply. **I'm sorry.**

>**Sorry? What have you got to be sorry about? It's me who should be apologising,** Annette typed, although her lips moved as she did so.

>**I've been off, sulking. You know me. It was just the thought of... well, you know.**

>**Look, nothing happened. Terry, I love *you*.**

>**And you love him as well.**

>**No, I—**

>**Yes... but Annie, it's okay. I've had a lot of time to think, and things have gotten a lot clearer for me. The fog's lifting.**

>**I don't know what you mean.**

Annette bit down on her lip, hard, after saying the words out loud this time.

>**While we're doing this, neither of us can move on. And we need to, we *have* to, sweetheart – as much as it hurts. He can offer you what I can't anymore. As much as I'd like to, as much as I'd give anything in the world to be able to.**

She could feel the pricking at the corners of her eyes again.

>**He's a good man. I've seen it. Seen so much, you wouldn't believe... You'll be happy, he'll be a good dad to Hayley. You're going to have a long, long time together.**

There was a pause and then Terry typed: **Old farts on a beach.**

Was he just guessing that, or... *I've seen it; I've seen so much.* She could have sworn she'd heard the words then. The tears were breaking free now again, she couldn't hold them back – just like the night of Terry's birthday, and so many after that until he came back to her.

>**Terry, no.**

>**Yes, darlin'. It has to be like this. I'm going travelling, just like I used to.**

Annette could picture his face, see him speaking the words back to her. It was almost, for a fraction of a second, as if he was there in the room with her.

>**But... will I ever see—** She broke off, then rephrased the question: **Will I ever hear from you again?**

There was another pause.

>**Perhaps, someday. I'll always be around, though. Now, I really have to go.**

At that moment Annette could *feel* his presence, his hands on her shoulders – her imagination, she realised, but it didn't stop it from feeling real.

"Terry..." she said one last time, not even bothering to type anymore. The words came up on the screen from him, which she didn't read until later on, the tears coming too strong to even see. But she heard them as well, a whisper in her ear.

"Goodbye my love. And remember," said Terry, before vanishing again, just as swiftly as he did the first time:

"Life is sweet," he told her. "Life is sweet."

Presence
Written by Paul Kane
Based on the short story by Paul Kane

<u>INT. BEDROOM — DAY.</u>

An ordinary bedroom, with a double bed. A woman, late 30's - ANNETTE GRIFFITHS - dressed in a baggy sweater and jeans, with blonde hair tied back in a ponytail, is rummaging around in a wardrobe.

She takes out a man's jacket, pauses — almost puts it back — then folds it lovingly and places it in a box.

Annette looks across sadly at the bed, sniffing back tears.

<u>EXT. DRIVEWAY — DAY.</u>

ANNETTE carries the box, now full, to the end of the drive - placing it down next to a few more.

A van pulls up from a charity shop, and two men start to load these boxes into the back.

Annette stares at this, miles away. It reminds her of something.

<u>INT. FLASHBACK/CREMATORIUM — DAY.</u>

Now we see what that is, a coffin being loaded onto a set of rollers - facing the huge black tunnel where it will end up.

And we see ANNETTE, standing at a lectern,

looking across at the coffin, then facing
front. Facing us. She takes a breath and
continues on with her eulogy.

ANNETTE
Terry... Terry used to have a saying,
one he borrowed from his grandfather.
He... he used to say...
(beat)
Life is sweet, Annette. Life is sweet.

Tears well in her eyes and track down her
face, as she finally breaks down...

And the coffin starts to move over the
rollers towards the blackness.

CUT TO:

EXT. DRIVEWAY — DAY.

ANNETTE breaks down as the van drives off
along the road. She rushes back to the
house with her hand to her mouth.

INT. LANDING - DAY.

ANNETTE at the top of the stairs. She's
finished dabbing her eyes with a tissue,
stands on the landing and looks sideways
towards:

A closed door at the end.

She makes her way to it, hesitantly, then
stops. Annette shakes her head.

                    <u>ANNETTE</u>
                 (resolutely)
          Enough now. You've left it long
                    enough...

She nods to herself and strides towards the
door, taking hold of the handle and turning
it. Opening the door to reveal...

                                        <u>CUT TO:</u>

<u>INT. FLASHBACK/SPARE ROOM - DAY</u>

We're in the spare room, a smaller room
than the other one - with shelving that's
only half full of books and magazines. A
desk is in front of us, with a monitor and
mouse on top of it.

And sitting behind the desk, with papers
strewn around him, is a smiling man in his
early 40s with receding hairline to match -
TERRY. He has a kind face, which we see
when he looks up at us.

                    <u>TERRY</u>
          Thanks again love for helping me get
                 set up in here.

When the reply comes, we realise we're
looking at him from the POV of ANNETTE and
her memories.

<u>ANNETTE (O.S.)</u>
I still don't understand... writing?

<u>TERRY</u>
It's something I've always wanted to
try, but never had the time. And I want
to help bring in some money.

<u>ANNETTE (O.S.)</u>
Wasn't your fault you were made
redundant.

<u>TERRY</u>
I know. But, well, I <u>want</u> to help. Then
you wouldn't have to do so much of that
book-keeping stuff of an evening.

<u>ANNETTE (O.S.)</u>
I don't mind. I've always been good
with figures, you know that.

<u>TERRY</u>
(smiling)
I know. Always the practical one.
Solving problems. But I want to feel
useful...
(beat)
I want to help look after you and
Hayley. I love you both so much.

CUT TO:

<u>INT. SPARE ROOM - DAY.</u>

We're back on ANNETTE's face, as she
whispers:

ANNETTE

I love you too.

Then we get the reverse shot and see that
the seat TERRY had once occupied is empty.
The room is still in a similar state,
nothing much has changed.

Breathing in deeply, Annette shakes her
head - she knows she has to get on.

As she comes around the side of the desk,
she catches sight of a photo on the wall of
her, TERRY and a young girl of about 8 -
HAYLEY - a carbon copy of her mother.
They're on holiday somewhere, all looking
happy.

Annette backs into the desk and acciden-
tally jars the mouse. The monitor flashes
into life with a beep, making her start.
The computer must have been on standby all
this time, Terry never having had a chance
to turn it off.

Skirting around the desk, grateful for the
distraction, she takes a look at the
screen, eyes narrowing as she reads.

Annette sits down in the seat, and then we
see what she is seeing: Terry's page on a
social networking site.

CUT TO:

INT. FLASHBACK/LIVING ROOM - DAY.

TERRY again, on the sofa, looking up from a
WRITING MAGAZINE.

TERRY

I know you don't really like the
things, computers and all that, but it
says here that it can really help your
chances of getting published if you
have an online presence these days...

INT. SPARE ROOM - DAY.

Back to the present. A profile photo of
TERRY's happy face stares back at her, and
ANNETTE's eyes are misting up once more.
She hesitates, then finds herself reaching
for the mouse.

Annette clicks the button that takes her to
Terry's wall. He only has a handful of
people added, 30 or so. There are some
posts from well-wishers saying they hope
Terry has had a nice Christmas with his
family.

Annette frowns, not recognising any of
them.

Scrolling down, she spots the last message
left by Terry himself: 'It's so cold and

dark now. I don't like it.' We see a time
and date next to it.

Her hand goes to her mouth.

> ANNETTE
> (whispering)
> No... it can't be... that was after...

Another pinging noise startles her. Annette
glances at the side of the screen, where
she sees a message has come in.

She frowns again, then begins to move the
arrow across to messages. Annette hesitates, looking terrified. Then she clicks
on the link.

There are several in that section, but not
in the INBOX - instead they're all in the
OUTGOING folder.

> ANNETTE (CONT'D)
> What... Who's been using...

She can't resist any longer, and clicks on
the first, dated a day after the post on
his wall.

It says it's from Terry:

'Hello... Annie? Annie, sweetheart...
are you there? Please. I'm so, so
scared.'

Annette grinds her teeth together, breathes
out through her nose. There are tears
again, but of anger this time.

She clicks on more:

    'Please... please Annie, talk to me. I
    need to hear your voice. I'm so
    alone.'

    'Darlin', where are you? I'm lost...
    I'm not sure what's happening to me.'

    'For the love of Christ, please say
    something! Answer me!'

Then one final mail:

    'Darlin', it's me. It's really me. I
    don't know what's happened or why you
    won't talk to me.
    But... Look, I can prove it. Remember
    the juggler. The one we saw on our
    first date, when we were walking
    through the city?'

There's a sharp intake of breath and
Annette's hand is covering her mouth again.

She shakes her head.

                    ANNETTE
          No... How could they know...?

She continues to read:

                    'He was rubbish, remember? Dropped all
                    his clubs and we laughed, so hard?'

                              ANNETTE (CONT'D)
                         That was when we...

                    '...kissed for the first time, while we
                    were laughing,'

the message finishes for her.

Annette pushes back in the chair,
rushes out.

                                                  CUT TO:

INT. BATHROOM - DAY.

ANNETTE throws up in the toilet. Then she
stands, goes to the sink and splashes water
on her face.

She looks in the mirror, shakes her head
again. Then the angry face returns. She
storms back out.

                                                  CUT TO:

INT. SPARE ROOM - DAY.

Back into the room, letting the door slam
behind her. Back down in the seat, brushing
a strand of wet hair out of her eyes.

ANNETTE hits REPLY. Types:

>   'I don't know who this is, but I'm
> going to find out. You're evil and I'm
> going to make sure you pay for what
> you've done!'

She sends it.

Annette switches off the screen with a click. She looks around and then starts to gather books and other belongings, to put these in more boxes and bags.

INT. KITCHEN - EARLY EVENING.

ANNETTE is sitting at the kitchen table with HAYLEY, the evening meal in front of them. Hayley chats away, but Annette isn't really taking much notice, she's staring off into space.

                    HAYLEY
          ...and then Bobby Townsend said...

                    ANNETTE
                    U-huh.

                    HAYLEY
          ...and you know what Kerry Walter did
                    then? She...

The sound fades out as we concentrate on Annette's face, as she thinks again - remembering.

INT. FLASHBACK/MORGUE - DAY.

ANNETTE is walking through a white, sterile
corridor with a male MORGUE ATTENDANT,
looking pensive and confused.

ANNETTE
...must be some mistake, I mean he only
popped out to the newsagents for one of
his magazines and—

MORGUE ATTENDANT
Here we are.

They've pulled up short at one of the huge
drawers.

MORGUE ATTENDANT (CONT'D)
Are you ready?

ANNETTE
(nodding)
It won't be Terry, because—

The drawer slides out and she stares down,
shocked now, all the colour draining from
her face.

MORGUE ATTENDANT
Is... is this your husband, Mrs
Griffiths?

She starts to shake her head, but then
nods.

ANNETTE
(hitch in her voice)

> People... people don't just die like
> that, do they? They die in car
> accidents, of cancer, of... Not like
> this. Not like this... I never even got
> a chance to...

She turns away, begins to sob as she flees
the morgue.

INT. LANDING — NIGHT.

ANNETTE closes the door on her sleeping
daughter, looks across the landing at the
door to the spare room.

Swallowing dryly, she makes her way back
along and reaches for the handle.

                                    CUT TO:

INT. SPARE ROOM - NIGHT.

ANNETTE sits behind the desk, in the dark,
with the light from the monitor reflected
on her face.

We get the reverse shot of this now, to see
there's been a reply to her message.

Her shaking hand moves to the mouse and,
biting her lip, she clicks on it.

We read it as she does:

> 'Sweetheart, it *really* is me. I don't

know how or why, but I'm able to talk
to you this way. It's been very...
confusing. It's only the thought of you
maybe replying that's kept me going.'

Annette is frowning again, but reads on:

'I know what you're thinking, how do
you *know* it's really me? Okay, if the
juggler didn't prove it, how about
this...'

Now we see her reaction, mouth falling
open. She recovers, begins typing immediately.

We see her open up a chat box and start
talking to Terry.

<u>INT. SPARE ROOM — DAY.</u>

Montage sequence, showing ANNETTE at the
desk typing with different clothes on, in
the daytime, and at night-time.

Dissolves show the passage of time, while
we see snatches of conversation on the
screen at first:

'How did Hayley do in her test today?'

'Fine, she's worrying about the next
one now.'

'How are you doing for money?'

'Okay for now, there's still a little left out of the insurance policy...'

'How was the movie, sweetheart?'

'Oh, same old romantic rubbish that you used to hate.'

'Ha ha, you know me too well...'

'Did... did you get any more replies from the ad in the paper?'

'Yeah, a few more clients - nice people.'

In-between, we see photos being posted, of Hayley in school uniform, at the park, at her 10th birthday party, her 11th — in her new school uniform, starting secondary school now.

As it goes on, we hear their voices instead of reading the messages:

<u>ANNETTE (V.O.)</u>
Terry, look - I really think we need to tell Hayley.

<u>TERRY (V.O.)</u>
She can't know about any of this, I'm not sure she would understand.
(beat)
I'm not even sure I do myself.

<u>ANNETTE (V.O.)</u>
That makes two of us...

Finally, we come back to Annette typing again, in her pyjamas with a glass of red wine - at last getting round to the question she's been wanting to ask - what we're all thinking:

'What's... what's it like where you are, Terry?'

He replies:

'It's difficult to explain. It's like being in some kind of limbo. In a sort of fog or something. A thick mist.

'It's all still so confusing. But I don't think this is normal, sweetheart; what's happened to me. I don't think this happens to everyone, y'know?'

She nods, but her frown tells us she doesn't really know at all.

<u>FADE OUT.</u>

<u>INT. LANDING - DAY.</u>

ANNETTE stands on the landing, dressed quite smartly this time, glances sideways at the spare room again. She's as hesitant as she was the first time she went in.

She takes a few steps, stops. Shakes her
head, with tears in her eyes.
Remembering...

CUT TO:

INT. FLASHBACK/SPARE ROOM — EVENING.

ANNETTE's at the desk, dressed casually
again. She's frowning, typing over and over:

   'Terry? Terry are you there?'

and

   'I need to talk to you.'

At last he answers:

   'I know, Annette. I *know*.'

She leans back in the chair, blowing out a
breath, eyes misting up again. Then she
sits forward and types:

   'Terry... Terry? Please wait...'

There is no reply.

ANNETTE
Terry, please...

Annette sits back in the chair again and
begins to cry.

<u>INT. FLASHBACK/HALLWAY - DAY.</u>

ANNETTE opening the door to a handsome 30-
something with wavy hair and a kind face:
JAMES. He smiles.

<u>ANNETTE</u>
James?

<u>JAMES</u>
Annette, I presume?

They shake hands, the touch lingering a bit
longer than it should.

Annette smiles back.

<u>ANNETTE</u>
Please, come in.

<u>INT. FLASHBACK/LIVING ROOM - DAY.</u>

ANNETTE sitting with JAMES, there are cups
of coffee on the table in front of them. He
has a portfolio of photos he shows her.

<u>JAMES</u>
I really need someone to untangle my
finances, and you come very highly
recommended.

Annette smiles again.

<u>EXT. FLASHBACK/PARK BENCH - DAY.</u>

The couple are on a bench by a pond, feeding ducks. They're laughing, joking — have obviously got closer.

JAMES leans in to kiss ANNETTE, but she pulls away.

> ANNETTE
> I'm sorry... It's Terry.

James looks down sadly, nodding.

> ANNETTE (CONT'D)
> I'm so sorry.

He looks at her, attempting a smile.

> JAMES
> It's okay. Really. I understand.

INT. LANDING - DAY.

Back to the landing, to the present, and ANNETTE's hesitation again. Her fingers are reaching out for the handle. She bites her lip, but then gets a determined look on her face.

Annette grabs the handle and turns it.

INT. SPARE ROOM — DAY.

ANNETTE is back behind the desk, typing again.

'Can't we talk about this, sweetheart?
Please? Why won't you answer me? It's
been weeks now...'

She leans back and sighs.

There's a pinging noise, a message.

                    <u>ANNETTE</u>
        (hardly able to keep the joy from her
                      voice)
                     Terry!

She clicks on the message:

  'Yes, it's me... I'm sorry.'

Annette types:

  'Sorry? What have you got to be sorry
  about? It's me who should be apol-
  ogising.'

Terry:

  'I've been off, sulking. You know me.
  It was just the thought of... well, you
  know.'

Annette:

  'Look, nothing happened. Terry, I love
  you.'

Terry:

   'And you love him as well.'

Annette:

   'No, I-'

Terry:

   'Yes... but Annie, it's okay. I've had
   a lot of time to think, and things have
   gotten much clearer for me. The fog's
   lifting.'

                ANNETTE (CONT'D)
                  (out loud)
        I don't know what you mean.

She bites down on her lip, waiting for the
answer.

It appears on the screen:

   'While we're doing this, neither of us
   can move on. And we need to, we *have*
   to, sweetheart, as much as it hurts. He
   can offer you what I can't anymore. As
   much as I'd like to, as much as I'd
   give anything in the world to be
   able to.'

Tears are welling in Annette's eyes.

Terry continues:

'He's a good man. I've seen it. Seen so
much, you wouldn't believe... You'll be
happy, he'll be a good dad to Hayley.
You're going to have a long, long time
together.'

We switch now to hearing their voices.

                    ANNETTE (CONT'D)
                  Terry, no...

                    TERRY (O.S.)
          Yes, darlin'. It has to be like this.
                  It's right...

                    ANNETTE
                  Terry...

She closes her eyes, tears spilling from
them and running down her cheeks.

When she opens them again, Terry is behind
her - hands on her shoulders.

                    ANNETTE (CONT'D)
          But... will I ever see... Will I ever
                hear from you again?

                    TERRY
          Perhaps, someday. I'll always be
          around, though. Now, I really have
                    to go.

                    ANNETTE
                  Terry...?

TERRY
Goodbye my love. And remember...
(beat)
Life is sweet. Life is sweet.

Annette whirls around but Terry is already gone. She's crying freely now, but mouths the word:

ANNETTE
Goodbye.

END CREDITS

THE BACKGROUND TO...
PRESENCE

If I remember this rightly, I was putting together my collection of supernatural stories *Ghosts* – which eventually came out in 2013 – when Ian Whates asked if I wanted to do a story for a NewCon press anthology he was putting together called *Hauntings*. I saw the opportunity to do a tale for that, which I could also use in my collection, plus write a kind of 'ghost in the machine' thing that I'd had on my mind for a while.

Technology and social media has always fascinated me, and continues to do so. That might come as a bit of a surprise to those who know me, because I'm terrible at dealing with that side of things. I've always had trouble with computers, so I'm glad there are a few people in my life who understand all this much better than I do; my better half Marie for one. My first ever agent set me up with email back in the late '90s, as I didn't have a clue how it all worked. Still not that sure, if I'm being honest.

But with the wave of sites like Friends Reunited, Myspace and then Twitter and Facebook coming along, I began to think to myself, if it was that easy to talk to someone via a message who's on the other side of the world, why not someone who's on the actual *other* side? (You might notice I use this exact line in the story.) So the idea for 'Presence' was born, all about a woman who loses her husband and then begins talking to him through messages on a Facebook-esque site. And I must just mention here that the wonderful phrase 'Life is sweet' didn't come from me at all; someone way back in Marie's family used to say it, and of course it's true.

I read the story out for the launch of *Hauntings*, in an isolated little pub in Market Harborough in Leicestershire (the event included a Q&A/round table discussion about the paranormal, which was all recorded for Adele Wearing's *Un:Bound*). It was only really at this one that I realised what a tear-jerker I'd written, and it's reduced audiences to floods every time I've read it since – including as a Guest at the 2019 UK Ghost Story Festival in Derby (where someone told myself and Marie, who was also reading out a sad ghost story called 'In the Howling of the Wind', that we'd "Broken the audience"; there's no greater compliment than that).

The way I'd structured the story meant that it was quite easy to turn it into a short script, and when I was adapting some more of my tales into screenplays it seemed like a no-brainer to throw this one into the mix. There's a handful of characters, two main ones in essence, and only a limited number of locations, so it seemed ideal.

I got so far down the line with a couple of directors on this project. The first wanted to set it back in the '80s, which of course wouldn't have worked because we didn't even have social media back then – at least not in the way we think of it today – and the second had his own vision about what he wanted to do with the characters. I parted ways, quite amicably, with both.

I don't really remember where or how I first came across Dave Morgan, it was probably as I was searching around for short film directors as I tend to periodically. I do remember we were friends on Facebook, which somehow seems fitting. Dave was actively looking for short scripts that he could produce through his company DLM Media, and so I sent him *Presence* to have a look at. He loved it, and the next thing I knew we were signing contracts and he was casting the film, with Annabel Entress, Caitlin Bradley, Andrew Abrahamson and Vin Hawke starring in the pivotal roles of Annette, Hayley, Terry and James.

It was made during the first part of 2019, but of course ran into difficulties like everything else because of COVID. Due to work commitments and moving on to other projects, the film still remains in post-production at present, but I'm told there's light at the end of the tunnel – and after speaking again with Dave recently he gave me the go-ahead to include the script in this book anyway. Hopefully it'll be out before too much longer, and you know what they say about things being worth the wait...

I fully expect that when audiences watch the movie there'll be the same response as when I read it out, i.e. uncontrollable sobbing.

The anthology where 'Presence' was first published, Hauntings *from NewCon Press – with a cover by Ben Baldwin.*

The Hauntings Un:Bound event in Market Harborough, Leicestershire, with MC Katherine Heubeck.

Paul doing a reading of 'Presence' at the event.

'Presence' next appeared in Paul's collection GHOSTS from Spectral Press, cover by Edward Miller/Les Edwards.

The **Presence** *film script.*

The auditions for Presence, *with director/producer Dave Morgan (second from right)*

Filming outside for the first outdoor scene.

Director Dave Morgan on location.

Getting ready to shoot a scene with Caitlin Bradley playing daughter Hayley.

Dave again, prepping an indoors landing scene.

Filming Presence.

Dave (left) getting ready to direct a scene in the spare bedroom.

Andrew Abrahamson as Terry, working in his 'office'.

Annabel Entress goes through her lines as Annette.

Another location shot, this time at the front door.

Vin Hawke, playing James.

Variant concept poster for Presence.

Director: Jacob Osborn
Screenwriter: Paul Kane (based on his own short story)

BLACKOUT

THE SHORT STORY

When Kelly awoke, everything was black.

To start with she thought perhaps she was in bed and it was the middle of the night. But everything was so, so dark. Not even the streetlights outside were shining.

And she was alone.

It wasn't until she raised herself up and something heavy dropped from her lap that she realised where she was. Where she *had been* before she'd fallen asleep. Reading on the sofa, curled up enjoying her book.

Damn, I must be getting old, she thought, *nodding off without warning just like Mum used to do.* Or maybe it had something to do with the fact that she'd been up since six, dutifully seeing Jeff off at the station.

In any event it was a shock to wake up and find such a stifling gloom bearing down on her. She couldn't see her hand in front of her face, let alone any of the familiar, comforting objects in her living room.

Her phone! She'd had that with her, hadn't she? Though where was it now? Had it fallen as well, got lost down the side of the couch again? She couldn't feel it anywhere…

Kelly never had liked the dark. As a child she'd pleaded

with her parents to leave the table lamp on for her at night, and they had done so... for a time. But as she got older they said it was a waste of electricity. Kelly was a big girl, and big girls weren't afraid of the dark. It couldn't hurt her. It wasn't alive or anything. And the daytime Kelly agreed with them, there was nothing to be frightened of.

It was the night-time Kelly who was the problem – whispering lies in her ear, forcing her to see things that weren't there.

Oh, but it is alive! And so are the things that lurk within.

Was there any wonder she'd wet the bed until she was almost in her teens? The fears didn't go away just because you were older. The blackness didn't go away – ever.

Of course Kelly hadn't thought about any of this for ages. Her nights were no longer sleepless ones. No more tossing and turning. For one thing she'd been married six years and with her husband beside her at night she was perfectly safe. Her childish fallacies had finally been laid to rest.

But waking up here and now had stirred some of those dormant memories.

Kelly's sofa was next to the window, so she only had to look over the top to see outside. Everything was in shadow. The other bungalows; the streets branching off from her close; the town in the distance. Total blackout. It was as though someone had covered the entire area with a blanket.

Or a shroud.

Trust Jeff to be away when she needed him most. He'd probably be enjoying himself in the hotel bar right about now – she knew what these so-called conferences were like. While she was here, on her own. In the dark. Kelly leaned in closer. No, not a light to be seen. Not—

There was something moving at the window.

Startled, Kelly pulled back. She could only see a vague outline, but that was enough. She inched forwards again. Was there someone outside? A face at the window?

It moved again. Sweet Jesus, it was behind her! Something with protruding eyes and a wide, gaping mouth. Kelly lost her balance and fell backwards. She landed awkwardly, the hardback novel jabbing into her spine.

Cursing, she flung it away into oblivion. *Get a grip on yourself. It was just your reflection, that's all.* But that doubting little voice was talking to her again, reminding her that reflections don't move of their own accord.

Saying that something was coming for her.

After a quick feel around on the floor again for her mobile – nothing! – Kelly started to rise, slowly, carefully. Dammit, this was all her own fault. She should have taken up her sister's offer. Gone to stay with her for the weekend. But it would have been like admitting she couldn't cope. Fran would just love that. She'd been bad enough to live with when they were little. Kelly wasn't about to give her the satisfaction. Although by this stage even Fran's company was starting to look pretty appealing.

What to do now? A light! She should go and get a light.

As she staggered around the living room, trying to work out in which direction the door lay, an unwelcome thought crossed her mind. Why had no one else in her neighbourhood done the same? When Kelly had looked out of the window she'd seen none of the usual flickering of candles. No erratic torch beams flashing. What did this tell her? That the electricity had only just gone off. Or maybe, just maybe, something had happened to those people before they could—

She was doing it again. Scaring herself silly for no reason. It was all in her imagination. Now she'd get to the kitchen, find the torch, and shed some light on the situation.

Kelly followed the wall around, fingertips tentatively reaching out, half expecting to touch something nasty and slimy despite what she'd just told herself. Before she had too long to dwell on this, she came upon the open door and sighed with relief. She was no longer trapped in that room, in a confined space. Here was the hallway, and further up, the kitchen.

Still Kelly hesitated before stepping out into what felt like a dank, empty cavern, or some kind of disused railway tunnel with no beginning and no end. Perhaps *it* wanted her to come out. That might be part of *its* plan.

Stupid! Stupid!

Kelly dug her nails into the palms of her hands, the pain taking her mind off things for a blessed moment. She pressed on regardless, dragged into limbo. Kelly couldn't see the floor, so was it still there? For all she knew she could be falling into a pit and at the very bottom, waiting for her, would be—

Something brushed her arm as she moved through the hall. Kelly rounded on it and heard a crash as an assortment of objects fell to the floor. The plastic clatter of a telephone, coins jangling in a collection box, the tinkling as a photograph frame shattered. She'd bumped into the hall table.

Calm down. Have to calm down. Kelly's heart was fluttering and she felt sick. What the hell was wrong with her? She was falling apart, and all because of a tiny power cut. Kelly bent down and groped around for the phone. The line was dead. But whether it was due to the fall or not, she had no way of knowing.

Steeling herself, she carried on down the hallway. Her bedroom would be on the right coming up any second, with the spare room directly opposite. Ignoring these, Kelly made for the open space of the kitchen. She lost her grip on the wall for a second and found herself wading in a sea of nothingness.

She collided with the edge of a work-surface and stepped back, only to bang her head on the extractor fan. But this was a good thing. Now she could work out where the overhead cupboard was in relation to the oven. Inside there was the torch, a really powerful one Jeff had been given for joining that motor rescue service. In addition to an ordinary beam there was also a fluorescent strip down the side, which had the capacity to illuminate an entire room.

Smiling, Kelly opened the cupboard door. Everything would be all right once she had the torch in her hands. She could chase away her demons in no time. Standing on her toes, Kelly searched around inside. The torch wasn't where it was supposed to be. *No, this isn't happening, we always keep it in here!*

Wait. Now she remembered. Not two weeks ago Jeff had used it to poke about up in the loft, clearing some space for his old junk. But what had he done with it? Bloody hell, she was forever telling him to put things back when he'd finished with them.

Access to the loft was through the spare room, so she'd try in there first. Knowing Jeff he'd probably left it on the sideboard or something. *But not up* in *the loft, please not up there!* She heard laughing. *It* knew she would have to double back, and *it* was mocking her. Watching, safe in the knowledge that she could see nothing. *It* had come when she was at her most vulnerable, just like when she was a kid.

But she'd show *it*! Kelly could beat this thing yet. Wasn't far to the spare room, a few short metres. She could run if she had to.

Kelly turned and started to move forwards. Again it was hard to tell where she was going. She prayed that her internal radar would guide her, take her safely to her destination.

She had only managed a few steps when she heard the noise. A rough scratching – like that of sharpened claws – echoing all around. The laughing grew louder. Kelly made a dash for the spare room. This wasn't her imagination, this was real. There was something in here with her, fuelled by the energy of the night; the thing from her youth that would not leave her alone. Images returned to plague her. *It* had waited so long for the chance to savour her spirit. So long. Now that opportunity had arisen.

Kelly began to panic and took short, sharp breaths. Without realising, she plunged headlong into sorrow's arms. *It* grabbed her by the shoulders. She felt hands there, clutching. Strong hands. The blackness given form. Kelly twirled out of *its* grasp, swinging her fists round until they struck something. Tumbling, she caught a glimpse of *its* contours. The monster groaned. Kelly heard the flapping of wings, could picture those appendages which grew out of the black.

You're dreaming. Can't you see that it's all a dream, you're still on the couch in the living room and none of this is happening? None of this is real, Kelly!

But dream or no dream, she couldn't just wait for this thing to attack again. On the floor she crawled backwards to avoid *its* talons.

"Kelly," *it* whispered, coming closer, closer.

She put her hand out, feeling for something she could use as a weapon. Kelly's fingers came across a shard of glass from the ruined picture frame. Quickly, she grabbed the makeshift dagger and brought it up with all of her might. A warm wetness jetted across her face and she realised her aim had been true. The shape gurgled, then seemed to be absorbed by *its* dense surroundings.

She'd done it. The monstrosity was defeated. She felt stronger than she'd ever felt in her life.

That was when the lights came back on, and Kelly slipped even further into madness.

The scene was unreal, still part of her nightmare. On the floor was Jeff's prone body, his raincoat flowing behind, a bloody pool welling beneath his chin where the glass jutted out. Behind him was the open front door, his key still in the lock, scratch marks around the wood. She could imagine what he'd been trying to say: *"Kelly, guess what? The conference was rubbish so I thought I'd surprise you. I know how much you hate being on your own at night."*

To her left was the discarded book she'd been flipping

through when she dropped to sleep. One of those pulpy horror stories Jeff warned her about reading because they always made her so jumpy: the latest Herbert Lynch. Next to it was the broken picture frame. Her wedding photograph.

Kelly sat there on the floor, rocking back and forth. She wept, but they were more than just tears for Jeff. She cried for herself, because she knew that after all these years the darkness, the *shadows*, had finally won. She'd never sleep with her husband beside her again. Never be safe again.

As if to underline this fact Kelly heard the laughing again, inside her head.

And it wasn't long before she too began to black out.

<u>BLACKOUT</u>
Written by Paul Kane
Based on the short story by Paul Kane

<u>INT. BEDROOM - MORNING.</u>

Everything is black. Suddenly an alarm
beeps, we see a digital clock on the
bedside table which tells us it's 6:30 AM.

Two bodies are in bed, a woman's hand
reaches out to switch off the alarm, then
turn on the bedside light. We see KELLY,
late 20s, in shorts and a vest, serious
bedhead, yawning and swinging out of bed.

Beside her, husband JAMES is still snoring.
She gives him a shake.

                    JAMES
                   Wha...?

Kelly rises, rubs her eyes and wanders out
of shot.

                                    CUT TO:

<u>INT. KITCHEN - MORNING.</u>

KELLY and JAMES are dressed now, her in T-
shirt and jeans, him in a suit. She's
standing at the back pouring coffee, still
yawning; he's at the table wolfing down
cereal.

                    KELLY
          I really wish you didn't have to go
                  this weekend.

                    JAMES
       Me too, it's be boring as anything.
          You know what these business
             conferences are like.

                    KELLY
        Yeah right, James. I'm sure you'll have
          a horrible time in the hotel bar
                    tonight.

James grabs a final spoonful, rises, and
goes over to Kelly, wraps his arms
around her.

                    JAMES
        You know I'm really going to miss you,
                    Kelly.

                    KELLY
        I'll miss you too... Hate sleeping
                    alone.

                    JAMES
                   (laughs)
          The only reason you married me.

He glances at his watch.

                 JAMES (CONT'D)
        Look at the time, my train's in half an
          hour... Thanks for the lift by the way,
                    love.

<u>INT. HALLWAY - MORNING.</u>

KELLY and JAMES walk through the hallway,
past the phone table on the right, with the
stairs on their left. He carries his raincoat over his arm.

The door slams and the table wobbles. We
can see there's a phone and a framed photo
on it, but not what this is yet.

<u>INT. LIVING ROOM - LATE AFTERNOON.</u>

KELLY is on her mobile as she enters the
living room, carrying another mug of coffee
which she places on the table. She's
partway through a conversation.

                    KELLY
     ...no, it's fine. I'll be <u>fine</u>, Ali.

                  ALI (O.S.)
     You sure, sis? You're welcome to come
            over. Stay the weekend...

Kelly sits down on the sofa, next to the
window. She places the coffee on the table
in front of the sofa. The sun is already
getting quite low, so she flicks on a
standing light beside her.

                    KELLY
              (slightly irritated)
                  I'm sure.

                    ALI (O.S.)
        Because I know how you hate being all
        alone. Even when you were a kid, you—

                      KELLY
                  (more firmly)
        I'm not a kid anymore, Ali. I'll be
                      fine.

                    ALI (O.S.)
            Or I could come to you.

                      KELLY
                    (sighs)
            Honestly, I'm fine.

                    ALI (O.S.)
        Well, you know where I am if you
                    need me.

                      KELLY
        I do... Thanks, sis. Talk soon.

She ends the call, lets out another long
breath. Then plugs in the phone which is on
really low battery, leaves it on the floor.

She picks up a hardback book from the
table, a thriller, lays back on the couch
and starts reading.

INT. BEDROOM/FLASHBACK - NIGHT.

A little girl, KELLY, is in bed under the

covers. KELLY'S DAD sits on the edge next
to her.

                    KELLY
              (visibly upset)
But <u>why</u> can't I go back in with Alison,
                   Daddy?

Kelly's dad rubs his forehead.

                  KELLY'S DAD
We've been through this, Kelly
sweetheart. Ali needs her own space,
        she's a teenager now and—

                    KELLY
But I don't want to be in a room on my
  own. Can I come in with you and Mum?

                  KELLY'S DAD
Don't be silly, love. You're too big
for all that. You're not a kid anymore.

He gets up off the bed, walks towards the
door. Then he reaches up to turn off the
light.

                    KELLY
Dad, can you leave the light on?
              <u>Please?</u>

                  KELLY'S DAD
You'll never get to sleep that way.

KELLY

But the dark, there's something—

KELLY'S DAD

There's nothing there that wasn't there
in the light... Tell you what, I'll
leave the door open a little. Okay? Now
close your eyes and it'll all go away.

Before she has time to say anything else,
he turns off the light and has closed the
door practically shut.

Kelly pulls the covers up, eyes wide open.
Terrified.

She hears something moving, turns her head
in its direction. The shadows loom menac-
ingly beyond the end of the bed.

KELLY

(to herself)

There's nothing there... Close your
eyes, Kelly.

She closes her eyes.

There's a creak, then a sound almost like
the flapping of wings and...

CUT TO:

<u>INT. LIVING ROOM - EVENING.</u>

Back to the present, and the living room

has been plunged into darkness. The
standing light is off and there's no light
coming in from outside.

KELLY'S eyes snap open, she wakes from a
dream — a nightmare. As she sits bolt
upright, the book falls from her lap onto
the floor.

                    KELLY
          Wha...? What's...?

Kelly looks around, can't work out what's
happened to the light. She reaches down,
snatches up her phone from the floor,
lights it up.

It's still on low battery — and isn't
charging.

                KELLY (CONT'D)
          Power cut... Great.

She tries to turn on the torch app, but the
phone switches itself off.

Kelly groans, turns to look out of the
window and we get the view outside: a scat-
tering of houses — also in darkness — the
streetlights extinguished.

Something moves on the other side of the
glass, the briefest flash of a face — something ugly, possibly demonic.

KELLY (CONT'D)
Shit!

Kelly sucks in a breath, pulls back from the window.

Standing, she walks backwards and bangs into the table — almost falls over it.

She tries to slow her breathing, then tentatively moves towards the window once more. Kelly kneels on the sofa to look out.

We see her own face hove into view where the other one was.

KELLY (CONT'D)
Stupid, stupid! Just your reflection,
Kelly. Scaring yourself like when you
were...
(beat)
You're not a kid anymore.

She gets up, tutting.

KELLY (CONT'D)
Light. That's it, I should go get a
light.

We follow her as she navigates the living room, arms and hands out in front of her. At the door she tries the main light switch, but it doesn't work.

                    KELLY (CONT'D)
                  Worth a shot.

                                        CUT TO:

<u>INT. HALLWAY - EVENING.</u>

We're still with KELLY, who moves into the
hallway. There's a glimpse of a shadow
moving past her.

Or at least that's what she thinks she
sees.

                                        CUT TO:

<u>INT. BEDROOM/FLASHBACK - NIGHT.</u>

The young KELLY again, as she remembers —
the shadows growing in front of her,
creating a shape: a FIGURE.

She pulls the covers up even higher.

                                        CUT TO:

<u>INT. HALLWAY - EVENING.</u>

Back to the present again. KELLY spins,
crashes into the table, knocks it over.

Sound of the phone clattering to the
ground, a tinkling noise, glass smashing.

> KELLY
> Fuck!

She crouches, searching the floor. Lets out a cry as her fingers brush the broken glass, then sucks her bleeding finger.

Kelly picks up the phone and puts it to her ear. It's dead, no dial tone.

> KELLY (CONT'D)
> Damn it... Calm down, Kelly. Just calm the hell down.

She gets up, feels for the wall, feels her way along it.

> KELLY (CONT'D)
> Kitchen. Need to get to the...

Kelly trips — and suddenly it's like she's falling into nothingness, hands out in front of her.

> CUT TO:

<u>INT. BEDROOM/FLASHBACK - NIGHT.</u>

The young KELLY in bed again, the darkness spreading out in front of her, almost like it's growing wings.

She closes her eyes.

                    KELLY
              (under her breath)
    Not real... You're not real. You can't
              hurt me, you can't—

Kelly opens them again, and the thing in
the dark is clawing at the bottom of her
bed, at the wood.

                  DARKNESS
                (whispering)
            Alone. All alone...

Eyes wide, she opens her mouth to scream
but nothing comes out.

                                    CUT TO:

INT. KITCHEN - EVENING.

Close-up on a hand slamming down on a work
surface in the kitchen. It's KELLY, as she
pulls herself up.

Her fingers sweep across the cupboards,
finding the knobs to open them.

                    KELLY
    Torch... If I could just find the...

Her hand reaches forward, about to go into
a cupboard, into the black empty space.

She pauses.

Then reaches inside slowly, carefully.
Kelly lets out the breath she was holding.

                    KELLY (CONT'D)
          What did you do with it, James?
                    (beat)
          The loft. You had it up in the loft
          last week. I bet you didn't put it back
                    when—

A noise behind her, and Kelly whirls
around.

                    DARKNESS
                    (whispering)
          Alone. All...

                    KELLY
          No. Nothing there. You're not here,
                you're not real, I—

She squeezes her eyes shut.

                                        CUT TO:

<u>INT. BEDROOM/FLASHBACK - NIGHT.</u>

Opens them again as the younger version of
herself.

The dark thing is crawling up the bed now -
and KELLY swings out to escape it, tumbles
to the floor.

                    KELLY
      No! Get away, get out! Leave me—

                  DARKNESS
                 (whispering)
             Alone... All...

The scratching sound is following her, the
sound of wings flapping behind.

                                        CUT TO:

INT. HALLWAY - EVENING.

KELLY makes her way back down the hall.

                    KELLY
      Upstairs, Kelly. The torch. The torch...

She stumbles again, but steadies herself
using the wall this time.

                  DARKNESS
                 (whispering)
                  Alone.

The scratching noise returns, the claws.

The flapping of the wings - this time in
front of her, blocking her path. She can
see the shape there for definite this time,
opening up those wings.

A hideous face, the one she saw briefly
through the window.

                    KELLY
                (to herself)
              No. Not real.

She closes her eyes.

Opens them, and the thing is even closer.
Kelly lets out a half-scream, stumbles
backwards, falls.

                    DARKNESS
                (whispering)
              All alone.

                    KELLY
              No. Get out, get away!

Her hands reach around for something,
anything she can use to fend it off.

Kelly's fingers find a piece of glass from
the shattered photo. She grabs it, rises,
and lashes out with it.

                    KELLY (CONT'D)
              No, I won't let you... You're not
                going to—

                                        CUT TO:

<u>INT. BEDROOM/FLASHBACK - NIGHT.</u>

Young KELLY on the floor, crawling, with
the shadow looming over her.

                    KELLY
                   ...win.

She gets to her feet, gets to the light-
switch and turns it on. The bedroom is
flooded with light.

The thing in the darkness has vanished.

                KELLY (CONT'D)
          Nothing there... Nothing...

Kelly slides down the wall, crying.

                                    CUT TO:

INT. HALLWAY - EVENING.

The present again, and the lights suddenly
come on as KELLY steps backwards.

And we see the figure in front of her is
JAMES, wearing his raincoat which is spread
open, still holding his key in one hand,
flowers in the other.

The door is open and there are scratch-
marks around the lock.

There's a piece of glass sticking out of
his neck. He makes whispering sounds, takes
a step, and begins to fall.

Kelly closes her eyes.

                                        CUT TO:

<u>INT. HALLWAY/IMAGINED - EVENING.</u>

Quick flash as she imagines JAMES coming in
with the flowers.

                    JAMES
        Kelly, guess what? The conference was
        rubbish so I thought I'd surprise you.
         I know how much you hate being all
            alone, especially at night...

                                        CUT TO:

<u>INT. HALLWAY - EVENING.</u>

KELLY opens her eyes again, sees JAMES on
the floor spread out - looking more like
the thing from the dark than ever.

Blood is pooling around him. We see the
fallen table, close in on the phone which
now has a dial tone. And the broken picture
frame which is from their wedding day.

                    DARKNESS
                  (whispering)
        Alone... All alone. You'll always be...

                    KELLY
                  (to herself)
        Close... close your eyes and it'll all
                    go away.

Kelly's eyelids flicker, she staggers backwards, slides down the wall, crying.

Then closes her eyes one last time as she
herself blacks out.

ENDS

THE BACKGROUND TO...
BLACKOUT

We're starting to come full circle now, with the most current projects. This is based on one of the first stories I wrote and sent anywhere back in 1996 or '97. I've always been afraid of the dark, which is why I write about it so much I guess. You only have to look at the name of my site – which comes from another early story – 'Shadow Writer'! And the most frightening thing to happen to someone who can't stand night-time is probably a blackout. We used to get a lot of these where we lived when I was growing up, which wasn't so bad because Mum or Dad would go and get the candles out. In fact it would be quite cosy in the living room, because we also had a real coal fire going; my dad was a miner. What wasn't so great was heading upstairs to go to the loo on my own, taking the torch or a candle with me, jumping at the shadows. This story originated from all of these experiences.

Kelly's childhood is a lot like mine was, nobody really understood why I was so frightened when the sun went down – people just thought I was being silly. I'm not sure I understand it myself, actually; perhaps it was as simple as having an overactive imagination? Back then *and* now. Even as an adult, I know I should have grown out of this, but I definitely haven't. Maybe that makes me a better horror writer, I don't know. It's certainly a source of material for my stories, that is true.

Once I'd written 'Blackout', which didn't take that long I don't think – it's a fairly short and simple tale after all – I entered it into a competition. I have a bit of a love-hate relationship with those, and didn't send stories to that many even when I was first starting out. Indeed, if I'd sent 'The Cave of Lost Souls' off to a competition as I'd originally intended, then I might not have a career at all. It was a last minute switch, seeing *Terror Tales* advertised in a magazine, that led to my sending it there instead. Not only did the editor John B. Ford accept it, but he also invited me to my very first gathering of writers – and I was off and running! But I digress, as you've probably noticed I often do...

This particular competition was in a magazine I subscribed to called *Graveyard Rendezvous* – the fan magazine of the late author Guy N. Smith. Along with the likes of King, Herbert, Campbell, Rice and Barker, Smith's books were a big part of my horror reading when I was growing up. I'd eventually pay homage to books like *The Crabs* in my own short novel *The Storm*, which came out from PS Publishing in 2020. And weirdly enough, the last publisher to include 'Blackout' in a collection of mine, Sinister Horror Company, have published quite a lot of Guy N. Smith's books. But more on that in a bit.

I sent in the story, then promptly forgot all about it as you do. Next thing I knew, I was being contacted to say Guy had handpicked my story as runner-up and it would be published in Issue 20, Summer 1999. There was even a small cash prize. To say I was delighted would be an understatement. Things like this mean a lot to young writers and in some cases – like this one – even keep us going. The story ended up being reprinted in my second collection, *Touching the Flame* from Rainfall books, and gave me the perfect excuse to read it out at events – like World Horror Day at Chesterfield Library in 2006 alongside Simon 'The Night of the Triffids' Clark, who wrote the intro for *Flame*.

By the late 2000s a lot of my stories were being published in a magazine called *Estronomicon*, the flagship of a publisher called Screaming Dreams, which was run by a thoroughly nice bloke called Steve Upham. I have a lot to thank Steve for, not least for giving 'A Chaos Demon is for Life' an Editor's Choice Award and bringing out the original edition of my novel *The Gemini Factor* (reprinted for its 10th anniversary by Encyclopocalypse in case you want to track it down; that also contains the pilot script for the TV series that almost got made of *Gemini*). Steve encouraged me to gather together my 'Order of the Shadows' tales in ebook form, though he also printed off a bound version just for me. There were only two really at that time, 'Shadow Writer' and 'The Convert', but because I thought it would be a good fit here, I figured I might as well include 'Blackout' as well. It was at this point I brought in the connection to 'Shadow Writer' by making it one of Herbert Lynch's novels Kelly was reading before she nodded off. Lynch is the titular 'Shadow Writer' of that story, controlled by beings that dwell in the dark. It allowed me to hint that they might have had something to do with what happened to Kelly… or did they?

Right, back to the Sinister Horror Company. I'd had one collection published by them, namely *Death* – notable for the first ever appearance of my horror superhero Mortis-Man! – and when I saw the owner Justin Park at an Edge-Lit event in Derby, he mentioned that he wanted to work with me again. I began thinking about what I had available, and realised that a short novel of mine called *Of Darkness and Light* – introduced by Mike 'The Girl with All the Gifts' Carey – had been out of print for some time, maybe a decade or so. I always like to try and keep my stuff in circulation, so people don't have to pay a fortune for it second-hand, so I suggested putting this together with the 'Order of the Shadows' tales – even adding a couple of new ones, 'Shadow Boxer' and 'Shadowplay', the latter drawing all of them together. Mike kindly allowed us to re-use the intro, and suddenly *Darkness & Shadows* was born in 2021 – looking very snazzy with a photo on the cover by none other than Michael Marshall Smith (he of *The Straw Men* and *Intruders* fame).

Naturally, 'Blackout' was included in the line-up again, which got me thinking about the short script I'd penned of this a few years ago. It was originally in response to a callout on social media for short scripts, but didn't make the cut. I'd tried a handful of directors with it since then, including a friend of mine Andy Berriman who I'd met when I was doing the iShorts Creative England thing – another competition coincidentally, where a script based on Alison Littlewood's story 'About the Dark' reached the latter stages. *Blackout* sadly never appealed to any of them.

Then I was doing one of my periodic searches for new directors around November 2022 – after attending the fantastic 'Monsters' event which Grimm Up North film festival put on (including guests like *Wolf Manor*'s Dominic Brunt, *Gangs of London*'s Corin Hardy and my old friend Mick Garris, who directed *The Stand* miniseries amongst other things) – and I came across a talented young American guy called Jacob Osborn. His movies include *Ian* and *Wake Up*, which you can find on YouTube just like I did. I was so impressed I dropped Jacob a line and to my delight, he replied straight away with a wonderfully enthusiastic mail. Yes, he was interested in making *Blackout*, and even fired back a bunch of questions about what inspired the script, how I saw the film looking and so on. It wasn't long after that we signed contracts.

You'll probably have seen for yourself that the script and the story are quite different. In the screenplay, we get to spend a bit of time with Kelly's husband – who has changed from Jeff to James, because I had a Jeff in the already made *Life-O-*

Matic, although now I come to go through it again I realise a
'James' is also briefly in *Presence* – which just makes the
ending all the more tragic. And we see some of that childhood
of hers, switching between past and present which hopefully
adds to the tension and suspense. It's also the opposite end of
the scale to *Presence*, this one, which makes it a nice follow-up
– in that Kelly causes the death of her husband, albeit acciden-
tally, rather than losing him to natural causes.

At the time of writing, Jacob hasn't begun filming yet
(which is why sadly there are no behind the scenes photos or
stills included here) but just from his previous work I can tell
he'll do a terrific job and I have every faith in him.

Watch this space!

Horror Day at Chesterfield Library where Paul read out 'Blackout'.

Paul reading out 'Blackout' from the Touching the Flame *collection at
Horror Day.*

Bestselling author Simon Clark, who did the introduction to Touching the
Flame, *at Horror Day in Chesterfield.*

The Shadows Trilogy, *featuring 'Blackout', produced as an ebook and one-off physical copy by Screaming Dreams – cover art by David Magitis.*

Paul Kane

Blackout

When Kelly awoke everything was black.
To start with she thought perhaps she was in bed and it was the middle of the night. But everything was so, so dark. Not even the streetlights outside were shining.

And she was alone.

It wasn't until she raised herself up and something heavy dropped from her lap that she realised where she was. Where she *had been* before she'd fallen asleep. Reading on the sofa, curled up enjoying her book.

God, I must be getting old, she thought, *nodding off without warning just like mum used to do.* Or maybe it had something to do with the fact that she'd been up since six, dutifully seeing Jeff off at the station.

In any event it was a shock to wake up and find such a stifling gloom bearing down on her. She couldn't see the hand in front of her face, let alone any of the familiar, comforting objects in her living room.

Kelly never had liked the dark. As a child she'd pleaded with her parents to leave the table lamp on for her at night, and they had done so for a time. But as she got older they said it was a waste of electricity. Kelly was a big girl, and big girls weren't afraid of the dark. It couldn't hurt her. It wasn't alive or anything. And the daytime Kelly agreed with them. There was nothing to be frightened of.

It was the night-time Kelly who was the problem; whispering lies into her ear, forcing her to see things that weren't there.

'Oh, but it is alive! And so are the things that lurk within...'

Was there any wonder she'd wet the bed until she was almost in her teens? The fears didn't go away just because you were older. The blackness didn't go away - ever.

Of course Kelly hadn't thought about any of this for ages. Her nights were no longer sleepless ones. No more tossing and turning. For one thing she'd been married six years and with her husband beside her she at night had

The story itself in **The Shadows Trilogy.**

Where 'Blackout' appeared last, Darkness & Shadows *from the Sinister Horror Company – cover photography by Michael Marshall Smith.*

EXTRAS

Life-O-Matic

Confidence

Life-O-Matic
BLACKEYED CAT FILMS PRESENTS A FILM BY JIM PHILLIPS JOE PAULSON CHRISTINA NATIVIDAD "LIFE-O-MATIC"
MIKE BURNELL ADAM SHELDON AND JIMMY PHILLIPS MAGGIE CASIDY PORTIA GREGORY CHRIS PEARSON
WRITTEN AND DIRECTED BY JIM PHILLIPS DIRECTOR OF PHOTOGRAPHY ALEX NIKNEJAD STORY BY PAUL KANE PRODUCTION DESIGN MARY-ELLEN ARSENAULT
ASSISTANT DIRECTOR CASEY PRICE PRODUCED BY JIM PHILLIPS CASEY PRICE MARY-ELLEN ARSENAULT

CREDITS
Director: Jim Phillips
Script: Jim Phillips (based on the story by Paul Kane)
Co-Producer/Assistant Director: Casey Nicholas Price
Director of Photography: Alex Niknejad
Gaffer: Wayan Morales
Sound: Austin Winnie
Production Designer/Associate Producer: Mary-Ellen
Arsenault
1st AC: Trina Pham
Grips: Andrew Cormier & Alex Lalanagan
PAs: Anna Phillips & Matthew Tiltlon
Make-up: John Aviles
DIT: Neal Halford

CAST
Joe Paulson: Jeff
Christina R. Natividad: June
Mike Burnell: Norman
Adam Sheldon: Andy
Portia Gregory: Office Manager
Chris Pearson: Office Intern
Jimmy Phillips: Jamie
Maggie Cassidy: Janet

LIFE-O-MATIC
THE SHORT STORY

Jeff woke rested.

But then he always did. Why wouldn't he? He was sleeping on the Snooze-away adjustable bed, which, as he had explained to his wife June just last night, could be adjusted to any position, plus the mattress moulded itself to the sleeper's body – thus allowing for a deep and satisfying sleep.

But something was different today, something...

June was already awake, and was lying beside him staring emotionless at the ceiling. Then a smile broke on her face, a big fake grin, and she seemed to rise up sideways out of the bed, her hair immaculately permed using the latest in home hair-styling technology from Bevnon, simultaneously curling and nourishing each lock of hair – as she'd explained at great length when she'd been demonstrating how it worked.

"Morning Jeff," she trilled, as she got out of bed and stretched. Then she ran her hands down her long nightdress, not in any kind of seductive way – more's the pity – but rather to illustrate that the material hadn't creased overnight. "Can you believe it? I've been in bed seven hours and it's stayed silky smooth," she said, beaming. But not to him... never *to* him. To the thin air over his shoulder as he himself rose: using the remote to lift his side of the bed. It was how they always talked, off past each other's shoulders, never directly looking at each other. "And all for only nine-ninety-nine. Now that's what I call a real bargain!"

Jeff nodded. The Deluxo Teasmaid was already percolating, and June gestured to it with her hands like a model on a game show, waving them around it as she explained all the special features: just press this button for milk, this one for sugar… After pouring him a cup, she went into the adjoining bathroom and he heard the shower begin.

Something was different, he felt *different…*

Jeff got up off the incredibly comfortable bed, and went through to join her. He got a start when she peeked round the side of the curtain, raving about the new Aquatonics shower gel they'd invested in. June was so impressed in fact, that she began making strange noises in there, the kind of noises Jeff couldn't ever remember her making with him. "Yes, yes, *YES!*" she shouted.

Shaking his head, Jeff squeezed a length of toothpaste onto his electric toothbrush, talking to the mirror as he cleaned his teeth. "It's the triple stripes, you see," he burbled, "that tackle bacteria and bad breath. And the Yaun vibrating triple-action brush that dislodges plaque from your teeth, leaving them shining so white…" he gave a little chuckle, "you'll dazzle everyone!"

"What was that, sweetheart?" June asked, taking a break from her orgasmic pleasures with the gel.

"Oh, nothing," said Jeff.

You're *different…*

Back in the bedroom, Jeff went over to the wardrobe. As he dressed in his shirt and trousers, he felt an uncontrollable urge to walk up and down parading them in front of June, explaining about the anti-crease cut and the liquid-resistant thread. A freshly dried June, for her part, did the same: first walking up and down in her camisole and shorts set, hands on her hips, explaining that it was part of the Janice Pickard Intimates collection: a fabulous designer, she assured him. "The camisole top can also be worn on an evening out," June said to Jeff, again shooting for well over his shoulder.

Next, she put on a light summer dress, which she told him was practical for either inside or outside on days like this.

The kids, Jamie – five – and Janet – eight – were already up by the time they made their way into the kitchen. Jeff and June found them sitting at the kitchen table.

"Good morning, children," June said in that ever-so-happy voice.

"Good morning, Mum. Morning, Dad."

Jeff waved a hello as June went to the cupboards and took out bowls and cereal for them. "With these," she confided in Jeff, once more looking to the left of his head, "we can give them their recommended daily intake of vitamins C, B12..." Jeff tuned out for a moment or two while she reeled off a bunch of numbers and chemicals, just like she did every morning – *every* single morning – coming back only when she got to the 'whole grain' announcement. "Plus we can make breakfast-time fun!"

He watched as she poured the star-shaped things into the bowls, then went to the fridge for milk – a fridge, she informed him again, which kept everything chilled to the proper degree using science developed in the space programme.

For them, she popped slices of toast into their multi-slot toaster. "See, it has space so that everyone can have a slice, if they want one." Then she went through the whole procedure of cooking their breakfast, using "This stylish, but affordable oven with grilling function, ideal for those of us who want to keep an eye on our health." June winked at him, same as always. Then she cracked eggs into the frying pan, though not before holding the pan up to show Jeff the revolutionary hot-spot in the middle that "tells you when your pan is hot enough to cook. Imagine, no more guessing, Jeff! Just imagine!"

Jeff didn't have to, he saw it *every* day. And it was explained to him *every* day.

As he sat down, he felt himself doing the same, talking to Jamie and Janet about the virtues of the particular brand of orange juice they were drinking. "So you see, children," he said, looking past them into empty space, "you can get one of your five a day just by drinking up all your sweet and tasty Sunfilled Delish juice!"

The kids smiled and nodded vigorously.

During breakfast, nobody spoke much – except June, to preach about the merits of their new Senko instant decaffeinated coffee, smelling the cup and going: "Ahhh!" Then, afterwards, she took the pots, scraped them, and placed them inside their dishwasher – which, she warned, you have to look after by destroying the limescale periodically – and then praised the tablets she was using for their ability to deal with grease and really dried on food.

Why are you telling me this again?

By the time the kids were ready for school and Jeff was ready for work, June had her ironing board out, complete with steam-powered Murphy Pritchard's iron, which left clothes already smelling lemon-fresh from the machine, shop new! June gave him a peck on the cheek and wished him a nice day.

As Jeff walked outside and waved off the children – who were singing about the processed cheese in their packed lunch as they made their way to the bus-stop at the end of the street – he noticed his retired neighbour, Norman, was cutting his hedges.

"Morning, Norman," said Jeff, looking past him to the garden beyond. "That's a mighty fine piece of equipment you've got there, if you don't mind me saying so."

"Good morning to you, too, Jeff. Indeed it is! Part of the Master Gardener Collection, it retails for about fifty pounds and will slice through just about anything. Other equipment in the range includes the Master Gardener lawnmower – which can tackle even the most overgrown of lawns…" He laughed at this, as if he'd just heard a particularly funny joke. "Precision strimmer, electric tiller…" Norman went on to list every single item available in the Master Gardener Collection, then finished off by saying Jeff should come round and see his shed sometime. "A steal at just under £400!"

Somehow Jeff knew he had already seen Norman's shed more times than he cared to remember. But he thanked him anyway and promised he'd be round soon for the tour. Then Jeff went on at length about the mileage and manoeuvrability of his new family car, running his hands down the side and finishing off by tapping the top.

Why do I always do that? he asked himself. *Why do I do that every morning?*

Jeff shook his head, climbed in, and started the car. He pulled out of the drive and headed off to work at the insurance company.

—————————

Jeff's working day – as always – was punctuated by people in his office telling him how competitive their own rates were, or by snacking on chocolates that they kept promising him (as if he cared) contained less than a 100 calories per bag.

I just don't give a shit.

"Andy," he said finally at about half past two in the afternoon, to his colleague who sat opposite – a balding man even though he was only in his early thirties, "do you ever think that—"

"Sorry to stop you there, Jeff, but I've just been informed that we're slashing our prices. Yes, that's right: be a part of the Mutual Alliance family and you could benefit from all kinds of rewards." How Andy had 'just been informed' from was anyone's guess, as he wasn't even on the phone, but Jeff held up his hand to stop the patter he'd been hearing all day long.

"Listen to me, don't you ever feel that things…" he attempted to shift his gaze sideways, to look directly at Andy, but couldn't manage it, "I don't know, should be different to this? That life should be about more than deals and… things. What about friendship? I mean, when was the last time we went down the pub for a drink or—"

Andy shook his head, looking firmly past Jeff at the window outside. "Not quite following you, there, buddy. We went out not long ago and sank a few of those cold, refreshing beers that reach the parts other—"

"Forget it," said Jeff, looking down at his desk. The papers on it were blank, the screen on his computer – a top of the range Bell one, with printer and scanner thrown in – a mess of jumbled letters and numbers that didn't make sense. He couldn't remember doing any actual work today, but then he couldn't remember the last time he'd done any work for this firm *at all*. "Look, I don't feel so well."

Immediately, Andy was reaching into his pocket for the solution. "You should try these. New 'Pain Away Extra'. They get rid of your headache and give your tired muscles a massage as well!"

Jeff ignored him and got up, leaving his desk to go home.

When he walked in through the front door, he found June in the living room, exercising to a DVD made by some celebrity Jeff couldn't remember the name of. She was dressed in a leotard, complete with headband, and was jumping up and down in time to the music.

"Er… Hello…" Jeff ventured.

June paused for a moment from her endeavours, suddenly grinning – though Jeff suspected it was more because she'd suddenly got an audience than she was pleased to see him. She never asked what he was doing back so early, or whether he was sick, just simply said: "Jeff, this workout is fantastic! It tones not only the stomach muscles, thighs and buttocks, but also gives the cardiovascular system a good going over. You should really try it sometime."

"Yes, er, maybe… sometime." Jeff was about to leave when June called him back again.

"Next I'm going to have a go on our new elliptical trainer," she said, pointing to a piece of equipment that looked like it had come out of the dungeons of the Spanish Inquisition. "It provides a low impact workout, unlike using a treadmill, because your feet don't leave the ground and impact during exercise." Once more, she was looking over his shoulder when she talked.

"June," he asked her, his tone serious, "do you remember our wedding?"

She looked at him, or rather beyond him, blankly. Then, suddenly, she blurted out, "My dress was an absolute bargain. Designed by J. Hourier, it was the perfect addition to any bride's day."

"What do you remember about *us*, about you and me. About how you felt?" he asked, desperately trying to drag his eyes across to focus on her.

She looked puzzled. Then she smiled a broad smile again, and said: "We were given lots of presents, including a deluxe sandwich maker which had little trenches to prevent overspill of any melted cheese and—"

"Forget it," Jeff told her. "Doesn't matter." He walked away, head slumped.

"Wait, Jeff sweetheart… I haven't told you about the special features on our new rowing machine yet!" he heard June call as he headed up the stairs to the bedroom to lie down.

By the time Jeff came back downstairs again, the kids were home from school and June was already preparing the dinner. Chopping up vegetables for the meal using her Ultra-blades, which, as she'd demonstrated to him time and again, could cut through anything, even metal tins. She offered to do this once more, but Jeff declined politely. June smiled and did it anyway. Then she demonstrated how her Peel-O-Matic device saved her time and effort in the kitchen by shaving the skins from her potatoes. "You just pop the spud on the spike and voila, the Peel-O-Matic does all the work for you. And we can finish off the mash by using our handy Bowlinix Blender."

I think... I think I'm going mad... thought Jeff.

When he took a seat beside the kids at the dinner table, they both expressed their hope to him that they were having fish fingers from Captain Codeye's table.

"They're full of Omega-3, Daddy," said Janet, resting her chin on her hand and looking over his shoulder, "essential fatty acids, also known as polyunsaturated fatty acids, these play a crucial role in brain function as well as normal growth and development."

What... what kid talks like that?

June brought over the mash, fish fingers and veg for their dinner. "And the whole thing took only half an hour to prepare," she said, looking directly at the wall, "bon appetit!"

Jeff forked the food into his mouth, but it tasted oddly bland tonight.

When the kids were tucked up in bed, he turned on the TV – their superb, high definition television set that hung on the wall 'with picture and sound quality so real, you'll think you're actually there!' – but June, excited, wanted to tell him all about the set of books that had arrived from Life and Times: "Buy the first volume, *History of the Incas*, and get the second one absolutely free," June promised.

Something... something's wrong here, very *wrong*.

When they were getting ready for bed, he couldn't contain it any longer. "June," he said, "I'm starting to think that things aren't how they're supposed to be."

She frowned, but not at him, at the dresser beyond. "I don't know what you mean," she replied. "We have everything we could ever want. Including these flame retardant pillow cases, only—"

"June, would you look at me!" He grabbed her arms. "Please..."

She blinked several times, but couldn't do it. He, on the other hand, was looking directly at *her*. He kissed her then, not as they did in the morning when she was seeing him off for work, but hard, urgent, on the lips. When he pulled back, there was no reaction whatsoever from June. Then she smiled, and Jeff's heart skipped a beat. "I think someone's got a touch of indigestion from dinner. Now if you just take one of these Easers, they'll bring express relief to—"

Jeff shook her. "I haven't got indigestion, for Heaven's sake! June, I can't remember the last time we made love, can you?"

His wife frowned again, but said nothing.

"In fact, I can't remember *ever* making love to you! We have the kids and everything, so we must have..." *But they never get any older, do they? None of us ever get any older. And we do the same thing, day in, day out.* "June, I'm beginning to think none of this is really real."

"Nonsense," she told him, still looking over his shoulder. "You just need a good night's sleep on the Snooze-away adjustable bed." June nodded, then waited, as if it was his turn to speak. When he said nothing she prompted: "Aren't... aren't you going to explain about how it can be adjusted to any position and the mattress moulds itself to the sleeper's body to allow for a deep and satisfying sleep?"

Jeff let her go, and climbed into bed. It was surprisingly uncomfortable.

"Goodnight darling," said June, switching off the light, and for a moment or two he could imagine he actually had a wife that cared about him more than she did about the furnishings... but then she explained about how the energy-saving lightbulbs they were using would shave pounds off their next electricity bill.

It took Jeff a long, long time to get to sleep, and he knew in the morning he would feel anything but rested.

———————

It was like that the next few days. Jeff was starting to notice more and more things about the world around him, more and more that simply didn't add up. For one thing the place was always spotless; no litter, no mess, not even in the kids' rooms. And yes, as June kept telling him, they had dozens of cleaning implements that could reach even into the smallest nooks or crannies, but Jeff never actually saw her using any of them, only on tiny sections of the carpet which she would spill wine on deliberately just to show him how easy it was to 'foam-away'!

There were no family photos in their house, either, nor albums in drawers. He had vague memories of them all going to Puntlins for holidays, but these seemed to be just fleeting images of them on rides, at a show, splashing around in a pool. Nothing more substantial than that. And when he tried to think harder about it all, the memories just slipped through his fingers and floated off, like someone trying to keep hold of the string on a balloon.

The weekend came around as it always did, ahead of yet another week of 'work'. Jeff still couldn't get to the bottom of what he did exactly, but he must get paid for it; how else were they affording all of this stuff they didn't really need?

In spite of June trying to coax him out of bed with tea or coffee from the teasmaid, Jeff pulled the covers over his head. If she'd pushed it he might just have grabbed the pot and thrown it all over her – see what kind of reaction he got then. See if she looked over his shoulder or actually *at* him? He eventually surfaced around noon, bags under his eyes. Beaming, June told him that she was taking the kids out to the mall and they'd be back around teatime. "You can fix yourself something to eat using the—"

Jeff held up his hand for her to stop. He couldn't take another reeling off of the appliances in their kitchen.

"But I was just going to—"

"Go," he told her. "Just *go!*"

June's smile slipped a little, but it was soon back, and the kids never even flinched. She bundled them out of the door and into the car, telling them about the amount of space in the boot for all their shopping.

Jeff sat down at the kitchen table, head in his hands. *What's happening to me?* he asked himself. *I used to be happy.* But that was it, wasn't it? He used to be *too* happy. Life wasn't meant to be all sunshine and roses. It was meant to be about endurance and getting through the day, which made those special moments all the more special.

And what about love? Jeff hadn't really thought about it until lately. He should love his wife, love his kids, and they should love him... shouldn't they? They should care, he should care.

But he didn't.

He didn't because none of this mattered. None of this felt real.

Jeff banged the table with his fist; the salt cellar tipped up and he watched as the tiny white grains spilled over the red chequered pattern of the table cloth, then onto the floor. Then he looked around at his oh-so perfect abode and sneered. Jeff grabbed the ketchup bottle – the sauce that 'splatters where it matters' – and threw it across the room. "Now we'll see what matters," he muttered. It made a satisfying shattering sound as it hit the wall and Jeff felt… good. Better than he had in days; better than he ever had, really. Because he actually felt *something*.

He got up, walked across to the wall and touched the redness there with his fingers. They came away wet and he rubbed his lips with the sauce.

———

Norman was outside waxing his car when Jeff came round.

They exchanged hellos, though Norman said nothing about the fact Jeff was still in his dressing gown. Then Norman attempted to tell him about the new miracle waxing treatment for cars he'd just discovered that protected the paintwork against some of those irritating scratches that can occur when you're out and about, but he didn't seem to want to know.

Jeff was more interested in taking that tour of the shed. Norman's smile widened, if that were at all possible, and he told him: "Of course, of course. Just follow me."

Once they were at the shed, and he'd unlocked it, Norman heard Jeff say from behind him. "Now I have something to show *you*."

Norman turned and saw the knife in Jeff's hand. "They can cut through tin cans, you know." Norman smiled and nodded. He knew all about them, had some of his own indoors. What he wasn't sure about was why Jeff was choosing this particular moment to—

The knife slid effortlessly into Norman's gut, and his smile turned into a grimace.

But all he could think about was he wouldn't be able to finish waxing the car now.

When June arrived back with the kids, she opened the front door and got a shock. They dropped the shopping and stood there, mouths gaping wide.

The house had been trashed. Not just the hallway, which looked like a herd of stampeding elephants had trampled through it, but the living room too, on their right. Someone had smeared paint all over the walls in there, upending the chairs and couch, knocking the TV off the wall and smashing it.

Though she didn't go upstairs, June suspected those rooms were in a similar state. When they came through into the kitchen, they saw Jeff. His hair was wild and he still hadn't had a shave with the new Five Blade contour razor she'd bought him, which clung to every curve of his chin.

The first words out of June's mouth were, "Jeff, how could this have happened when we're protected by Securisense? The 24 hour alarm system that rings through to a special centre when triggered, alerting the police to—"

"We haven't been burgled, June," Jeff said evenly, though his look was just as wild as his hair. "*I did this.*"

He was studying her for some kind of reaction. So June smiled. "Honey, that's okay. We can soon get the place looking ship-shape again; that paint will come right off with some Grime-Gone."

"Don't you want to know why?" he asked her.

June's brow furrowed, then she smiled. "You need to sit down and take it easy, have an instant Creambury's Hot Chocolate."

"I don't want a *fucking* hot chocolate!" Jeff shouted suddenly. "Now stop *fucking well* grinning – and look at me!"

June continued to smile, staring over his shoulder as she offered another solution: a soothing bath with aromatic oils.

"Look. At. Me!" snapped Jeff. "Or so help me I'll…"

June continued to gaze past him, not even properly facing him when she heard the motor start up.

Jeff pulled something out from behind his back and held it up. "Norman's kindly lent me this," he said. "Would you like to see how it works?"

Strangely, June and the kids all nodded.

That's what's wrong with this place. They can't resist a demonstration. He'd given them a chance to get away...

"Okay," said Jeff, coming towards them with the chainsaw. When he dug the teeth into June's shoulder, he added, shouting above the cries, "See how easily it cuts through human flesh and bone?"

June looked at him now, finally *looked* as her blood sprayed across his face, and he saw fear in her eyes.

How? How... and why?

But it was too late. It was all too late. First June, then the kids: who, instead of running, were watching their father as he talked them through it all.

Then him.

Afterwards they'd wake up somewhere else, somewhere normal. Escape from all this. Wake up... rested. He ignored the screams because this wasn't real, was it? None of this was life.

Not real life. It couldn't be. This was all simply life-*o-matic*, a pale imitation. He nodded, continuing his labours, trying not to wince at the sounds the blade made as it cut into his family. They sounded disturbingly real.

He shook his head. It was Life-O-Matic, that's all. A show. Just Life...

Life-O-Matic.

Just Life.

O.

Matic.

<u>LIFE-O-MATIC</u>
Written by Jim Phillips
Based on the short story by Paul Kane

<u>INT. BEDROOM - MORNING</u>

A fit, attractive middle-aged couple, JEFF and JUNE, are lying in bed. The bed is neatly made, and the couple are lying side-by-side on top of the covers. Both have a neutral expression, eyes open, staring at the ceiling. JEFF is wearing a neatly pressed pajama top and bottom. JUNE is wearing an elegant, demure camisole and short set.

JUNE breaks into a big smile, and stands up out of bed.

>   JUNE
>   Good morning!

JUNE turns directly towards the camera and runs her hands down her camisole.

>   JUNE (CONT'D)
>   Seven hours in bed, and this wonderful
>   camisole and short set from the Janice
>   Picard Intimates Collection is still
>   silky smooth and unwrinkled! And for
>   the low price of just $9.99, I can have
>   a different color for every night of
>   the week.

JEFF smiles and stands up out of bed.

>   JEFF
>   I feel so wonderfully rested, that was
>   the best night's sleep I've ever had!

JEFF turns and looks directly into the camera.

> JEFF (CONT'D)
> This Snooz-A-Way Adjustable Bed really works. It can be raised or lowered to any position, and the mattress molds itself perfectly to my body. No more tossing and turning, no more disturbing my partner in the middle of the night.

INT. BATHROOM - MORNING

JUNE is taking a shower, the curtain drawn and water running. JEFF walks into the bathroom, and just as he does JUNE pokes her head out the side of the curtain. JUNE's hair is dry and she is perfectly made up.

> JUNE
> Hello darling!

JUNE pokes one hand out of the curtain holding a bottle containing a bright blue gel, label directly towards the camera. JUNE looks directly into the camera.

> JUNE (CONT'D)
> Our new Aquatonics Shower Gel leaves my hair shiny and full of body. It satisfies me in a way I never thought possible!

JUNE withdraws back into the shower.

                    JUNE (CONT'D)
          Oh yes! Ah, oh, oh! Yes! Yes!

JEFF stares briefly at the shower, blinks,
and shakes his head before walking to the
sink. He picks up a toothbrush with the
toothpaste already applied and holds it
directly in front of his face, looking
directly into the camera.

                         JEFF
          Tooth-Too-Clean! Its triple power
          formula tackles plaque, tartar, and
                     gingivitis!

JEFF brushes his teeth for a moment, before
bending down out of sight. He comes up a
moment later, mouth dry and teeth shining.

                    JEFF (CONT'D)
          Leaving your teeth sparking clean and
            so white you will dazzle everyone!

<u>INT. KITCHEN - MORNING</u>

Two school-age children, JAMIE and JANET,
sit at the kitchen table. Both are neatly
dressed and well made-up, with beaming
smiles. JEFF and JUNE walk into the
kitchen. JEFF is wearing a neatly pressed
business suit, and JUNE is wearing a bright
sun dress.

JUNE
Good morning children!

JAMIE (IN UNISON)
Good morning Mom! Good morning Dad!

JANET (IN UNISON)
Good morning Mom! Good morning Dad!

JEFF waves to the children.

JUNE
Are you ready for breakfast Jamie?

JAMIE
Yes please, Mother. I need a good
breakfast to start my day off right.

JUNE
And what would you like for breakfast,
Janet?

JANET
Wheatix! We want Wheatix!

JUNE walks to the cupboard and takes out a
cereal box. She holds the box up near her
head, and looks directly into the camera.

JUNE
Wheatix! It has a full day's supply of
vitamins and minerals in every bowl.
Just what every growing child needs to
start the day off right.

CUT TO:

JAMIE and JANET both have full cereal bowls
in front of them at the table. The box of
cereal and a carafe of milk stands next to
them. Both children are smiling directly
into the camera.

                    JAMIE
        And they make breakfast time fun!

                    JANET
        Look out world, here I come!

JEFF looks confused for a moment, shakes
his head, and moves to sit down at the
table. JUNE takes a shiny frying pan out of
the cupboard and holds it up.

                    JUNE
        How about some eggs, Jeff? They will
        come out perfect, just the way you like
                    them...

JUNE turns to look directly into the
camera.

                    JUNE (CONT'D)
        ...thanks to this wonderful new pan
                from U-Gal.
        It has this revolutionary hot spot
        right in the middle which tells you
        when the pan is hot enough. No more
                guesswork!

                                         CUT TO:

JEFF and JUNE are both seated at the table,
with a plate of eggs and toast in front of
each of them. JEFF has a large glass of
bright orange drink in front of him, which
he picks up and drinks from as he turns to
look into the camera.

                    JEFF
It's Delish juice, a full serving of
fruit in every glass. Just the thing I
     need to power through my morning.

JEFF's smile falters as he sets the glass
back down on the table, and he looks around
at his family in brief confusion before
shaking his head and picking up a fork to
begin eating.

INT. LIVING ROOM - MORNING

JUNE stands by the front door as JAMIE and
JANET, each carrying a school bag, walk
past. JUNE leans towards each and kisses
them briefly on the cheek just before they
walk out the door.

                    JUNE
Goodbye children! Have a good day at
              school!

                    JAMIE
Goodbye Mother!

> JANET
> See you after school!

JUNE looks out the door after the children have left and waves to them. JEFF walks towards the door carrying a briefcase. JUNE kisses him briefly on the cheek as he walks out.

> JUNE
> Have a good day at work dear!

<u>EXT. DRIVEWAY - MORNING</u>

JEFF walks out of the front door. A shiny and clean sedan sits parked in the driveway.

Next door an elderly man, NORMAN, wearing neatly pressed casual clothes is pruning a rose bush with a hedge trimmer.

> JEFF
> Good morning Norman! That's a mighty fine piece of equipment you've got there.

NORMAN looks up and smiles.

> NORMAN
> Good morning to you too Jeff.

NORMAN turns to look into the camera, still smiling.

                    NORMAN (CONT'D)
This is part of the new Master Gardener
  Collection. It retails for just $50,
   and will slice through just about
  anything with the greatest of ease.
   Other items in the Master Gardener
   range include a quiet and efficient
   lawn mower and a precision trimmer.

NORMAN turns back to JEFF.

                    NORMAN (CONT'D)
You should come by and see my brand new
   Master Gardener shed, a steal at
                under $400.

JEFF walks forward past the car and towards
Norman.

                       JEFF
Certainly Norman, I will be over just
   as soon as I can. But right now...

JEFF turns and looks into the camera,
running his hands over the sedan.

                    JEFF (CONT'D)
I must get to work in my comfortable
  and fuel efficient Baird Traveler. It's
   as pleasant to drive as it is to look
    at, a quiet and soothing cabin with
  heated seats and premium stereo system.
     Just the thing for those hectic
                commutes!

JEFF taps the top of the car as he
finishes, then blinks and shakes his head
in confusion.

JEFF looks around at NORMAN, who is staring
at JEFF in rapt attention and with a big
smile. NORMAN nods, as JEFF opens the car
door.

                    JEFF
              (Silently mouthing)
              Why do I ...

<u>EXT. OFFICE BUILDING - MORNING</u>

JEFF gets out of his car and walks towards
the building entrance.

<u>INT. OFFICE - MORNING</u>

JEFF sits quietly at a desk holding a
keyboard, monitor, and two boxes labeled
"In" and "Out" each of which holds a neat
stack of paper. A man walks up and stops next
to the desk. He is holding a cup of coffee.

               OFFICE WORKER #1
              Good morning Jeff!

                    JEFF
              Good morning.

The man turns and looks directly into the
camera, holding up the cup of coffee.

                    OFFICE WORKER #1
          Mmm! Sanko Coffee. Certified organic
         fair trade beans, perfectly roasted for
            a smooth and creamy texture. The
                 perfect start to my day.

<u>INT. OFFICE - MORNING</u>

JEFF is standing near a coffee machine
waiting for it to finish brewing as a woman
walks up and stops next to him.

                    OFFICE WORKER #2
                 Good morning Jeff!

                        JEFF
                   Good morning.

                    OFFICE WORKER #2
          I don't know about you, but I'm ready
              to save people some money.

The woman turns and looks directly into the
camera.

               OFFICE WORKER #2 (CONT'D)
           Here at Mutual Alliance Life and
         Casualty, we not only have the lowest
          rates around, but also the friendliest
          and most caring agents. Because we know
           how difficult shopping for insurance
                      can be.

JEFF sighs and shakes his head.

<u>**INT. OFFICE - AFTERNOON**</u>

JEFF sits quietly at his desk as a man carrying an open box of chocolates walks up to him and holds it out.

> OFFICE WORKER #1
> Good afternoon Jeff!

> JEFF
> Good afternoon.

> OFFICE WORKER #1
> Would you like one of these Hear's
> Candies?

The man turns and looks directly into the camera.

> OFFICE WORKER #1 (CONT'D)
> Made from the finest free-trade cacao
> beans and the freshest cruelty-free
> dairy. Guaranteed to be all-natural and
> preservative-free.

JEFF takes a chocolate from the box and pops it in his mouth.

<u>**INT. OFFICE - AFTERNOON**</u>

JEFF stands next to a photocopier, looking somewhat puzzled. A woman walks up to him.

> OFFICE WORKER #2
> Good afternoon Jeff!

                    JEFF
              Good afternoon.

              OFFICE WORKER #2
          Isn't this a wonderful day?

The woman turns and looks directly into the
camera.

         OFFICE WORKER #2 (CONT'D)
But of course every day here at Mutual
   Alliance Life and Casualty is a
   wonderful day. We have the most
competitive rates around, and the most
helpful agents standing by for all your
             insurance needs.

JEFF has a pained expression on his face
and walks away.

INT. OFFICE - AFTERNOON

JEFF sits at his desk staring into the
computer monitor. The screen displays a
partially-written document, but all the
words are nonsense jumbles of letters.
JEFF has a confused look on his face and
picks a stack of papers from a box
labeled "In" and begins to flip through
it. All the pages are blank. He takes
another stack from a box labeled "Out",
and flips through those. These pages are
also all blank. JEFF looks over to ANDY,
a middle-aged man sitting at the desk
opposite his.

                    JEFF
        Andy? Do you ever think that...

ANDY turns to JEFF.

                    ANDY
    Sorry to stop you there, but I have
    just been informed that we are slashing
               our prices!

ANDY turns directly into the camera.

                 ANDY (CONT'D)
      That's right, become a part of the
    Mutual Alliance family today with our
    best rates ever. And for this week only
    receive a brand new Deluxe-O-Teas-Maid
    tea maker with every new account! It's
               programmable and...

JEFF holds up his hand.

                    JEFF
    Listen to me Andy! Don't you ever feel
      that things should be...I don't
    know...different? That life should be
      about more than deals and new tea
    makers? I mean...when was the last time
      we went out after work for a drink
                    or...

ANDY looks confused for a moment, his eyes
darting briefly away from the camera. He
nods quickly and then returns to looking at
JEFF.

                          ANDY
           Why of course, we're going to go right
             after work to watch the big game.

ANDY turns directly into the camera.

                      ANDY (CONT'D)
            And nothing goes better with the big
           game than Sudsmeiser! Brewed cold from
           artisanal spring water and organically
                        grown hops.
            Sudsmeiser! It's the prince of beers!

JEFF groans and holds his head.

                          JEFF
              Oh my god, Andy! Forget it.
           Just...forget it. Look, I don't feel so
                           well.

ANDY looks around briefly, confused, before
a smile comes over his face.

                          ANDY
            Well I'm very sorry to hear that.

ANDY reaches into his pocket to pull out a
pill bottle, which he holds up with the
label facing the camera. ANDY faces into
the camera as well.

                      ANDY (CONT'D)
            You need new Pain-Away Extra! Headache
           and muscle pain relief for 12 straight
                          hours!

JEFF groans louder, stands up, and walks away.

<u>EXT. FRONT DRIVEWAY</u>

JEFF gets out of his car and walks towards the front door of the house.

<u>INT. LIVING ROOM - AFTERNOON</u>

JEFF walks in the front door. In the room JUNE is dressed in a leotard, leg warmers, and headband. Music is playing, and JUNE is exercising in time to the music.

> JEFF
> Hello?

> JUNE
> Jeff? Oh hi honey, I'm so glad you are home!

JUNE turns to look directly into the camera.

> JUNE (CONT'D)
> This new workout from Amber Autumn is fantastic! It tones the thighs and buttocks, flattens the abdomen, and provides a complete cardiovascular workout in just 20 minutes a day.

JEFF looks frustrated, almost angry.

> JEFF

                    June...please. Do you remember our
                              wedding?

JUNE's face goes blank as she looks off
camera briefly. She then nods slightly as
she brightens into a big smile.

                              JUNE
                Why of course dear, how could I ever
                              forget?

JUNE turns and looks directly into the
camera.

                         JUNE (CONT'D)
                My dress was an absolute bargain!
                Designed by J. Huriea, it was the
                perfect addition to any bride's day.

                              JEFF
                No, June! What do you remember about
                us? About you and me? About how you
                              felt?

JUNE's face goes blank again, before once
again brightening into a big smile.

                              JUNE
                Oh it was delightful, my parents gave
                              us...

JUNE turns directly into the camera.
                         JUNE (CONT'D)

> ...a new Deluxe-O-Toast toaster! With
> four slots so...

JEFF grabs JUNE roughly by the arms.

                         JEFF
              June! Look at me!

JUNE turns her head away from both JEFF and
the camera looking confused. JEFF kisses
JUNE hard on the lips. JUNE does not react
until JEFF pulls back.

                         JUNE
         Oh dear, I think someone has a touch of
                   indigestion.

JUNE pulls out a roll of tablets from somewhere and holds it up with the label facing
the camera.

JUNE turns directly into the camera as
well.

                     JUNE (CONT'D)
         You need to take one of these Easers
            Stomach Remedies! For quick relief
                       of...

JEFF growls, yelling at JUNE.

                         JEFF
            I haven't got indigestion for god's
            sake! June! I can't remember the last

> time we kissed. Or the last time we
> made love. Can you?

JUNE looks confused, but does not react.
JEFF growls in anger and walks away.

<u>INT. KITCHEN - AFTERNOON</u>

JEFF walks into the kitchen. The dining
table is set neatly for four people, and a
bottle of ketchup stands in the center.
JEFF walks to the table and picks up the
ketchup, looks at it for a moment, and
holds it up while he turns to look directly
into the camera.

> JEFF
> Trapps Ketchup, the perfect
> accompaniment to any meal. Made from
> real whole...

JEFF falters and grimaces.

> JEFF (CONT'D)
> No! This is wrong! This is all wrong!

JEFF hurls the bottle at the wall. The
bottle smashes apart, leaving a large
splotch of ketchup dripping down. JEFF walks
up to the mess and looks at it for a moment.
He draws a finger through the ketchup and
looks at the red liquid on his finger.

<u>EXT. FRONT DRIVEWAY - AFTERNOON</u>

JEFF walks out of the front door and
towards his neighbor's house.

<u>EXT. TOOLSHED - AFTERNOON</u>

NORMAN stands in front of the open toolshed
holding a shiny and new-looking hedge
trimmer as JEFF walks up to him.

> NORMAN
> Jeff! How are you?

> JEFF
> Not...not good...something's going on
> Norman. I don't...June, she...

> NORMAN
> Well, I'm sorry to hear that. I'm
> having a wonderful day though, since I
> was just going to trim my rose bushes
> with this wonderful new hedge trimmer
> from the Master Gardener Collection.

NORMAN turns to the camera.

> NORMAN (CONT'D)
> It slices through the toughest...

> JEFF
> Damn it! Not you too! Stop it!
> Just...just stop all of this! Please!

> NORMAN
> But really, it slices right through the
> thickest and toughest...

                    JEFF
              No! I said stop!

JEFF swings and punches NORMAN across the
jaw. NORMAN cries out and collapses to the
ground. JEFF jumps on top of NORMAN,
pummeling him. NORMAN's body twitches
briefly, but then stops moving.

JEFF stands, looking down first at
NORMAN's body and then at his own bloodied
hands.

                 JEFF (CONT'D)
              You stopped. That's
            it...you're...you're free.

JEFF looks around, looking back towards his
house.

                 JEFF (CONT'D)
         June. The kids. They...we can all be
                    free.

JEFF looks down to see the hedge trimmer
lying near NORMAN's body. He reaches down
and picks it up.

EXT. FRONT DRIVEWAY - AFTERNOON

JAMIE and JANET, both carrying their
schoolbags, walk up the driveway and into
the house. A moment later JEFF comes around
the corner and follows them in, carrying
the hedge trimmer.

INT. KITCHEN - AFTERNOON

JUNE, JAMIE, and JANET are standing in the kitchen looking at the ketchup stain on the wall. JUNE is no longer in her leotard, but instead is wearing a neat summer dress. JUNE gestures toward the stain and holds up a spray bottle while looking directly into the camera.

> JUNE
> It's no trouble at all children, this will come right off thanks to Grime-A-Gon and...

JEFF walks in holding the hedge trimmer behind his back.

> JUNE (CONT'D)
> Darling! You'll want to see this too, it's the power of oranges and...

> JEFF
> I don't care, June. I have something much better here.

JEFF holds up the hedge trimmer.

> JEFF (CONT'D)
> Norman has kindly lent me this lovely trimmer from the Master Gardener Collection. Would you like to see how it works?

JUNE, JAMIE, and JANET all smile and nod.

                    JEFF (CONT'D)
                    Okay then.

JEFF starts the hedge trimmer and advances
on JUNE. He swings the trimmer up over his
head and then down towards JUNE's shoulder.
Blood sprays out onto JEFF. JUNE screams in
pain.

CUT TO BLACK.

JUNE cries out in pain, as we hear the
sound of a hedge trimmer cutting into her.
JUNE's body falls to the floor.

                                        CUT TO:

JAMIE and JANET look up at JEFF, smiling
and impassive. Their faces are splattered
with blood. JEFF turns towards them,
crying, and lifts the hedge trimmer.

                    JEFF (CONT'D)
                It's okay. It'll all be okay.

CUT TO BLACK.

The sound of a hedge trimmer cutting into
JAMIE and JANET, followed by the sound of
two bodies falling to the floor.

                                        CUT TO:

JEFF looks down. He is crying and shaking,
his face a mask of blood.

                    JEFF (CONT'D)
       We can all be together, the way we're
                 supposed to be.
       We just need to get out of here. This
       isn't real. This is all just...just...

JEFF looks directly into the camera.

                    JEFF (CONT'D)
                 Life-O-Matic.

JEFF swings the trimmer up and towards his
own head.

CUT TO BLACK.

The sound of a hedge trimmer cutting
through flesh and bone, and then silence.

END

THE BACKGROUND TO...

LIFE-O-MATIC

This one came about because of a bunch of audio readings from my stories that appeared on the excellent *Tales to Terrify* podcast. I think the first was 'Guilty Pleasures', all about a day in the life of a guilt demon, then 'Remote', 'Keeper of the Light' and finally 'Life-O-Matic' if I'm remembering this correctly.

Jim Phillips, who's a long-time listener and has even done some narrations for the show, heard the last one and dropped me a line in – appropriately enough – October of 2016 asking if anyone had the film rights to the story. Jim explained that he was a screenwriter and director working out of San Diego, CA; a lovely place I'd visited a couple of years previously for a World Fantasy Convention, where I was on a panel about – believe it or not – Faustian Pacts.

Obviously, mails like this out of the blue are very rare but also extremely welcome (I'm putting that out there in case anyone reading this wants to get in touch about something they've read or heard). As luck would have it, I hadn't sold those rights yet, so we got chatting and I found out Jim was looking for a short project to direct as a SAG film (with himself and his wife producing) while he was waiting to start work on a TV series. Something in the 10-15 minute range, that he could make with a budget of $3,000-$5,000.

We came to an agreement, with Jim optioning the work for a year, and quickly signed the paperwork. Then, as with so many of these projects, Jim went off and started putting it all together. I've included *Life-O-Matic* in the extras section at the back of this book because Jim adapted it himself, so although it got made and it's my story, it's his script (presented here with his kind permission).

The idea itself came to me when I was staying over at a friend's house. We'd had a few beers, as you do, and were watching late night TV. A horror movie had just finished – I'm fuzzy on what exactly that was – and the infomercials had started up. We began taking the mickey out of these, mainly because every channel we hopped to had one of them playing – either that or the only thing we could find were home shopping networks. As tipsy as I was, the writing part of my brain was still taking notes and I began to imagine what a nightmare it would be to live in a world like that. Trapped inside a place where you had no control of your actions and had to try and sell everything that was in front of you.

And what if you were suddenly aware that was happening, you knew something was wrong but nobody else did?

I'm a big fan of *The Truman Show* – I mean, who isn't? – so that one's clearly an inspiration as well. But in that film, Jim Carrey's character is the only one who doesn't know what's going on – everybody else does. In mine, there aren't any cameras, actors, directors, producers. You're just in this strange alternate universe of 'selling', but even I have no idea who you're selling things *to*. I'm not even sure there's an audience!

Being a horror writer, my mind went straight to the old 'being the only sane one in the asylum' thing. So my character – who has a family, friends, co-workers – finally snaps and tries to think of a way to free the people he loves from all this.

To my mind, *Life-O-Matic* actually benefits from being an American production, as they were the pioneers of flogging stuff like this on TV. And Jim gathered together a group of very talented actors to pull it off, including Joe Paulson (as Jeff) and Christina R. Natividad (as his wife, June), but a special shoutout should go to the kids in the production who did a sterling job: Jimmy Phillips (as Jamie) and Maggie Cassidy (as Janet).

A series of clips were put up on Vimeo as teasers in the early part of 2017, like the breakfast scene and Jeff talking to his neighbour Norman (Mike Burnell), then the movie itself took to the festival circuit, where it won Best Horror Short at the Los Angeles Independent Film Festival Awards, Best Horror/Thriller/Sci-Fi Short at the London Independent Film Awards, was a Silver Award Winner at the Spotlight Horror Film Awards, won the prize for Horror Short at The Wayward Festival, and was an official selection at the Bucharest ShortCut CineFest, Another Hole in the Head festival, The Lost Sanity Horror & Sci-Fi Film Festival, GenCon Film Festival and the Oceanside International Film Festival, where some of the cast and crew were present for a Q&A alongside the screening.

In 2018, the Birmingham Horror Group also included it as part of their movie marathon which was raising money for Diabetes UK. And in 2023, it was screened as part of a Q&A with me about my career in film and television, at HorrorConUK in Rotherham (as mentioned in *The Opportunity* section). The packed crowd at that gathering seemed to love it!

Jim and I subsequently worked on an adaptation of my short YA novel *The Rainbow Man* as a feature, but like a lot of work in the film and TV industry it didn't pan out into anything. Yet. Maybe someday…

Variant poster featuring Joe Paulson as Jeff. Photo credit: Mary-Ellen Arsenault.

Variant poster featuring Christina R. Natividad as June. Photo credit: Mary-Ellen Arsenault.

Variant poster featuring Mike Burnell as Norman. Photo credit: Mary-Ellen Arsenault.

Variant poster featuring Adam Sheldon as Andy. Photo credit: Mary-Ellen Arsenault.

Variant poster featuring Portia Gregory as the Office Manager. Photo credit: Mary-Ellen Arsenault.

Variant poster featuring Chris Pearson as the Office Intern. Photo credit: Mary-Ellen Arsenault.

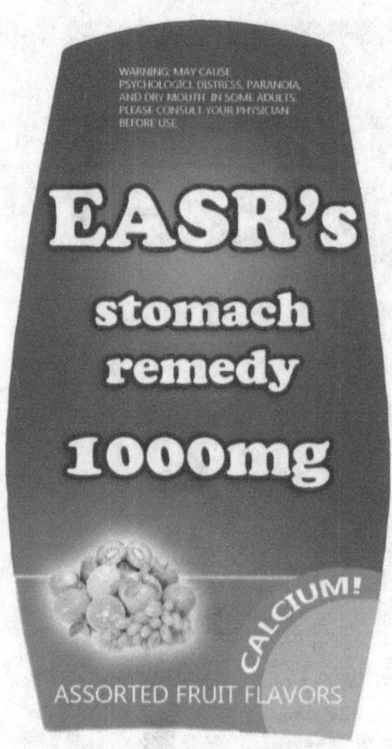

One of the brands created especially for the film.

One of the brands created especially for the film.

One of the brands created especially for the film.

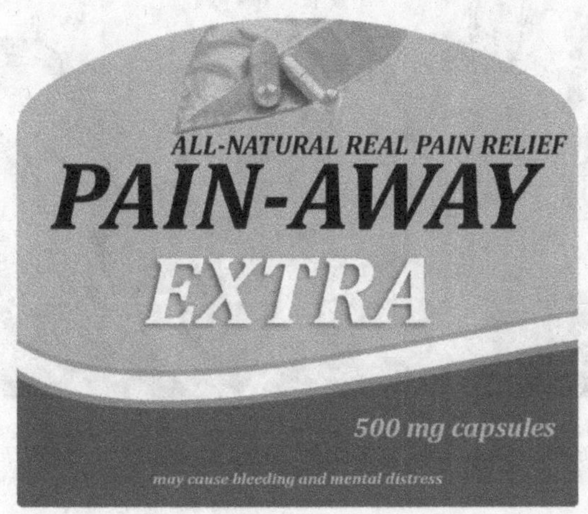

One of the brands created especially for the film.

One of the brands created especiaily for the film.

The Life-O-Matic team attending the Oceanside Intl Film Festival. From left: Adam Sheldon (Andy), Joe Paulson (Jeff), Maggie Cassidy (Janet), Jim Phillips, Jimmy Phillips (Jamie), and Christina R. Natividad (June). Photo credit: Mary-Ellen Arsenault.

Life-O-Matic's *Silver Award win at Spotlight.*

Life-O-Matic's *win at the LA Independent Film Awards.*

Life-O-Matic's *win at the London Independent Film Awards.*

Selected for a screening at the massive Gen-Con.

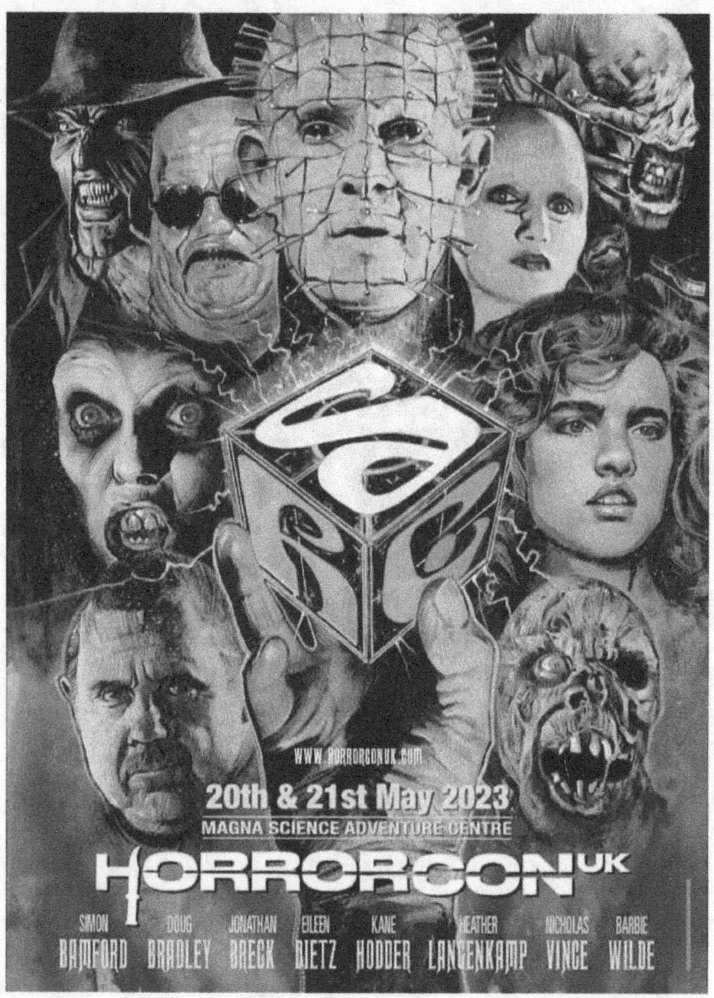

HorrorConUK in Sheffield where Life-O-Matic *had a screening in May 2023.*

The start of the movie, screening to a packed audience at HorrorConUK.

Paul being interviewed about the film and his career by Ben Warren.

Poster Credit: Mike Clarke.

Scary Bits by Committee presents a Mike Clarke film

CREDITS

Director: Mike Clarke
Script: Paul Kane
Producer: Luke Greensmith
Cinematography: James Twyman
Editor: Mark Nugent
Sound: Luke Parkinson
Music: Nicolas Iaconis IV

CAST

Simon Bamford: Therapist/Teacher/Father
Phil Gwilliam: Fretwell
Rachael Skerritt: Group Member/ Schoolgirl/Office
Woman/Mother
Jay Giblin: Group Member
Luke Greensmith: Group Member

Confidence
Written by Paul Kane

INT. THERAPY ROOM - DAY

The scream that has been heard throughout the credits is revealed to be coming from one man's mouth. We pull back from this to see an ordinary room with drab walls and a couple of windows. Somewhere on one of the walls is a print of Magritte's 'The Therapist'.

There are orange plastic chairs arranged in a semi-circle on the outskirts of the room, with a handful of shocked-looking men and women welded to them, eyes wide open in surprise. One or two are even clapping their ears to block out the noise of the scream.

We focus on one particular seated man who appears to be much more uncomfortable than the rest, if that's at all possible. He is gripping the sides of his chair tightly, looking nervously from side to side at the rest of the group, then back to the man at the front, screaming. He is wriggling around in the seat, twitching as if he'd get up and make a dash for it if he had the courage.

The door to the room opens sharply. A panic-stricken man and woman rush inside, expecting to see some kind of calamity on the other side. When the screaming man sees them he smiles and raises a hand to wave hello - but doesn't stop screaming. The man and woman, a puzzled look on their faces, smile and tentatively wave back. Then, after looking quickly around and seeing that everything appears to be okay, they depart again.

The screaming man continues to smile as he turns back to the group. Finally, after what seems like a lifetime, the man stops on a final assured note, nodding to put a full stop on the scream. The rest of the group give a communal twitch on this note, and the nervous man from before jumps in his seat. The screaming man closes his eyes slowly, before opening them again.

                    SCREAMING MAN/THERAPIST
                         (hoarse)
                        And relax.

He coughs to get his voice back.

                    THERAPIST (CONT'D)
                      (claps hands)
            Well, I don't know about you guys but I
                     feel <u>fan-tastic.</u>

The group looks anything but fantastic. Still wide-eyed, they are even more tense than before.

                    THERAPIST (CONT'D)
                      (with relish)
            The primal scream, folks. A release of
             tension, a cleansing... But it's also a

> way of reaching deep inside yourself,
> finding your core.
> An empowering thing, putting you in
> touch with your basic animal urges and
> instincts.

He looks enthusiastically from face to
face, hoping to see some kind of positive
feedback in them, something that shows his
words are having an effect.

What he sees is more bewilderment than
anything.

>   THERAPIST (CONT'D)
> (smiling a confident, if false, smile)
> Ah, you'll understand what I mean when
> you have a go yourself. This is the
> first step to a different life for you.
> Trust me. Okay, so if you'd all just
> stand up now.

The members of the group remain in their
seats.

>   THERAPIST (CONT'D)
>   (more forceful)
> Well, come on then boys and girls,
>   shake your tailfeathers!

They all look at each other. Nobody wants
to be the first to get up and make a fool
of themselves.

>   THERAPIST (CONT'D)

                    (on the verge of shouting)
         Oh, for Pete's sake, just get up! Come
            on, come on! Move it people.
            You want to spend the rest of your
            lives being told what to do? No, of
                course not. So stand up!

This time they all get up, more or less at
the same time. The extremely nervous man
is just a shade more hesitant than the
rest.

                    THERAPIST (CONT'D)
         Good, good. That's better. Now, all go
         together. On the count of three, I want
            you to give it everything you've got.
            Don't worry about the noise. Right,
                        one...
            (looks expectantly round the group)
            ...get ready... two... nearly there,
            you excited? I can't wait... Here it
                    comes now... three!

The Therapist clutches his fists, braces
himself, and prepares for an enormous
outburst. He is greeted by silence. The
Therapist sighs, closes his eyes,
unclenches his fists and shouts:

                    THERAPIST (CONT'D)
            Screeeeeeeaaaaaaaaaaaaaam!

Bullied into it, the group attempts to do a
primal scream. But as the Therapist's own
shouting dies out we discover that theirs

is much less forceful. In fact it's quite
pitiful.

                    THERAPIST (CONT'D)
          Come on, put your lungs into it!

His encouragement doesn't get him very far,
and the scream dies out pretty quickly,
with a whimper rather than a bang. The
Therapist walks up and down in front of
them like a sergeant major inspecting his
troops. He stops and singles out the
nervous man.

                    THERAPIST (CONT'D)
                  You... Mr...?

                    FRETWELL
                  (weakly)
                  Fretwell

                    THERAPIST
          Let's hear you, Fretwell. Your chance
          to show us what you're made of. Start
                  from here...
                  (points to Fretwell's stomach)
          ...and let it all out. One...
                  (the Therapist nods on each number,
                  Fretwell nods with him)
                  two, three... Go!

A terrified-looking Fretwell lets out the
strangest whine you've ever heard, like a
timid woodland creature in pain.

                    THERAPIST (CONT'D)
No, no, no. What was that supposed to
be? I've never heard anything like it
in my life. Pathetic. Do it again, do
                  it again...

<u>INT. CLASSROOM - DAY</u>

On the last word the scene changes to a dingy
classroom and Fretwell sees a grouchy school
teacher saying exactly the same thing,
hovering over him as he tries to work.

                      TEACHER
        (slamming a cane down on his desk)
No, no, no. Do it again, do it again...

The young Fretwell is on the brink of tears
as he looks around at the rest of the
class, but the teacher doesn't care. If
anything he seems to be enjoying humili-
ating Fretwell in front of them.

                  TEACHER (CONT'D)
  Are you an idiot, Fretwell, or just
      plain ignorant? I can't decide.

                      FRETWELL
                      But I...

                      TEACHER
Don't you ever dare answer me back!
                  Get up.
          (grabs him by the jacket)

              Get up and go and stand in the corner.
              Go on...

The other children laugh as Fretwell does
as he's told, the teacher smirking.

                    TEACHER (CONT'D)
          I don't know whatever we're going to do
          with you. You're pathetic, Fretwell.
                    Pathetic.

<u>INT. THERAPY ROOM - DAY</u>

The group is seated again with the
Therapist at the front. His arms are folded
and he's walking up and down once more.

The group's eyes follow him, Fretwell swallowing dryly.

                    THERAPIST
          Believe it or not, I used to be just
          like you guys. Wouldn't say boo to a
          gooseberry. But I learned the hard way
          that it gets you zip. Nobody respects a
          wimp. You're here because you want to
          increase your confidence, and that's
          what you're going to do. By the time
          I've finished with you, you won't
          recognise yourselves. Hell, not even
          your own parents will recognise you...

He smiles that big false smile again.

                    THERAPIST (CONT'D)

> Assertiveness, it's all in the mind.
> Think your way to confidence, then act
> it and do it. Sounds easy, don't it.
> That's because it is.
> Inside each of you there's a strong,
> assertive person itching to get out. I
> can show you the door, I can give you
> the key. But only you can turn it and
> let them suckers free. So, how's about
> a bit of role- playing... You.
> (points to one of the women in the
> group)
> Yes, you there. Come up and join me at
> the front. Come on, that's the way.

The woman he's singled out reluctantly goes
to join him.

> THERAPIST (CONT'D)
> Now, I'm going to pretend to be a
> salesman calling at your house, trying
> to sell you something you don't want.
> Okay?

The woman nods her head quickly several
times. The Therapist goes over to the door
and steps outside. A few seconds later
there's a knock. The woman looks round at
the rest of the group in confusion,
hoping for some help or maybe encouragement?

The knock comes again, louder this time.
When no-one answers, the Therapist lets
himself back inside.

                THERAPIST (CONT'D)
                (slightly annoyed)
All right, so what went wrong there,
honey? Perhaps I didn't make myself
clear. It's your house, you have to
answer the door. Remember, key, lock...
                (he mimes turning a key)
Hey presto: confidence!

A man on Fretwell's left wearing a neck-
brace raises a shaky hand.

                THERAPIST (CONT'D)
Yep, that's what I like to see.
Interaction. What's on your mind?

                MAN
I was... that is... I...

                THERAPIST
Spit it out.

                MAN
Would... er... wouldn't it... er...
just be better not to let the... er...
salesman in?

The Therapist knits his eyebrows together.

                THERAPIST
How would that help, Einstein?
                (to rest of group)
I'm trying to build bridges here
people. I'm Simon, you're Garfunkel.
Work with me. What if you didn't know

who it was at the door, eh? What then?
You just gonna leave everyone who comes
to your house standing outside?
(beat as he looks at them)
On second thoughts don't answer that.
Okay, start again. Let's pretend
you've already answered the door.
Now, my name's Chaz Hannigan ma'am.
I'm here to tell you about the
amazing benefits of owning one of
our revolutionary vacuum cleaners.
How's about I come inside and give
you a free, unique, once in a
lifetime, not to be missed
demonstration?

WOMAN
I-I don't really—

The Therapist holds up his hand.

THERAPIST
Now, I know what you're thinking. You
don't need another vacuum cleaner,
right?
(he nods, she nods with him)
Wrong.
(he shakes his head and she shakes
hers)
You need this one. It's the vacuum
you've been searching for all your
life, sugar.

WOMAN
Erm... maybe just...

                    THERAPIST
          (out of the corner of his mouth)
     No, no. Stand up for yourself, lady.
     Geez. Just tell me where to get off.

                     WOMAN
     Erm... no? I don't... I mean... I don't
                     know...

                    THERAPIST
     You don't know? <u>You don't know</u>! For
     Chrissakes, make up your mind about
                   something.
                    (shouting)
     No wonder he's turned out the way he
                     has...
             (points at Fretwell)

Fretwell frowns, amazed.

               THERAPIST (CONT'D)
          (Therapist's accent changes)
     No wonder he's always getting picked
     on. Useless, bleeding useless, the pair
                    of you!

<u>INT. FRETWELL FAMILY LIVING ROOM - DAY</u>

The Therapist turns into Fretwell's father
and the woman becomes his mother. He's
watching as his father shouts and raves,
wagging his finger aggressively. His mother
can do nothing but stand and take it,
barely able to fight back.

                    FATHER
I'm ashamed to call him my son. You've
done that to him, molly-coddling him.
        He's nothing but a pansy.

                    MOTHER
                   (weakly)
        Don't... don't call him that.

                    FATHER
        Aye? And why not, it's true.

                    MOTHER
        (finding strength from somewhere,
           although still a whisper)
     It... it was you... He doesn't have...
                     any—

                    FATHER
        Is that right? Well, we'd better try
           knocking some back in then.

Off camera we hear the sounds of slapping
and screaming. We focus on Fretwell's
scared face. When his father is finished,
he turns on the young boy, winding a belt
around his hand.

                FATHER (CONT'D)
        Going to teach you to stand up for
           yourself. Come on, stand up for
              yourself, stand up—

<u>INT. THERAPY ROOM - DAY</u>

Fretwell jumps when he realises the
Therapist is hovering over him.

                    THERAPIST
          I said stand up, Mr Fretwell.

Fretwell is returned to the here and now,
but is still a bit disoriented. He touches
his finger to his chest and the Therapist
nods.

It's Fretwell's turn to have a go at role-
playing. The Therapist helps him up out of
the chair with more force than is
necessary.

                THERAPIST (CONT'D)
          Okay, so in this particular scenario
            someone's run into your car.

Fretwell holds up his finger.

                    FRETWELL
          I... I don't have a car. I don't drive.

                    THERAPIST
                  (to himself)
            Not a massive surprise.
                  (to Fretwell)
          Doesn't matter, we'll just pretend,
          okay? And look, you can choose the car
            of your dreams. Ferrari, Porsche,
            BMW...? Use your imagination.

Fretwell stares at him blankly.

                    THERAPIST (CONT'D)
          Right, well I've just hit your car.
          I've smashed up the back end, caused a
                  hell of a lot a damage.
             It's all my fault, see, but I'm
            refusing to admit culpability. Got the
                         picture?

Fretwell nods.

                    THERAPIST (CONT'D)
                 (getting into character)
          Would you look at my bumper here. Why
          don't you watch where you're going, eh?
          Pulling out in front of me like that,
                    you stupid asshole.

                        FRETWELL
               A-a-actually I think...

                        THERAPIST
          You think, do you? That's a relief, I
          was startin' to wonder. Someone's gonna
          pay for all this and it ain't gonna be
                    me, catch my drift?

Fretwell nods again, his eyes brushing the
floor.

                    THERAPIST (CONT'D)
          Okay, big mistake there. You never agree
          with a guy like me... I mean a guy like
          that. And you don't break eye contact;
          stare the guy down, show him who's boss.
          That you won't be pissed on by anyone.

> Got it? You gotta take control of the
> situation, strike while the iron's hot
> and don't let anyone get in your way...

<u>INT. OFFICE - DAY</u>

The words ring out as Fretwell remembers
another incident. He's in the bank at work,
a single corner-desk with papers in neat
piles on it. He's glancing nervously across
at a woman with glasses on sitting at
another desk. Fretwell bites his lip.

Once or twice she catches him and he looks
away. He's obviously trying to work up
enough courage to go over and say something. He's looking at the clock - it's
almost time for lunch. But before he can
get up, another much more confident worker
arrives and starts to chat her up.

They flirt and she goes off with him for
lunch. The man laughs as they leave
together, one hand slipping around her
waist.

<u>INT. THERAPY ROOM - DAY</u>

THERAPIST

> ...sure as hell ain't going to pay for
> it, I'll tell you that right now.

FRETWELL

> I... It wasn't—

                    THERAPIST
      Hey, what's this, the worthless piece
        of crap wants to speak. So come on,
            what ya gonna do about my car?

Fretwell looks like he's about to say something else, but then decides not to. The
Therapist picks up on this and tries to
provoke him further.

                THERAPIST (CONT'D)
      I said, what are you gonna do, pal?
      I'll tell you what, first things first:
      let's have an apology out of you. Come
        on, say you're sorry for wrecking
                    my car.

                    FRETWELL
            But... I... I didn't...

                    THERAPIST
      I must be going deaf. Because I didn't
      catch that too well. Didn't sound like
                  sorry to me.
          (addressing the other members of the
                    group)
                  Did it you?

The rest of the group shake their heads.
Fretwell looks around at them, then back at
the Therapist.

                THERAPIST (CONT'D)
      There, see? Nothing like it. Come on, I

clap, then chant the word 'loser' over and
over again. Fretwell looks from face to
face as the Therapist prods him again in
the chest.

                    FRETWELL
          No, stop it... Stop...

                    THERAPIST
              Or what, eh?
          (carries on prodding)
          Come on, show me.

                    FRETWELL
              Or... or...

The room is spinning, the faces from the
group a blur. They change into children in
a playground, spinning the young Fretwell
around.

The chants continue as we cut to the couple
from work throwing their heads back and
laughing at him in an overemphasised way.

The Therapist's face changes alternately
into that of his old teacher, his father.
It becomes unclear as to what is real and
what's not.

                    THERAPIST
          Use your imagination... you're
          pathetic... I don't know what we're
          going to do with you here...
          Useless, bleeding useless...

                         FRETWELL
                     (more forceful)
                      Shut up...

The room is still spinning with bits from
other scenes intercut, including Fretwell
wetting himself in the school playground -
or his bed at home.

Then at work he sees the ad in the paper:
'Increase Your Confidence!' with prices
underneath. He rings this with a red pen.

The chanting continues.

                    FRETWELL (CONT'D)
                 Shut up, shut up. Shut up!

                       THERAPIST
                Show me! For Chrissakes show me!

He sees a door, the Therapist miming
turning a key in a lock. A real key clicks
somewhere, and a door opens. Fretwell's
expression changes to one of anger and
hatred, everything he's ever had to put up
with in his life bubbling to the surface.

We see the finger prod him one last time,
then more hands grabbing. The scene becomes
confused, and we finally settle on
Fretwell's face.

We pull back and the room looks like a
bomb's hit it, with bodies lying all around

and chairs upended. The Therapist lays at
Fretwell's feet.

The door is open and the two people from
the beginning are there. The woman puts her
hand to her mouth in shock.

Fretwell looks around him at the devasta-
tion, hardly believing he is capable of
this. Then the realisation that he is
responsible dawns on him.

                    FRETWELL
          I... I'm sorry...

And he starts to scream.

We close up on his mouth and the credits
roll with Fretwell's primal scream as the
soundtrack.

THE END.

THE BACKGROUND TO...
CONFIDENCE

The journey of *Confidence* – which remains one of the few original scripts I've ever written, as opposed to being based on a short story or novel of my own (so this is the first time it's ever seen print) – begins around 2001 or 2002 when I was interviewed for a documentary called *Assembly of Rogues*. Director Martin Roberts and his partner Helen Hopley were going around and filming informal chats with horror authors such as Ramsey Campbell, Mark Morris, Tim Lebbon, Carol Anne Davis, Paul Finch, Mark Chadbourn and many others. My interview took place at the late author Derek M. Fox's house, alongside John B. Ford, and we even did some inserts in a local graveyard because, y'know, horror writers.

I recall being terrified on the day itself, rambling on about my work, but apparently I did okay enough to be included in the finished thing, parts of which we screened at the big Terror Scribes convention in Birmingham in 2002. During the course of all this, though, I became good friends with Martin and Helen, even staying over at theirs for film marathons and what we termed 'Indie-Chis', which were a mix of Indian and Chinese takeaways.

Anyway, during some of our late night discussions –

fuelled by probably way too much vodka – we started talking about working on something together. And I thought it might be quite nice this time if it was something totally original, rather than having that safety net of fiction already there to fall back on. This was something I hadn't really done since my uni days for Film Writing modules (you'll find an example of this elsewhere in the book). I said this just recently in a meeting, but I do like to have a roadmap of sorts to follow when scripting – and this was the only time professionally I hadn't really done that. I guess I sort of had half an idea of where I was going or what I was doing when I started penning *Confidence*, but nothing concrete, so really it had altogether the wrong title. Or did it? Because the whole theme of this one was to *gain* confidence, that's why the main character has gone to the group in the first place.

Full disclosure, and contrary to how I might come across, I've never been a particularly confident person – although I've never had the kind of problems Fretwell (note the gag in the name) has to work through. It did put me in a position where I could relate to him, however, and I've always been fascinated by those sort of therapy sessions where they do primal screams or whatever. Especially if they might not be on the level.

I've also been a fan of *Monty Python* since I was a kid, and there's definitely more than a whiff of *Python* about both the Therapist and the execution of this story, though perhaps I do go even darker than those guys, especially with my ending. I recall from my childhood as well, an episode of the old sitcom starring Michael Crawford, *Some Mothers Do 'Ave 'Em*, where Frank Spencer causes chaos during a training session which uses role-playing...

I struggled a bit to write *Confidence*, I'll be honest, but I was pretty happy with the final draft of it, even though it was and remains a bit rough around the edges. Happy enough to hand it over to Martin and Helen at any rate, and they began looking into how they could film it; even scoping out a local school where their friend worked so they could capture that flashback scene.

Time passed, and life got in the way of things for all of us – not least both of my parents passing away within two years of each other, meaning I had to clear out the family home and also move into a bigger place with Marie so we could accommodate some of the stuff that I had stored there. We were also busy helping to run, or chairing, various conventions – which Martin and Helen were involved in too – like World Horror, FantasyCon and World Fantasy. When it became apparent that Martin wouldn't be able to make the movie, I dusted it off and went through it again with a fresh eye.

This coincided with our Guesting at Liverpool HorrorCon in 2015, which artist Ilan Sheady kindly invited us to. In-between being on panels and such, I was interviewed for a podcast or TV thing by a guy called Luke Greensmith, who gave me his card. Luke was just starting out as a producer and asked if I had any scripts that were short, so he could cut his teeth on them. A light-bulb went on over my head, as they do sometimes, and I remembered *Confidence* – so when I got back home again I sent it over.

Luke loved it, and suddenly the project was a 'go' again. I think it was Luke who brought Mike Clarke on board, as he'd directed shorts like *A Hand to Play* and *Paper and Plastic*, which Luke sent me to have a look at. And I think I suggested Simon Bamford for the role of the Therapist; I'd got to know Simon through his connection with *Hellraiser* (he played Butterball in the original, not to mention Ohnaka in *Nightbreed*). I asked him, he read the script, and then said yes. Indeed, he ended up playing the Teacher and Father as well! With a producer, director and star now in place, it was just a matter of raising the cash to film it all and Luke set up a Kickstarter that was shared by the likes of the Clive Barker Podcast, HorrorNews.net and various other film news sites.

Sadly, we only managed to bring in about £300 of the £4k goal, which was disappointing. However, Luke bumped this amount up to a point where the film could get made guerrilla-style, and filming took place in February and March of 2016. Now, I've heard audio and seen clips from the shoot – plus pictures obviously, some of which are presented here – and Simon was simply amazing. Everyone on set agreed with that, which makes the fact we never got a finished film all the more heart-breaking.

I don't know all the ins and outs about what happened, and it's not really for me to speculate, but the film was shot and something was wrong with the sound and/or some of the footage (I was told it was corrupted), for which Luke – who I have worked with since, on some of the *Ghost Story Guys* audio adaptations of my work like 'A Nightmare on 34th Street' and 'Bounty' – has apologised profusely to both myself and Simon. I still live in hope that at some point it can all be brought together and fixed, but at the time of writing that doesn't seem likely anytime soon.

Just one of those things with film, I suppose – and especially low-budget movie-making. Such a shame, but at least you can read the script now and see what was intended.

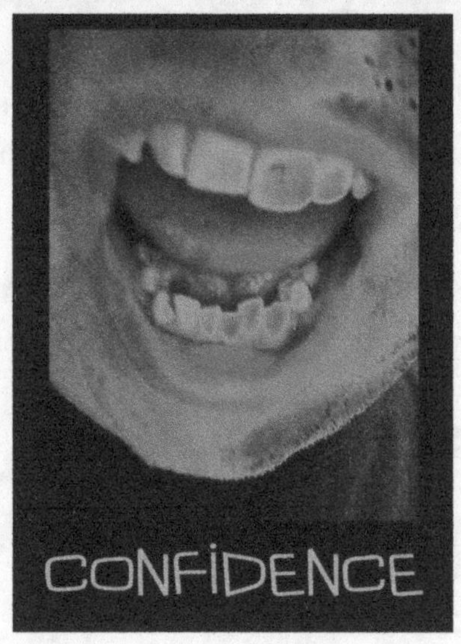

An early Confidence *poster concept by Paul, used in the online Kickstarter campaign.*

Simon Bamford as the Teacher in the classroom scene.

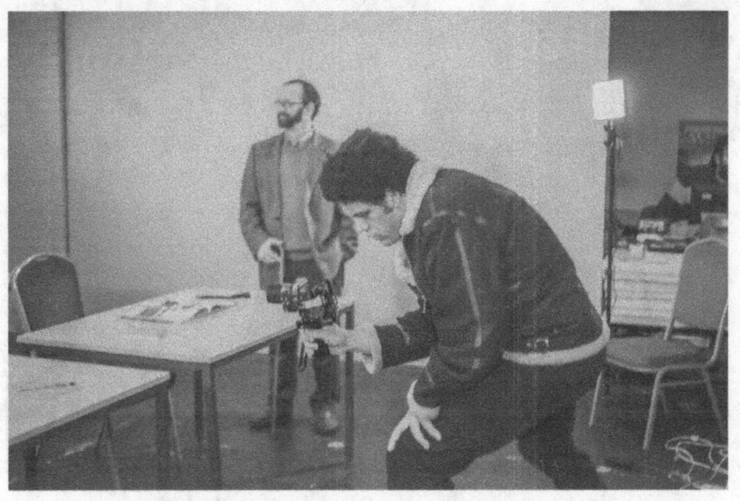

James Twyman, the DP, getting ready for a take with Simon.

Another classroom shot.

Rachael Skerritt in one of her multiple roles as the 'little schoolgirl'.

Simon Bamford as the Teacher – publicity still.

Director Mike Clarke with Rachael Skerritt and Simon Bamford as the mother and father, while DP James Twyman (far right) lines up a shot.

Rachael and Simon in the tense mother and father flashback scene.

Close-up of the mother and father scene.

Mock-up flyers asking people if they have 'Confidence'.

Cast and crew on the set of Confidence.

Variant poster for Confidence *featuring Simon Bamford as the Therapist. Credit: Mike Clarke.*

BONUS MATERIAL

Graduation Day

The Buzz

Graduation Day
Written by Paul Kane

SC. 1. INT. DAY — Wentfield University Hall

A medium-sized hall with a few people inside, milling around. Some seats are occupied by students in caps and gowns, and a couple of early parents are finding their places at the back.

TOM, one of the graduates, is sitting on the end of a row of seats. Jeans and a T-shirt are clearly visible beneath his gown, and he has a rough beard.

He looks down the row to his left where a couple of students, SAMANTHA and RICHARD, are sitting several places away. SAMANTHA — blonde, curly hair falling around a pretty face — looks back shyly.

TOM and SAMANTHA gaze at each other until RICHARD — a man with aquiline features, gelled down black hair poking out from under his cap, and an obviously expensive suit on underneath his own gown — pulls her back sharply in the chair.

RICHARD glares at TOM, then says something to SAMANTHA.

TOM leans back in his chair and sighs.

OPENING CREDITS

The screen goes black, then a series of old photographs emerge slowly. They show two

children, about eleven years old, standing
together. One is a girl in pigtails
(SAMANTHA), the other is a scruffy lad with
close-cropped hair (TOM). They are both
wearing the same school uniform.

In some of the pictures the unlikely pair
are holding hands. The photographs show
them getting older and one in particular
has them in a photobooth, kissing. Now they
become more recognisable as the people we
have just seen.

Somewhere in the middle of this comes the
title, GRADUATION DAY, and the whole
sequence is set to the tune of Queen's
'Under Pressure'.

<u>SC. 2. EXT. DAY — City</u>

A bustling city-scape from above. The area
is dotted with office blocks; the roads are
littered with cars nose-to-tail. The sound
of car-horns competes with that of the
engines.

In the centre of the city, one building
stands out from the rest because of its
shape. A grey concrete square with other
smaller buildings joined onto it. A large
sign on the metal gates says 'WENTFIELD
CITY UNIVERSITY'. We travel up the stone
steps into the main building itself.

<u>SC. 3. INT. DAY — University Hallway</u>

The entrance hallway of the university.
Some students are standing against the
wall. As we approach, we see they are the
students from scene 1, only at an earlier
time. TOM has no beard now and has signifi-
cantly shorter hair, but still sports the
jeans and T-shirt.

SAMANTHA, or SAM as she likes to be called,
is next to him. She constantly brushes the
hair out of her face with her free hand.
The other arm is around TOM's shoulders.
She watches him as he reads a history book.

Across from them are RICHARD, still looking
suave, clean-shaven with a light blue shirt
on, and BECKY, a mousy yet excitable girl,
who is looking fixedly at TOM. BECKY seems
particularly restless.

BECKY
So, where are you going this summer,
Tom?

TOM looks up from his book reluctantly.

TOM
What?

BECKY
(giggling)
Are you going away after your finals?

                    TOM
                 (shrugs)
Not really thought about it, Becky.
Just wanna pass 'em really. I'll make
    it up as I go along, as usual.

                   BECKY
        I'm sure you'll pass, Tom

SAM is annoyed at this obvious flirting and
turns to Richard.

                    SAM
Are you off anywhere Ricky — parents
           treating you?

                  RICHARD
Richard please Samantha, and if I go
     anywhere I will pay for myself.

RICHARD smirks and looks her straight in
the eye.

                    TOM
                 (laughs)
Yeah, but yer parents'll give you the
      cash to pay for yerself.

RICHARD glares at him. TOM simply smiles
back.

               TOM (CONT'D)
You know I'm only takin' the piss,
      mate. No offence meant.

TOM gets back to his book.

                    BECKY
       So, are you guys going to the party
              Friday night?

                    SAM
              I'm up for it!

                    TOM
          (without looking up)
   I'll 'ave to pass, I'm afraid. Got work
                to do.

SAM looks at him, frowning. It's obvious
she had planned to go with him and he's
sprung this on her. Her expression turns to
one of anger.

                  RICHARD
       I will definitely be there.

TOM doesn't hear any of this, he is
engrossed in his book again.

<u>SC. 4. INT. NIGHT — Tom's Digs</u>

TOM is in his room, lying back on the bed.
A large poster of Jarvis Cocker is hanging
over his head. The debris of lager cans and
history books lie scattered around him.

He is intently scrutinising one particular
book by the light of the bedside lamp. Then
he begins making notes on a pad.

The phone rings on the landing and a muffled voice shouts: 'Tom, it's Sam!'. TOM jumps off the bed and pelts through the door, nearly tumbling as he goes.

He picks up the pay-phone receiver, left hanging by its cord.

> TOM
> Sam, what's up?
> *(muffled voice)*
> Can't, I'm cramming tonight...
> *(muffled voice)*
> That's not fair, y'know I need to study more than you. This is important to me.
> *(loud click)*

After shouting SAM's name a couple of times, he hangs up himself and rings her number. He has no success, so goes back to his room, confused and angry.

SC. 5. EXT. NIGHT — Richard's Place

TOM is outside, banging on the door with his fist. The light comes on upstairs and then a few seconds later the sound of bolts and chains can be heard on the other side of the door.

The door opens and RICHARD is stood there in his dressing gown, a red silk affair. Even though it's obvious he's just got out of bed, RICHARD's appearance is immaculate.

                    RICHARD
        For heaven's sake Thomas, do you know
                 what time it is?

                      TOM
        I need to know if ya seen Sam. She
        disappeared after the exams and she's
        not at home… We bin fightin' a bit.

                    RICHARD
        How the hell should I know where she
          is? I am not her only friend!

                      TOM
                 Tried the rest.

                    RICHARD
        You know, you have only yourself to
        blame, 'mate'. Everyone's talking about
                 you and Becky.

                      TOM
        What yer on about? You know how I feel
        about Sam… We bin together fer years.

                    RICHARD
        It's late Thomas. Why don't you go
        home. Samantha will probably turn up in
                 the morning.

TOM, more confused than ever, reluctantly
goes. Behind RICHARD, on the stairs, SAM
comes down wearing only a night-shirt. She
peers out through the crack in the door.

                         SAM
                    Has he gone?

                       RICHARD
                    Yes, he's gone.

The door shuts.

SC. 6. INT. NIGHT — Tom's Digs

TOM is sat, crossed-legged, on his bed.
There is no lamp on, but in the half-light
from the window his face is quite visible.
His hair is now longer and he has started
to grow a beard.

Looking up at the twinkling stars, tears
well in his eyes.

SC. 7. EXT. DAY — University Steps

On the steps of the university, TOM is
looking anxiously around. He has a full
beard (to illustrate the passage of time)
and is dressed in cap and gown. Other
students begin to congregate here too,
wandering round as they wait for the cere-
mony to start.

BECKY arrives at the foot of the steps and
waves frantically to TOM. She dashes up to
join him and gives him a big hug. TOM
hardly responds at all, preoccupied as
he is.

BECKY

Tommy, I'm so pleased to see you! Have
you had a good holiday?

TOM
(snaps)
Brilliant!

BECKY
(babbling)
I hardly recognised you, what with the
beard and everything. It really suits
you, though. Are your parents here, I
bet they're so proud.

TOM

Already inside. Listen, 'ave you seen
Sam? I've been looking everywhere for
her. She's not at her digs or at home.

BECKY

I haven't heard from her but... my God
Tom, you don't know, do you?

TOM
What?

BECKY
I thought she might have had the
decency to tell you.

TOM puts a hand on her shoulder.

TOM
Told me what, Becky?

                    BECKY
     She's seeing Richard. They went away
              together this month.

TOM lets her go, devastated. His mouth
hangs open — eyes blank.

                    BECKY
            I'm so sorry Tom.

TOM doesn't hear a word she says. He walks,
like a zombie, to the entrance, away from
BECKY.

<u>SC. 8. INT. DAY — University Hall</u>

A return to scene 1 where the students are
arriving for the graduation, but RICHARD,
SAM and BECKY have not yet appeared.

TOM is already sat on the end of the row of
seats, but keeps looking around him; he
even stands up a couple of times to crane
his neck around.

BECKY comes in through the main entrance
and looks around for him. She comes across
when she spots him and takes her seat in
front.

Neither of them speak. BECKY looks as
though she is about to, but thinks better
of it because of TOM's gloomy face.

Then at the entrance SAM appears and stands

there for a while. When TOM notices her he
starts to get up. Just as he does so,
RICHARD joins her, standing very close, as
if he doesn't want to let her out of his
sight.

The pair make their way to the seats along
from TOM. For just a moment TOM and SAM's
eyes connect. She turns away when RICHARD
ushers her into a seat.

Despite this, SAM cannot help glancing to
her right at TOM. He still hasn't taken his
eyes off her since she came in. RICHARD
notices and keeps forcing her attention
back to him.

SC. 9. EXT. DAY — University Steps

Some of the students emerge from the cere-
mony, onto the steps. They pile out and
start to look for members of their family.
A couple have compact cameras ready to take
photos.

They congregate in a group like a murder of
black crows. In the middle of all this SAM
and RICHARD make their way out into
the day.

He has hold of her hand in a vice-like
grip. RICHARD's head swivels this way and
that looking, not for his family, but
for TOM.

TOM is not far behind, dogging their every step. BECKY isn't far behind him, following like a puppy after its master.

TOM soon catches up with the pair in front and when he gets within arm's reach, he taps RICHARD on the shoulder. RICHARD spins around quickly.

RICHARD
Thomas… I really feel I must explain.

TOM
Seems pretty obvious to me. Yer like some sort of ghoul, waitin' to pounce.

RICHARD
(laughing)
Is that what you think? Look at yourself, you couldn't even be bothered to get properly dressed, today of all days. She's well shot of you!

TOM
Unlike yerself, I make me own way in life 'Dick'. And Sam's got a name.

RICHARD
Don't split hairs, Thomas. Samantha and I are perfectly happy together. You're only showing yourself up in front of everyone

TOM
I don' t care abou' that.

> (*turning to SAM*)
> I luv you Sam. Always have, always
> will!

RICHARD
Maybe you should have thought about
that before you jumped into bed with
Becky.

TOM grabs hold of RICHARD by the arms.

RICHARD
Let go of me!

RICHARD starts to shove TOM backwards, an
angry expression on his face. SAM takes
hold of RICHARD'S arm but he easily shrugs
her off.

SAM
Richard, no! Please don't—

TOM starts to push back, harder. This esca-
lates fairly quickly into an all-out brawl.
Soon both the students are swinging at each
other. Cameras are flashing, caps are flying,
and RICHARD and TOM begin to wrestle.

It isn't long before they've attracted a
few spectators. Students in full graduation
regalia stand round in a circle, cheering
them on, like a crowd at a boxing match.

SAM, despite being brushed off several

times, still tries to hold RICHARD back.
BECKY, at TOM's side, attempts to do the
same with little success.

Suddenly RICHARD catches TOM in the face
with his elbow, purely by accident. SAM
manages to drag RICHARD away now as TOM
collapses onto the steps. RICHARD then
takes hold of SAM's arm and starts to whisk
her away from the scene. He stops only to
pick up their fallen hats.

TOM is sprawled out on the steps, his nose
bleeding profusely. He dabs at it with the
back of his hand, wiping blood onto his
gown. BECKY has a handkerchief out, ready
to tend to the wound.

TOM's parents rush over to him when they
realise what has happened. His MUM, dressed
in a loud flowery frock, instantly begins
to fuss over him.

MUM
Love, oh love. Are you all right? Look
at that blood on yer gown, and yer only
'ired it fer the day. It'll never come
out, y'know!

TOM holds up his hand in mock protest.

TOM
Mum, it's okay, really. Go on ahead,
I'll meet yer later.

MUM begins to argue but BECKY cuts in.

                    BECKY
                   (kindly)
        I'll take care of him, don't worry.

TOM is helped up by BECKY and they stagger
up the steps. The other students look on in
bemusement.

<u>SC. 10. EXT. DAY — Street</u>

SAM is still being herded along the high
street by RICHARD. She stops, tugging
against his arm. He turns defiantly to
face her.

                   RICHARD
              Yes, what is it?

                    SAM
        Don't you think we ought to see how
                  Tom is?

                   RICHARD
        He's a big boy. Anyway, why are you
        interested? I'm sure Becky is taking
                good care of him.

                    SAM
                  (scowling)
        You might have really hurt him.

                   RICHARD
        Oh I do hope so! He deserves it, loud

               mouthed... If it wasn't for me you
               would still be with him. I shudder to
                         think what—

SAM slaps him hard across the face. The hat
he has just put back on is knocked off
again.

                         SAM
               (tears running from her eyes)
               Maybe that wouldn't have been a bad
               thing. At least Tom treated me like a
               person, not a possession. Something to
                         flaunt.

                       RICHARD
               (rubbing his red face)
               Oh spare me! Everyone knows about him
               and Becky. He wouldn't have done that
               if he thought anything about you.

                         SAM
               You bastard! Why did I ever listen
                         to you?

SAM turns around and storms off. At first
RICHARD cannot believe it. Then, regaining
his composure, he shouts after her.

                       RICHARD
               Go on, see if I care, you stupid bitch!
               You could have had it all with me.

A passer-by stops and gapes at his
outburst.

RICHARD
(angry)
What are you staring at?

The passer-by passes by. RICHARD stoops to
pick up his cap and places it on his head
at an angle.

SC. 11. INT. DAY — University Hallway

TOM is sat down on an orange plastic chair
in the hallway from scene 3. BECKY is
hovering over him, plugging up his running
nose with her hanky. He seems dazed, not
quite able to grasp what has happened
to him.

BECKY
I think it's stopped now. Can you
believe those two. You're far too good
for her, Tommy.

She places his head on her chest and gently
nurses him.

TOM
(mumbling)
No, no I'm not. I never was.

BECKY
(Ignoring him)
Now it's just you and me. Aren't you
glad I told people we were together.

TOM suddenly snaps awake, hearing her as if

for the first time. He releases himself
from her grip.

                    TOM
            (raising his voice)
You did what? Becky, what the hell were
            yer thinkin' about?

                    BECKY
            (genuinely surprised)
Don't be angry. I was thinking about
                us, Tommy.

                    TOM
There's no us, Becky. How could there
be? I'm in luv with Sam. I fell in luv
with her at school, made sure we went
      to the same uni together and
                everythin'.

                    BECKY
              Don't say that!

                    TOM
's true, Becky. You've always known,
  but that didn't stop yer, did it? I
    tried not to hurt you before, but...
                I'm sorry.

TOM gets up and walks out of the building,
leaving BECKY in floods of tears behind.

SC. 12. EXT. DUSK — University Steps.

TOM is sat on the stone steps at the

entrance-way, where he had the fight with
RICHARD. He holds his head in his palms,
his cap on his lap.

A slender hand snakes over his shoulders
and SAM sits down beside him on the steps.
TOM looks up at her with red eyes.

In the cold night air his breath steams up.

SAM

You'll catch your death of cold out
here. Are you alright?

TOM

SAM! Wha…? I mean, where's Richard?

SAM

Don't know and I don't care. Tom,
listen—

TOM

No, hang on a sec, I 've got summat to
say. There were never anythin' between
me an' Becky. She made it all up.

SAM
(softly)
Ssssh. I've… I've been a bit stupid.

TOM
(sighing)
Yeah.

                    SAM
                 (laughing)
      You don't have to agree with me, you
                    know.

                    TOM
      Sorry... I didn't mean to ignore yer
      Sam. Me degree would've bin fer nothin'
      wivout... I only came 'ere today to
                   see you.

SAM hesitates for a second then begins to
titter into her free hand. TOM looks at her
inquisitively, then starts to laugh too.

                    TOM
                   What?

                    SAM
      Just wondering what our folks are going
                to make of today.

                    TOM
      One fer the family album innit? The day we
                 'graduated'.
                 (pause)
            So what 'appens now?

                    SAM
                 (sighing)
      I dunno. Let's just make it up as we go
                   along.

She rests her head on his shoulder and they
look up at the night sky together.

PAUL KANE

FADE TO BLACK

SAM'S VOICE
Just do me a favour, will you? Shave
that stupid beard off.

CREDITS

Possible songs to go with the end credits:
The Cure, 'Friday I'm in Love'.
Tony Wilson, 'Just When I Needed You Most'.

END

THE BACKGROUND TO...
GRADUATION DAY

I debated about whether or not to include these, but in the end thought 'in for a penny' – hence the 'bonus' section on top of the 'extras'. The first of the two bonus pieces is one of my uni assignments from about 1995. I studied History of Art, Design and Film at Sheffield Hallam, after doing two years General Art and Design at Chesterfield College – so had already graduated from one course by the time I headed to university.

The GAD course was actually one of the best experiences of my life, the opportunity to experiment in all kinds of different media, from oil painting to life drawing, from photography (some of my photos even went on a touring exhibition abroad) and film to metalwork and sculpture. If I'm being honest, though, I was always better at the writing side of things, and so my theory tutor suggested I go for the HADAF degree. It was hard work, but I'm glad he did, because it not only increased my knowledge of art and design, but also taught me how to write critically about movies (something I enjoyed so much, I even went back and did an MA, which helped enormously with writing *The Hellraiser Films and Their Legacy*). There was even a 'Professional

Writing' module, which kicked off my whole journalism career and led to years of freelancing work.

There was a 'Writing for Film' module as well, however, which is where *Graduation Day* comes into things. I always got the impression that our tutor was only teaching it between actual film scripting gigs – which is never a great thing to do, for you or the students, because neither side will be invested – but I did pick up a few things from him, nevertheless. It also sadly put me off scripting for a long time. I just didn't seem to be able to get into the mindset of it, which is probably why I still like to adapt them more than write off the top of my head.

The assignment was to write a straight drama short – another reason why I was reluctant to include it here, because there are absolutely no genre elements to it at all. They say write what you know, and by the time I hit Hallam I'd already graduated from two places – albeit on a much smaller scale to the two graduation ceremonies I'd have for my BA and MA. I'd also been through a lot of heartache and seen friends who'd gone through the emotional wringer too, which meant there was plenty of meat for a love story script in my head. Although, I have to say, compared with what today's youngsters have to deal with – social media, especially – we got off lightly back in those days.

Okay, the formatting is all over the place; my characters are wooden, and the dialogue for Tom is as dodgy as anything; the story itself is a very slight 'love quadrangle' thing, and I was almost certainly channelling *Gregory's Girl* but without the football. Give me a break, I was still in my early 20s! But I still think in amongst all that, there is the germ of something that is halfway decent for its time. It certainly didn't deserve the panning my tutor gave it… probably.

Looking back, and with many short scripts behind me, some produced and some not, plus a few feature scripts, I'd be lying if I said it didn't cause me to wince going through it. I actually had to scan it in because whatever disc I might have saved it on has long gone the way of the Dodo, but I promise I didn't change anything other than a few grammar and spelling mistakes.

Unsurprisingly, *Graduation Day* never got made; the copyrights alone for those songs would have cost a fortune! Yet I'm including it regardless, in the hopes that you can at least see there was promise there.

And to show we all have to start somewhere…

CHARACTER OUTLINES FOR
GRADUATION DAY

Tom

He comes from a fairly poor, working-class family. He is not particularly good looking, but there is a certain something about him. He is a rough diamond. His appearance might be a bit untidy, perhaps even 'thuggish', but he is a very deep young man.

Because of this background he feels a greater obligation to study. It's his chance to make something of himself (probably being the first in his family to attend university). So he takes his studies seriously. This is partly the reason why Samantha thinks he is cheating on her. In contrast, it all comes so easy to her; she can find time to party when Tom can't.

Tom has known Samantha since secondary school, as the opening credits suggest, and cares very deeply for her. This is why he goes off the deep end when she splits with him. He is certainly not violent by nature but, when he feels motivated enough, he can stand up for what he thinks is right.

Samantha or Sam

A very pretty blonde girl, but extremely intelligent with it. She comes from the same background as Tom, but her parents have perhaps slightly more money. She is naturally gifted academically and cares for Tom as much as he does for her.

She is probably frightened that a relationship like theirs, which has lasted many years, is due to hit the rocks soon. This is why she is quick to believe the rumours about Becky and Tom. It is also why she falls for Richard's charm. She may also subconsciously need space away from Tom, to experience something different. But, as with many things, 'the grass is always greener'. It seems Tom and Sam are destined to be together.

Richard

He is diametrically the opposite of Tom, everything he is not. Richard and his parents are extremely rich and he flaunts it in his dress and mannerisms (speech, reluctance to shorten names). He has had quite a spoilt upbringing and has a fierce desire to possess things, even people. Sam, therefore, becomes just another possession in the end, something he must own; a novelty, being from a different class to him.

He also cannot stand to see people in a happy relationship. The rumours about Becky and Tom are just an excuse for him to move in on Sam, he doesn't care whether they are true or not. Indeed, he even feeds this gossip in order to 'get' Sam. Her confusion, anger and vulnerability combine to blind her to his true nature.

Richard can be quite violent without much provocation. He feels a deep urge to prove his manhood, whereas Tom has little to prove; all he is bothered about is being with Sam again.

Becky

A mousy girl and attractive with it, Becky is quite a one-dimensional character. She is totally smitten with Tom and every action she takes is geared towards them becoming a couple. It is quite malicious of her to start the false rumours, but she honestly believes she has a chance with Tom. She truly thinks she is doing it for the greater good.

Her infatuation with Tom makes her this way, although she is very 'clingy' in nature. We cannot judge her too harshly, as love can do strange things to the best of us. To some extent she is not to blame for her actions. And she gets away with it, at first, because of the time Tom is spending studying.

She is much closer to Richard's class than Tom, but the latter definitely casts some sort of spell over her. He fascinates her and this might be because of his 'rough' exterior.

THE BACKGROUND TO...
THE BUZZ

We're really scraping the bottom of the barrel now, I hear you cry. Not even a script this one, but a hand-drawn set of story-boards for a competition I entered not long after leaving university. So, you see I did find a way around writing a script, but still wanted to get my stuff made.

It's not really genre either, *The Buzz*, but is a kind of black comedy – and inspired by my hatred of insects flying around, particularly in the summer months. I could so easily have made the antagonist a wasp, because I really do hate those little f**kers! That comes from getting stung by a bunch of them when I was playing with mates at about age ten. It wouldn't have been a patch on what my old friend Matt 'Garth Marenghi' Holness did with *War of the Wasps*, mind. Besides, I figured flies are more annoying, and much, much harder to get rid of. Just ask Walt and Jessie from that classic episode of *Breaking Bad*.

In any event, I figured there was some mileage in following the antics of one obsessed bloke trying to bring down this specific fly. A kind of David and Goliath battle, which sees him going to extremes.

Like *Graduation Day*, this didn't go anywhere – I never

heard back from the competition, and so put the storyboards aside and promptly lost them, only to find them when we moved again a couple of years ago. I had to photograph them for this book, as they're in a bit of a state.

Unlike *Graduation Day*, I actually do still think this would make a quirky short. If anyone fancies having a go sometime, drop me a line – you know where to find me!

THE BUZZ

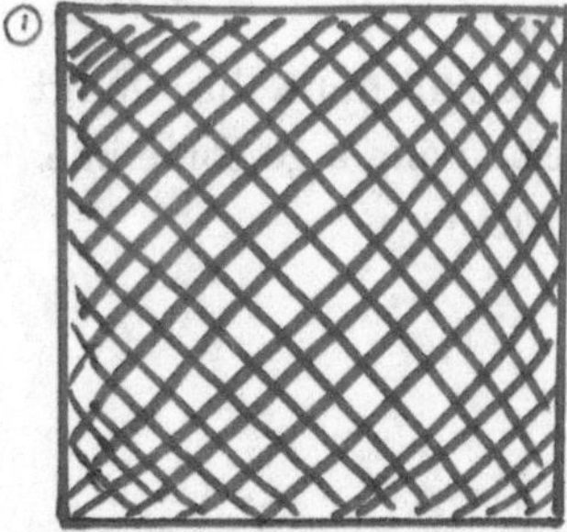

START : WHERE THE CAMERA
IS UP TIGHT ON THE BUG'S EYE

IT PULLS BACK SLOWLY,
THE BUZZING SOUND GETS
LOUDER

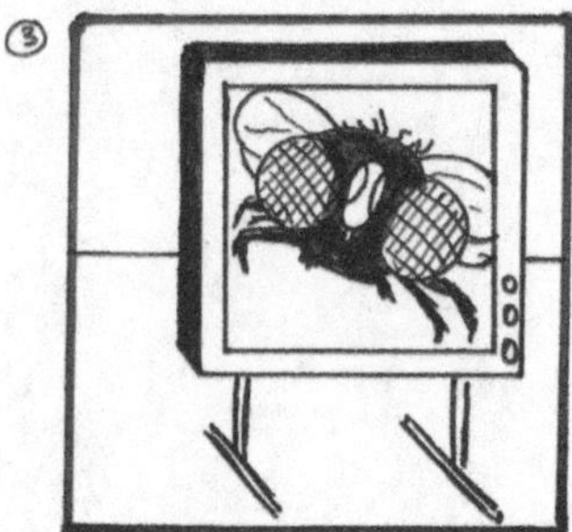

TO REVEAL IT IS A FLY ON
THE TV.

A MAN AND WOMAN ARE SAT
WATCHING THE NATURE
PROGRAMME

SHE IS ASLEEP - HE IS EATING
DINNER - OR TRYING TO!

HE TRIES OTHER STATIONS
USING THE REMOTE - THE BUZZING
NOISE CONTINUES.

THE MAN LOOKS AROUND FOR THE SOURCE OF THE BUZZ.

AND IT'S RIGHT IN FRONT OF HIM - A REAL FLY ON HIS BANGERS AND MASH.

WITH HIS FREE HAND, HE REACHES FOR A MAGAZINE

THEN BRINGS IT CRASHING DOWN ON HIS MEAL.

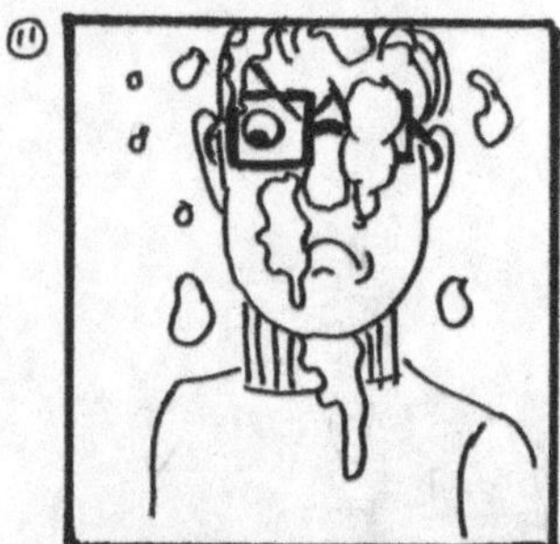

IT SPLATTERS EVERYWHERE - INCLUDING ON HIS FACE.

HE GOES AFTER IT IN A FIT RAGE, KNOCKING OVER HIS TRAY IN THE PROCESS.

HE TREADS ON THE REMOTE,
WHICH IS NOW ON THE FLOOR..

AND FLICKS THE CHANNELS —
(THE OLD INSECT SCI-FI FILM AND U2)
THE TV ROCKS AS HE DASHES AROUND
(CAN BE DONE BY CAMERA SHAKE)

THE MAN PAUSES, OUT OF
BREATH ...

HIS EAR TWITCHES, AND HE
SMILES WHEN HE CAN'T HEAR
THE BUZZ.

THE FLY'S P.O.V. — RESTING
ON THE CURTAIN

IT DIVE BOMBS INTO HIS EAR
WITH PREDICTABLE RESULTS

HE GOES OUT, AND RETURNS WITH SOMETHING BEHIND HIS BACK

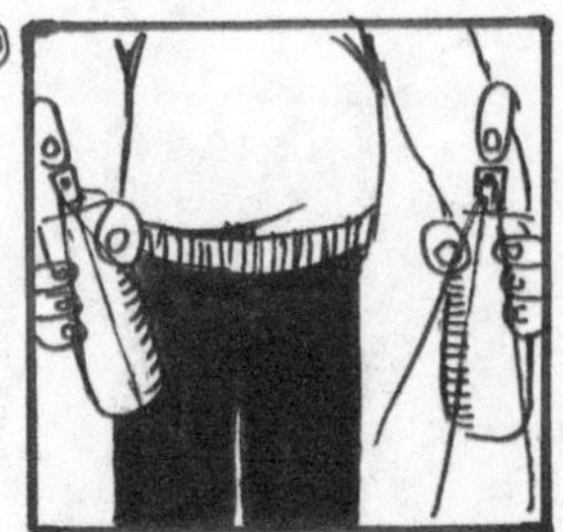

HE BRINGS OUT THE FLY SPRAY — GUNSLINGER STYLE — TO THE TUNE OF 'THE GOOD, THE BAD AND THE UGLY'

HE SPRAYS SO MUCH, THERE IS A CLOUD OF GAS IN THE ROOM

THE MAN SNEEZES AND BREATHES IN JUST AS THE FLY GOES UP HIS NOSE. HE SNORTS IT OUT EVENTUALLY.

THE MAN STARTS TO THROW ANYTHING HE CAN AT THE FLY.

HE'S ABOUT TO THROW A CARRIAGE CLOCK, THEN THINKS THE BETTER OF IT.

25

THE MAN APPEARS NOW IN ALL
KINDS OF PROTECTIVE CLOTHING

26

HE SWINGS HIS BAT AROUND
IN A VAIN ATTEMPT TO SWAT THE FLY.

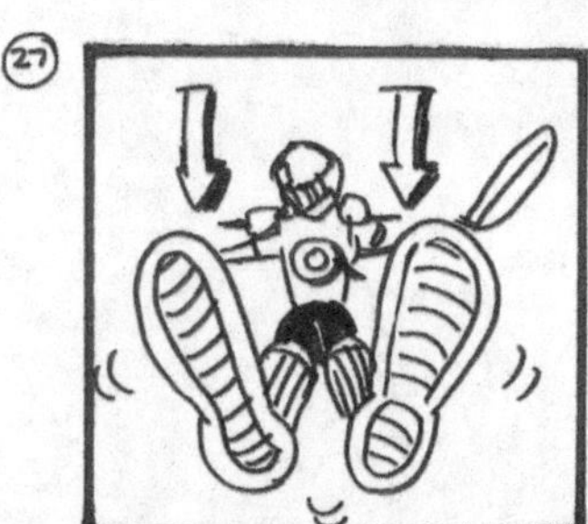

27

INDEED, HE SPINS AROUND SO
SO MUCH HE FALLS OVER
BACKWARDS.

28

THE BUZZING TURNS TO
LAUGHTER — BUT THE FLY
GETS SUCKED INTO THE WOMAN'S
SNORING MOUTH

29

SHE THEN APPEARS TO CHEW
AND SWALLOW

30

— THE BUZZING STOPS AND
ONCE AGAIN THE MAN'S
EARS TWITCH...

AS HE APPROACHES - IT STARTS
UP AGAIN SLIGHTLY MUTED

HE PULLS A FACE AS THE
BUZZING GETS LOUDER,
AND HE KNOWS HE
CAN'T GET TO THE FLY NOW.

THE END.

CLOSING CREDITS ACCOMPANIED BY THE OLD SONG 'THERE
ONCE WAS A WOMAN WHO SWALLOWED A FLY' — WITH BUZZING
STILL IN THE BACKGROUND.

ABOUT THE AUTHOR

Paul Kane is an award-winning (including the British Fantasy Society's Legends of FantasyCon Award), bestselling writer and editor based in Derbyshire, UK. His short story collections include *Alone (In the Dark)*, *Touching the Flame*, *FunnyBones*, *Peripheral Visions*, *Shadow Writer*, *The Adventures of Dalton Quayle*, *The Butterfly Man and Other Stories*, *The Spaces Between*, *Ghosts*, the British Fantasy Award-nominated *Monsters*, *Shadow Casting*, *Nailbiters*, *Death*, *Disexistence*, *Scary Tales*, *More Monsters*, *Lost Souls*, *The Controllers*, *The Colour of Madness*, *Traumas*, *Darkness & Shadows* and *The Naked Eye*. His novellas include *The Lazarus Condition*, *RED* and *Pain Cages* (a #1 Amazon bestseller). He is the author of such novels as *Of Darkness and Light*, *The Gemini Factor* and the bestselling *Arrowhead* trilogy (*Arrowhead*, *Broken Arrow* and *Arrowland*, gathered together in the sell-out omnibus edition *Hooded Man*), a post-apocalyptic reworking of the Robin Hood mythology. His latest novels include *Lunar* (which is set to be turned into a feature film), the short YA novel *The Rainbow Man* (as P.B. Kane), the critically-acclaimed and award-winning *Sherlock Holmes and the Servants of Hell* from Solaris, the sequels to *RED* – *Blood RED* and *Deep RED* – *Before* from Grey Matter Press, *Arcana* from WordFire Press, plus *Her Last*

Secret, *Her Husband's Grave* and *The Family Lie* from HQ/HarperCollins (as P.L. Kane)

He has also written for comics, most notably for the *Dead Roots* zombie anthology alongside writers such as James Moran (*Torchwood, Cockneys vs. Zombies*) and Jason Arnopp (*Doctor Who, Friday the 13th, The Last Days of Jack Sparks*) and as part of the team turning *Clive Barker's Books of Blood* into motion comics for Seraphim/MadeFire. His stand-alone comic *The Disease*, published by Hellbound Media, was also a 2016 Ghastly Award-nominated title in the 'One Shot' category. Paul is co-editor of the anthology *Hellbound Hearts* (Simon & Schuster) – stories based around the mythology that spawned *Hellraiser* – *The Mammoth Book of Body Horror* (Constable & Robinson/Running Press), featuring the likes of Stephen King and James Herbert, *A Carnivàle of Horror* (PS) featuring Ray Bradbury and Joe Hill, *Beyond Rue Morgue* from Titan (stories based around Poe's detective, Dupin), *Exit Wounds* – a crime anthology featuring the likes of Lee Child, Val McDermid, Dennis Lehane and Jeffery Deaver – *Wonderland* (a finalist in the Shirley Jackson Awards), *Cursed*, *Twice Cursed* and #1 bestseller *The Other Side of Never: Dark Tales from the World of Peter and Wendy*, the last five also from Titan.

His non-fiction books include *The Hellraiser Films and Their Legacy*, *Voices in the Dark* and *Shadow Writer – The Non-Fiction. Vol. 1: Reviews* and *Vol. 2: Articles and Essays*, plus his genre journalism has appeared in the likes of *SFX*, *Fangoria*, *Dreamwatch*, *Gorezone* and *Rue Morgue*. He also co-wrote the afterword to the limited edition of Stephen King's *Night Shift* collection. He has been a Guest at Alt.Fiction five times, was a Guest at the first SFX Weekender, at Thought Bubble in 2011, Derbyshire Literary Festival and Off the Shelf in 2012, Monster Mash and Event Horizon in 2013, Edge-Lit in 2014, HorrorCon, HorrorFest and Grimm Up North in 2015, The Dublin Ghost Story Festival and Sledge-Lit in 2016, IMATS Olympia and Celluloid Screams in 2017, Black Library Live

(Warhammer 40k) and The UK Ghost Story Festival in 2019, delivered the keynote speech at the 2021 WordCrafter conference, as well as being a panellist at FantasyCon and the World Fantasy Convention, and a fiction judge at the Sci-Fi London Film Festival. He is a former Special Publications Editor of the British Fantasy Society, has served as co-chair for the UK arm of the Horror Writers Association, and was co-chair of ChillerCon UK 2022 in Scarborough.

His work has been optioned for film and television, and his zombie story 'Dead Time' was turned into an episode of the Lionsgate/NBC TV series *Fear Itself*, adapted by Steve Niles (*30 Days of Night*) and directed by Darren Lynn Bousman (*SAW II-IV* and *Spiral*). He also scripted *The Opportunity*, which premiered at the Cannes Film Festival, *Wind Chimes* (directed by Brad 'Hallows Eve' Watson and which sold to TV), *The Weeping Woman* – filmed by award-winning director Mark Steensland, starring Tony-nominated actor Stephen Geoffreys (*Fright Night*) – *Confidence*, directed by award-winning Mike Clarke (*A Hand to Play, Paper and Plastic*) which stars Simon Bamford (*Hellraiser, Nightbreed, Starfish*), and *The Torturer* directed by Joe Manco of Little Spark Films. Loose Canon/Hydra Films have just turned Paul's novelette *Men of the Cloth* into a feature called *Sacrifice* (aka *The Colour of Madness*), starring *Re-Animator* and *You're Next*'s Barbara Crampton. His work for audio includes the full cast drama adaptation of *The Hellbound Heart* for Bafflegab, starring Tom Meeten (*The Ghoul*), Neve McIntosh (*Doctor Who*) and Alice Lowe (*Prevenge*), and the *Robin of Sherwood* adventure *The Red Lord* for Spiteful Puppet/ITV, narrated by Ian Ogilvy (*Return of the Saint*). You can find out more at his website www.shadow-writer.co.uk which has featured Guest Writers such as Dean Koontz, Robert Kirkman, Olivie Blake and Guillermo del Toro.

PREVIOUS PUBLICATION HISTORY

The Opportunity (*Hidden Corners*, Issue 1, March 2001)

The Opportunity screenplay (Original to this collection)

The Background to The Opportunity (Original to this collection)

The Weeping Woman (*Terror Tales E-Mail Magazine* Issue 2, April 2000)

The Weeping Woman screenplay (Original to this collection)

The Background to The Weeping Woman (Original to this collection)

Wind Chimes (*Read by Dawn Vol. 3*, May 2008)

Wind Chimes screenplay (Original to this collection)

The Background to Wind Chimes (Original to this collection)

The Torturer (*Touching the Flame*, Rainfall Books, 2002)

The Torturer screenplay (Original to this collection)

The Background to The Torturer (Original to this collection)

Presence (*Hauntings*, NewCon Press, 2012)

Presence screenplay (Original to this collection)

The Background to Presence (Original to this collection)

Blackout (*Graveyard Rendezvous*, Issue 20, Summer 1999)

Blackout screenplay (Original to this collection)

The Background to Blackout (Original to this collection)

Life-O-Matic (*Estronomicon* magazine, Spring/Summer Issue, June 2009)

Life-O-Matic screenplay by Jim Phillips (Original to this collection, used with
   permission)

The Background to Life-O-Matic (Original to this collection)

Confidence screenplay (Original to this collection)

The Background to Confidence (Original to this collection)

Graduation Day (Original to this collection)

The Background to Graduation Day (Original to this collection)

The Buzz storyboards (Original to this collection)

The Background to The Buzz (Original to this collection)

PICTURE THANKS

All photos used with permission.

Massive thanks to:

Lewis Copson, Kristie & Mark Steensland, Brad Watson, Dave Morgan, Joe Manco & Catalina Querida, Jim Philips & Mary-Ellen Arsenault, Luke Greensmith and Mike Clarke.

OTHER BOOKS BY PAUL KANE:

Novels

Arrowhead

Broken Arrow

Arrowland

Hooded Man (Omnibus)

The Gemini Factor

Lunar

Sleeper(s)

The Rainbow Man (as P.B. Kane)

Blood RED

Sherlock Holmes and the Servants of Hell

Before

Deep RED

Arcana

The Red Lord

Her Last Secret (as PL Kane)

The Storm

Her Husband's Grave (as PL Kane)

The Family Lie (as PL Kane)

The Gemini Effect

Novellas & Novelettes: Signs of Life

The Lazarus Condition

Dalton Quayle Rides Out

RED

Pain Cages

Creakers (chapbook)

Flaming Arrow

The Bric-a-Brac Man

The P.I.'s Tale

Snow

The Rot

Beneath the Surface (with Simon Clark)

Blood Red Sky

Confessions (as PL Kane)

Corpsing (as PL Kane)

Coming of Age (as PB Kane)

Murder on the Golden Sands Express (as PL Kane)

The Communion (as PL Kane)

Collections: Alone (In the Dark)

Touching the Flame

FunnyBones

Peripheral Visions

The Adventures of Dalton Quayle

Shadow Writer

The Butterfly Man and Other Stories

The Spaces Between

Ghosts

Monsters

The Dead Trilogy

Shadow Casting

Nailbiters

Death

The Life Cycle

Disexistence

Kane's Scary Tales Vol. 1

More Monsters

Lost Souls

The Controllers

White Shadows (as P.B. Kane)

The Colour of Madness: Official Movie Tie-In

Traumas

Darkness & Shadows

The Naked Eye

Tempting Fate

Nailbiters – Hard Bitten

Zombies!

Editor & Co-Editor: Shadow Writers Vol. 1 & 2

Terror Tales #1-4

Top International Horror

Albions Alptraume: Zombies

The British Fantasy Society: A Celebration

Hellbound Hearts

The Mammoth Book of Body Horror

A Carnivàle of Horror: Dark Tales from the Fairground

Beyond Rue Morgue

Dark Mirages

Exit Wounds

Wonderland

Cursed

Twice Cursed

The Other Side of Never

In These Hallowed Halls

Non-Fiction: Contemporary North American Film Directors: A Wallflower Critical Guide (Major Contributor)

Cinema Macabre (Contributor)

The Hellraiser Films And Their Legacy

Voices in the Dark

Shadow Writer – The Non-Fiction. Vol. 1: Reviews

Shadow Writer – The Non-Fiction. Vol. 2: Articles & Essays

Leviathan – The Story of Hellraiser and Hellbound: Hellraiser II (contributor)

Hellraisers

War is Hell: Making Hellraiser III: Hell on Earth (Contributor)

Stuart Gordon: Interviews (Conversations with Filmmakers Series) (Contributor)